Killer in Sight

A Tom Lackey Mystery

Other books by Sandra Carrington-Smith...

The Book of Obeah

While fulfilling the final request of her departed Grandmama, Melody Bennet, a young professional raised in the genteel suburbs of North Carolina, is plunged into the clandestine world of an ancient West African religion – via the Louisiana bayou. In unearthing a mysterious religious manuscript, Melody collides with those seeking powers believed to be contained within the text, from The Vatican to individuals claiming it as their legacy. She accepts the task of safeguarding the book and finds lives are threatened, including her own, sometimes from unexpected directions. As her knowledge grows and perceptions shift, Melody's path is fused with that of the sacred book. She risks body and soul to protect both and, unbeknownst to her, secures the future of an esoteric, divine prophecy.

"... captured me from the start and would not let me go."

Rebecca Cox, Reviewthebook.com

"An exciting, riveting novel with many twists, this book will surely satisfy mystery fans and paranormal/mystical fans."

Betty Gelean, "*Night reader*"

"A fine choice and a highly recommended read."

Midwest Book Review

"A psychological thriller filled with suspense."
Stephanie Rose Bird, author of *Stick, Stones, Roots and Bones*

Housekeeping for the Soul:
A Practical Guide to Restoring Your Inner Sanctuary

The first book to combine how-to, self-help and spiritual genres to address the needs of millions of readers as they strive to detach from the Culture of Chaos and embrace a life of balance. It is through this inner harmony and balance that one may then create a meaningful, authentic reality. With a down-to-earth approach, the reader is guided through the process of emotional healing and renewal of spirit through the familiar analogy of housekeeping: cleaning, organizing, and "airing out" our lives, room by room, task by task.

"...helps us clear out some spiritual cobwebs and make our next 'spring cleaning' apply not to our homes but to the deepest part of ourselves."

Victoria Moran,
author of international bestseller *Creating a Charmed Life*

"...overflows with important concepts presented in a style that is fresh and relatable. A unique, 'must read' debut from this eloquent author."

S.T. Underdahl,
Clinical Psychologist and author of *The Other Sister* and
Remember This

"A great soul gripping and informative book to live by."

Dr. Robert E McGinnis

Coming soon...

The Rosaries

Book two of the Crossroads series. After risking her life to safeguard the prophecy hidden within the pages of the famed Book of Obeah, Melody Bennet thinks her life has finally settled into normalcy. Now the tables are turning and Melody is once again thrust into uncharted territory. As the prophecy closes in, new dangers are lurking at the door...

Shadows of a Tuscan Moon

A beautiful mother of two mysteriously disappears without leaving a trace, apparently swallowed by the darkness of a frigid winter night. The local law enforcement gets right to work, but as time goes by every lead turns into a dead end. Has the woman decided to run off and turn her back on her too-tight family life, or is her disappearance the work of a skilled killer who has left no clues behind? Many shadows lurk in the timeless beauty of a small Tuscan town; one of those shadows, maybe the darkest one of all, holds the key to a terrifying truth...

Killer in Sight

A Tom Lackey Mystery

Sandra Carrington-Smith

First Edition

ISBN-13: 978-0-9855558-0-1

Crossroads Books

http://www.sandracarringtonsmith.com

To my guide and muse, P.L.,

thanks to whom I never walk alone.

Acknowledgments

Any time a new book hits the market, the name of the author is usually the one that stands out, but truth is that no author can produce a book alone.

There are many people working backstage, and although their faces will likely remain behind the curtain, the value of their work should share the spotlight.

I would like to thank my families, the Carrington-Smiths and the Faiazzas, and also Riccardo Panessa -- the uncle I always wished I could have – for always supporting me.

I would especially like to send a special thank you to all the friends who helped me: Sherrill Suitt-Craig, your wonderful graphic designing skills have saved the day; had I been doing this on my own, the cover would have featured stick people.

Julie Wall, as always I appreciate your eye for detail and your fantastic photographic skills which allow people to look at the author page without getting scared.

Jon Batson, I don't have enough words to thank you for helping me format the book files, as all who know me are also aware that I should probably receive disability for being so technically challenged.

Many thanks also to Dara Lyon Warner who helped me edit parts of the book, and to all the friends who read the story and offered critique and blurbs: Scott Schultz, Tracy White (the amazing sheriff deputy who helped me with police protocol), Ed Powers, Thomas Smith, Victoria Roder, Don Vaughn, Debby Marshall, Alice Osborn, Elaine Estes and my wonderful agent Natalie Kimber from Sunrae Literary Agency.

Special thanks also to Donna Freeman, Toni Overby and Pam Scarboro for the emotional support they are always ready to provide.

Tremendous gratitude must certainly be extended to my husband John and to my children, Stephen, Michael and Morgan, for always believing in me and for being eternally patient.
Last but not least, this book is dedicated to you, the unknown reader. Thank you for giving my work a chance; I hope you will enjoy the story.

Chapter 1

Tracey Newman held her breath, afraid the man could hear her. He was close now—she couldn't see him in the darkness of the stuffy room, but she could somehow detect his presence nearby. She closed her eyes, as if trying to delete this moment from her reality, and her nostrils picked up a pungent smell, but she couldn't decide what it was or where it came from. It was a strange, earthy scent—a mixture of mildew and something else—slightly offset by the fragrance of honeysuckle that filtered in through the open door.

Tracey shivered even though the temperature in the room was hot and the air was still, and she wanted to wrap her arms around herself in a gesture of comfort, but was too afraid to move. *Where is he? Has he left?* Her mind raced back to the last few days, and she thought of her family. Her mother had celebrated a birthday the previous weekend, and Tracey planned to fly home to St. Louis a week from today to surprise the whole family, especially her half-sister Alexis. It was hard for a physician assistant to get time off, and she had to sweet-talk the supervising doctor into allowing her to take five days of vacation. Now she wasn't sure her travel plans were going to work out after all. This was so surreal! She quietly opened and closed her fists just to feel movement, to know that she wasn't trapped in a nightmare. Unfortunately, she was awake and not at all sure she would still be breathing even a few minutes from now. The thought of dying made her head spin and her stomach tighten. Her ears were buzzing, and for a moment she thought she was going to faint. She could hear the sound of water dripping in the distance, but couldn't determine if it was coming from inside the cabin or outside. It wasn't raining when she came in, but the weather in North Carolina was crazy this time of year, and anything could be expected. March had left with a bang—violent storms and widespread power outages had dominated the greater part of the month— and April was already blistering hot, with temperatures that were a bit uncharacteristic so early in the season but quite welcome after the unusually cold winter. Rain was often elusive in this part of the country, and it usually showed up either on weekends when she and her friend Shannon planned to go kayaking, or when she washed her car.

A creaking sound exploded in the silence of the room, and Tracey's heart jumped to her throat. He was getting closer, she just knew it...what could she do now? She could remain hidden and hope he would not find her, or she could try to escape outside again. Maybe she would run into someone else out there, and she would be safe.

"I know you are in here, Tracey. It's not nice to hide."

Tracey did not respond, and swallowed hard to smother the deep scream which threatened to rise from her stomach. She could taste the salty, silent tears that ran unchecked down her face and over her lips.

"You are just making this harder for yourself, Tracey. I promise it will be fast. You will barely feel a thing." The man's voice was sickeningly condescending and fatherly, and Tracey was so distraught and confused that she almost considered his words for a moment; but as she glimpsed reflected light from the blade of a knife, something else came over her. A primal scream erupted from her pounding chest and ripped through her throat, as she ran past the man toward the door. He lunged to grab her and slid on the floor, the knife landing with a metallic clunk on the wooden surface. Tracey ran outside, unsure of where to go. She had jogged through these woods dozens of times, but now the trees appeared to connect together, forming a black wall that spread out in all directions. It was barely dusk when she ran into the unlocked cabin looking for a place to hide, after she noticed she was being followed, and now it was pitch dark—how long had she been in there? Her mother had warned her often about jogging alone, but Tracey always brushed off her mother's worried comments with a smile, believing in her heart that she could take care of herself. Maybe she should have listened.

She could hear the man's steps crunching leaves in his path, and his breathing was labored. Tracey wanted to turn around to see if he was behind her, but she couldn't risk stopping. The eerie silk of a spider web touched her forehead, but even though she was terrified of spiders, she kept running blindly through the dense forest. The path was gone, and all the trees looked alike; menacing hands seemed to be reaching out in the night, to capture her and deliver her to the man who was after her. An owl hooted frighteningly nearby, as if to signal the man of her whereabouts, and Tracey tripped on a root poking from the ground but didn't fall. Suddenly, she heard her name being called, and the voice was a familiar one...someone else was in the woods, someone who knew her! She thrust herself toward the voice, knowing her assailant was only steps behind and safety was near. She could feel branches scraping her ankles as she ran, but she was numb to pain.

"Tracey! Where are you?"

She could see a shadow in the woods, running toward her with a flashlight. She wasn't at all certain who the person was, but she was happy someone else was there. *Oh yes, thank you, God! Please watch over me. I'm coming...* Tracey ran faster, nearly throwing herself into the arms of the person who had come to rescue her. Her body shook with deep sobs as she looked up, and her eyes registered surprise when she saw who it was. It didn't matter. She tried to formulate words to convey what was happening. "He is coming after me! I don't know why he is doing this! He has a knife!" Her voice was so shrill she almost couldn't recognize it as being her own.

"It's going to be okay, Tracey. I'm here now, and I will take care of things."

Tracey nodded, and turned toward the man who was quickly approaching. He stopped and spoke, and his voice echoed in the stillness of the woods. "I'm sorry. I shouldn't have let her get away. I screwed up."

Tracey shook her head, struggling to grasp what was happening, but when she turned to look at her rescuer, her eyes locked with the cold mouth of a revolver pointed at her. Words jammed in her throat, and her legs almost collapsed beneath her.

"I'm sorry, Tracey. I didn't want to be the one to do

this, but you leave me no choice. Goodbye, Sweetheart."

Before Tracey could speak a word, even to ask why, the gun went off, and she fell into a heap on a bed of leaves. Before she died, she looked at the two people who were standing there—waiting for her to take her last breath—knowing she would never see anyone else again. Their features were photographed by her fading eyes, but sadly, nobody would ever see them.

Chapter 2

The phone rang just as Tom Lackey got ready to sit down for breakfast with Kathy Spencer, his girlfriend of over ten years. People often wondered why Tom and Kathy were not married after being together for so long, but neither worried enough about the opinions of others to actually care. Both in their mid-forties—Tom was going to be 45 in just another month, and Kathy had turned 43 in February—and both with failed marriages behind them, they had come to see marriage as chloroform when applied to a relationship. Tom and Kathy were happy just the way they were; Tom was confident that Kathy loved him and was attracted to him, even if his hairline was slightly receding and a small tire had begun to inflate around his midsection. Aside from those two age markers, Tom still had a good build and a handsome face devoid of wrinkles, and his full lips and deep brown eyes—a bit droopy and hauntingly soulful—were still his most attractive features. Despite his own good looks, Tom felt his lucky star had shone brighter the day he met Kathy. Aside from being a beautiful woman, with sparkling, sapphire-blue eyes, she was also extremely intelligent, and her voice was as soft and as smooth as velvet.

Kathy took a look at the caller ID and handed the phone to Tom. "It's for you…the station." That was his Kathy, a woman of few words.

Tom took the receiver, tucking it between his ear and shoulder while he buttered a piece of toast. "Lackey."

"Lieutenant, Sergeant Parker asked me to call you. A couple of joggers found the body of a young woman in Durant Park a short while ago. We have already taped the area."

"Have you identified the woman?" Tom hurried to spread some jelly over his toast, knowing that he was not going to have much time for breakfast today.

"No, Sir. We haven't looked around yet, but she doesn't appear to have any ID."

"Okay, I will be there as soon as possible. Keep everybody away, especially the media." Tom clicked the phone off, placed it down on the table, then he took a hurried sip of coffee and bit into the toast as he walked briskly toward the small table near the door to grab his car keys. "I don't know what time I will be home. They found a young woman in Durant Park. No ID."

Kathy arched her eyebrows and put down her coffee cup. "Oh, dear! That's awful, Tom…" She shook her head lightly, thinking of her own daughter who was away at college and whose safety she worried about from time to time. It was normal for parents to be concerned about their children, young and older alike, and for a moment her heart ached for the parents of this yet-unidentified young woman.

Tom blew a kiss her way, and Kathy smiled. Then he was gone. She took another sip of coffee and tried to focus on a newspaper article about the latest decisions of the Wake County school board, but she couldn't concentrate. So, she took her plate and cup to the kitchen sink and went upstairs to shower, and get ready for work.

#

Traffic at this time of morning was a beast, and Tom wondered about the possibilities of looking for a different type of job that would keep him off the roads so early in the day. He thought about his sister's husband, and the business he tried to convince Tom to join. Todd drove a tow truck, and in the last few months his business had taken off, leaving him short-handed and slightly grouchy from lack of personal time. The money was good, but Todd was rarely ever home, and Tom knew he couldn't do that to Kathy. Although he was fairly sure Kathy would support any decision he made, the long hours away from home would definitely affect their relationship, and Tom didn't want to take any chances on losing her. Besides, traffic was what he was hoping to get away from, so driving a tow truck at all hours of the day and night wasn't the answer to his problems. And of course, there was another thing to take into account: Even if he loved complaining about the randomness of his working hours—and the bullshit he and the other detectives had to sometimes put up with— Tom loved his job. He loved being the good guy, he loved getting the bad guys, and more than anything, he loved a happy ending, though in his profession it wasn't always guaranteed.

When he pulled into the parking lot adjacent to the entrance near the wooded area of the park, he noticed a small group of people talking. One man was pointing his finger toward the pathway leading into the forest; his face appeared flushed. Tom got out of his car and began to walk toward the group when a uniformed officer on the other side of the yellow tape called him. Tom headed in that direction, still studying the first man from the corner of his eye.

"Lieutenant Lackey, right through here." The uniform pointed toward a small trail veering off from the main path, which was almost hidden by decomposing leaves.

Tom nodded, and followed the officer after taking

one last look at the group of people standing beyond the tape, whose heads were now turned in their direction.

"One of the men standing there seemed sort of excited. Has he seen anything?" He asked the officer, a young fellow whose slowly fading acne betrayed his tender age.

"No, Sir. We have kept everyone away. The two joggers used his phone to call 911. They had left theirs at home because they were afraid of dropping them while running."

"Oh, okay. As soon as you show me where to go, go back and tell him that he can't disclose any information he might have heard."

"Yes, Sir. This way."

As they approached the area where the young woman had been found, Tom saw several uniforms standing around. Sergeant Gene Parker was already on the scene.

"About time you got here, Lackey!" The sergeant was being his usual non-charming self. "What kept you?"

Tom let it slide. "I got here as soon as I could. My

car is fast, but it still can't fly over other cars. Traffic is terrible!"

Parker snorted derisively, and Tom ignored him. The temperature was already high, even this early in the day and, given that it was only the end of April, Tom expected the upcoming summer to be one for the records. A light breeze barely stirred the leaves on the trees around them, and a faint scent of unidentified flowers mixed subtly with the smell of decaying wood in the distance. Under normal circumstances, Tom loved to inhale deeply and enjoy the almost tactile earthiness of the woods, but today the air smelled different: Death had come to mar the beauty of nature, and it had interrupted the flow of things. Today, the air in the woods was repulsive.

He and Parker walked together toward the body. Tom took one look and his heart dropped. The young woman was crumpled on the ground like a discarded doll, her silky blond hair spread like a fan around her head. She appeared to be about five feet, five inches tall, weighing around 120 pounds. A large blood stain radiated from a single wound on her chest near the heart. Her mouth was opened in a silent scream, and her blue eyes were fixed on the horrors they had witnessed before they could no longer focus on anything ever again. What had those eyes seen? Who had done this to her?

From the moment he first glimpsed the body, Tom knew who the young woman was. For the last five days, he had stared at her picture on his desk, after her family had reported her missing. Tracey Newman was a physician assistant at Wake Memorial, and her best friend, Shannon Brinkley, had called Tracey's mother after her roommate didn't show up for her shift at the hospital. The family called the police and filed a missing person report, but Tracey appeared to have vanished into thin air…until now.

Tom kneeled beside the body, careful not to disturb any evidence, and looked at Tracey's beautiful face. What could possibly motivate someone to take away such a young and promising life? A single gunshot to the heart suggested a premeditated killing, rather than a crime of passion. The body didn't appear to be injured in any other way, aside from a few marks on the ankles that were probably caused by the brushy, thorny ground cover characteristic of the area.

Tom stood up and walked toward the coroner, who was talking to a young lady busily taking notes. Dr. Greer looked up and nodded to Tom. He said something to the young girl; she went off still looking at her notepad. Greer was a sight to behold—at nearly 65 years of age he refused to retire—and he talked about his work the same way a besotted lover would discuss the virtues of his beloved. He was a short, round man, with a fluffy mane of snow-white hair, a bushy white mustache and eyebrows. The hair on his head and face always reminded Tom of the cotton fields he passed when he drove over to Smithfield to visit his mother. With a reddish complexion and benevolent blue eyes, the doctor looked like a miniature Santa Claus, minus the beard.

"Hey, Lackey…a clean job, this one."

Tom nodded. "Yes, I saw that. How long has she been dead, Doc?"

"Hard to say exactly, but I would say at least a few days. Strange how nobody has found the body before.

Lots of people go through these woods."

"They usually stick to the beaten path. It's pretty thick in here. I think I know who she is. We will have to compare dental records and bring in the family for identification, but I am pretty sure she is the young woman who was reported missing last week. Her family lives in Missouri. She was a physician assistant at one of the local hospitals."

Greer shook his head. "These young women never want to believe how dangerous it is to jog alone in these woods, until tragedies like this happen."

Tom looked at the doctor with a surprised look on his face. "You think she was attacked by a maniac while she jogged? Don't you think the gunshot wound is inconsistent with that? She is fully dressed, so sexual assault doesn't seem to apply. No marks other than what she might have inflicted on herself while trying to run."

"Lackey!" Parker's voice thundered from the left. "One of the uniforms just found a print from a man's shoe inside a cabin on the grounds. The print looks smeared, as if he slipped."

"I'm coming," Lackey turned back toward the

coroner and said, "I will call you as soon as I get back to my desk, Doc."

Tom rushed to meet Parker, who was already walking toward the cabin. Parker was making irritated noises, but this time it sounded more like the huffing and puffing was due to the uphill trail than to his grumpy attitude.

"It would be real good if we could nail him with the shoe print. Hopefully it won't be too smeared."

Tom nodded and walked on.

#

Kathy Spencer sometimes wished she had more than two hands: Today was one of those times. She tried her best to balance her handbag, camera, a tote bag and a large cup of skim latte in one hand while attempting to turn the key to open the door of her studio. Most of the items made it in; the cup of coffee, however, was not so lucky. As the cup fell from her hand, splattering its hot contents on the hardwood floor, Kathy knew this was not going to be a good day. The morning had already taken a turn for the worse when Tom received the call about the young woman who was found at Durant Park, and this latest incident only compounded Kathy's encroaching feeling of gloom. She wasn't sure why hearing about this young girl affected her so much— living with a police detective for the greater part of the last ten years had thickened her skin, and she didn't usually get involved with his work. But this case was different, and Kathy couldn't figure out what was different about it. She still didn't know what the young girl looked like or what her story was, but she felt close to both the girl and her family. The fact that Kathy's own daughter was probably nearly the same age as the young woman may have explained why her death had hit so close to home. She carried her armful of possessions to the desk, then went to the utility closet to retrieve a mop and clean up the coffee spill. After rinsing and putting away the mop, she sat at her desk and uploaded the photos from yesterday's shoot to her computer. In a few moments, the image of a smiling young woman appeared on the screen. She was stunning and youthful, and in the photo she smiled adoringly at her fiancé; the young man appeared just as happy and excited about their future together. *Did Tom's young girl have a boyfriend? Was she happy?* Here it was happening again...she couldn't get the dead girl off her mind. But why?

Kathy was very open to signs. Since early childhood she had experienced strange occurrences from time to time; her curiosity had led her to explore the possibility of alternate realities and the validity of little-known systems of belief. Given her passion for photography and anything related to cameras, it was no surprise to her that she had instantly fallen in love with the concept of iridology when it was presented during a discussion with a naturopathic physician. Of course, the main purpose of iridology was to detect illnesses in the body through a study of the iris, but Kathy was convinced—contrary to the tenets of current science—that the eye bore similarities to a camera. One of her secret dreams was to create a device that could be used to download images recorded by the eye. She conceived of digital cameras working along the same lines—images needed to be transferred to a computer, but even before being sent, they were recorded and preserved into a temporary memory slot in the machine; without an additional memory card, only few images could be saved in the camera at one time, but some could certainly be retrieved. Could the same process happen within the human eye? Might there be a way to view the last image captured by the eye in the moments before death? If the eye was indeed similar to a digital camera, Kathy reasoned, even if the main computer shut down before the images were sent to it, it should be able to retain at least a few impressions. *Tom's young woman saw her killer…*

Kathy's mind snapped back to the present, and she tried once again to focus on the photos of the girl smiling at her from the screen, but her mind was elsewhere. She picked up the phone and dialed her daughter's number, tapping her finger on the desk as she nervously waited for Caroline to answer. When she did, Kathy sighed in relief.

"Caroline, it's Mom. How are you, Honey?"

"Mom? Is everything okay?"

"Of course, Sweetie!" Her excited tone betrayed her

anxiety, "Everything is great. I just wanted to say hi."

"Oh, okay. It's just that you never call so early in the day. I thought something happened."

Kathy paused long enough for Caroline to wonder. "Mom, are you sure everything is okay?"

Again, Kathy hesitated for a moment. Her daughter hated to be treated like a baby; at nineteen, she felt grown up and all-knowing, and certainly able to take care of herself. "Everything is fine, Caroline. It's just that the body of a young woman was found today, not too far from here, and I was thinking of how devastating that will be for her family. I also thought of how lucky I am to have you."

"Oh Mom, you old sweet thing…you know I am the lucky one, to have you in my life." Caroline's voice was smiling; Kathy could tell. Although she didn't like to be babied, she did like to be the center of Kathy's world, and Kathy was instantly proud of herself for the way she had handled this—conveying her affection without sounding too smothering.

"Is Tom assigned to the case, Mom?"

"Yes, I think so. He got the call early this morning

while we were eating breakfast. For some reason I can't get this young girl off my mind. How awful for her, and for her whole family!"

"I'm sorry, Mom, but I promise you that you will have to put up with me for many years to come…at least until the day I have to push you around in a wheelchair!"

Caroline's words were a balm to Kathy's heart. "I know that, Sweetheart. I'm just being a mom."

"Well, I have to get ready for school; I have a class in 45 minutes. Can I call you tonight?"

"Of course. I'll probably be home after six."

"Okay, Mom, I will talk to you around dinner time, then."

"Caroline? I love you. I really do."

"I love you too, Mom."

A click marked the end of the conversation, and Kathy sat there for a moment, with the phone still close to her ear. At least she had told Caroline she loved her— had the other young woman's mother had a chance to do the same?

She tried to call Tom's desk and then his mobile

phone, but she got voice mail both times, so she got up from the desk and turned off the computer. She had plenty of work to do, but she just couldn't focus. She decided to take the rest of the day off and go home. Maybe she would stop by Starbucks to replace the coffee that got spilled earlier. Right now, for reasons still not known to her, Kathy needed something that would bring her comfort.

#

Tom stopped by the coffee machine before going to his desk. He was happy the department had installed one of the new machines that brew coffee from pods. He took a moment to decide whether he felt like Hazelnut or French Vanilla, but ended up choosing a non-flavored dark roast instead. Kathy had tried, over the years, to introduce him to a more exotic taste, but when he was alone Tom preferred to tap back into his old ways. Born and raised in Smithfield, North Carolina—population 13,000—Tom still preferred biscuits and gravy over eggs benedict any day.

He was getting ready to take the first sip, the aroma of strong coffee tantalizing to his nostrils and the steam rising up to fog his reading glasses, when Sergeant Parker appeared out of nowhere like a bad dream.

"We need to notify the family, Lackey. Wanna do it, or should we call St. Louis?"

"I haven't thought that far yet. I suppose it is probably better for them to deliver the news in person than for us to call. Would you want to find out about your daughter's death over the phone?"

Parker's face softened. He had a kid of about the same age, and his paternal instincts were stronger than his crusty attitude. Lackey had no children of his own, but over the years he had become close to Kathy's daughter, so he could sympathize.

"No, I guess not," Parker answered with a much more subdued tone. "I will get on the phone with them in a minute, and ask them to visit the family."

"Thank you, Parker. We can request dental records as soon as the family is contacted. After Greer is through with the autopsy, and if everything checks out, we can start with her apartment. We have a local name,

Shannon Brinkley. She was Tracey Newman's best friend and she is the one who called the family to let them know that Tracey didn't show up for her shift at the hospital."

"You think that's her, Lackey?"

"Look for yourself." Lackey tapped a few keys on his computer and clicked on the photo Tracey Newman's family had provided. "See the resemblance?"

Parker arched his eyebrow. "Shit…it sure looks like the same girl. Okay, I'm going to call St. Louis now."

When Parker left, Lackey took a sip of his coffee, but it was already lukewarm and not sweet enough, so he put the lid back on and dropped the cup inside his waste basket. Today, coffee wasn't in the cards and a cold-hearted killer was still on the loose. Sometimes he really hated his job.

Chapter 3

Rose Howard focused on watering her plants to hide her nervousness. According to the police in North Carolina, there had been no activity on Tracey's credit cards or debit card since the day she didn't show up for work over a week ago, but Rose refused to wrap her mind around the possibility that something could have happened to her daughter. The family had been on edge since Shannon called; preparations were being made for Rose and her husband Mike to fly to Raleigh by the end of this week, if something didn't turn up. Tracey was a free spirit—she always had been—and Rose preferred to think that her young daughter was gone to take care of a friend, and maybe she just didn't take the time to notify anyone. Yes, that had to be it.

The soft patter of Alexis' footsteps transported Rose back to the present moment, and she turned around to welcome her younger daughter with a smile. "Hi, Angel Face! I didn't hear the bus. How was school?"

Alexis wrinkled her miniature nose and shrugged. "It was okay, Mom…same old stuff."

Her expression made Rose smile in spite of the anxiety that kept her heart trapped in an ice chest. Alexis acted so grown up, and even if she was very petite for her nine years, her mind was far beyond her chronological age. There was something very wise about Alexis, and many people often commented that she was an old soul. The child was also extremely sensitive in a way that Rose considered a little strange, and she sometimes surprised her parents with questions that made them uncomfortable. Since a very early age, Alexis claimed she had a friend—an imaginary pal named Lily—who visited her from time to time, and told her all sorts of strange things. Rose and Mike worried about it at first, and they even took Alexis to see a specialist, but the diagnosis was that Alexis was a perfectly healthy child with a very fertile imagination.

"Is your stuff packed to go to Grandma's this weekend, Alexis?" Rose asked while she continued to water the plants.

Alexis pouted. "I don't want to go to Grandma's! I want to go with you!"

Rose's nerves were on edge, but she tried her best to maintain her cool. "You know that's not possible, Alexis. Dad and I are flying to Raleigh to look for Tracey...we've talked about that."

"Tracey is not coming back, Mom. Tracey is dead! Lily told me."

Rose's hand flew to strike her daughter's face before she could even acknowledge her reaction. "Stop it with this nonsense! Lily doesn't exist!" The moment her hand fell back to her side, Rose was aware of what she had done. Alexis just stood there looking smaller than ever, her big blue eyes filling with tears.

"Oh, Alexis, I am so sorry...I didn't mean to...I'm just a bit out of sorts, you know. Tracey is fine. We are bringing her home with us."

"No, you are not! Tracey is dead!" Alexis shot

through the room and ran up the stairs to her room before Rose could say anything else. Rose followed with her eyes, but didn't move, and as soon as Alexis was gone she burst into tears. She wasn't sure how long she sat there crying, and when Mike walked in from work he ran to her and wrapped his arms around her. "There, there…it's going to be okay, Darling."

Rose cried softly against his chest, the bulk of her tears now spent. "I'm sorry…Alexis came home from school and told me Tracey was dead. I couldn't handle it, even if what she considers facts are based on an imaginary conversation she had with Phantom Lily."

Mike's face darkened. "This is a lot for her to process, Rose. I'm not surprised she is seeking comfort in any way she can. Yet…she shouldn't say things like that. I will talk to her."

"No, you're right. She is upset. I shouldn't have reacted the way I did."

"Come on," Mike said. "Let's go make a cup of tea. It will make you feel better."

They stood up and were walking slowly toward the kitchen when the doorbell rang.

"Probably just a salesman," Mike suggested. "They always ignore the 'No Soliciting' sign at the entrance to the subdivision. I will get rid of him in a second. Why don't you get the kettle on the stove while you wait?"

Rose nodded and they separated in the hallway—Mike heading to the door, and Rose to the kitchen.

Rose filled the kettle with water and turned on the burner, then she sat down at the kitchen table to wait for Mike. After a few moments she wondered why he wasn't coming back and decided to go see if the salesman was gone, but as she stood up, Mike walked through the kitchen door, a thousand invisible bricks weighing on his shoulders. His face was pale, and Rose could tell his eyes were wet with tears, though he had done his best to wipe them before coming in.

"Mike? What's wrong?"

Mike didn't respond immediately, and Rose felt panic rising from the pit of her stomach until it constricted her heart. "Mike! Tell me what is wrong!"

Mike walked closer, and put his arms around her. His voice was eerily soft. "Sit down, Rose."

"Mike, you are scaring me…what is it?"

31

Mike looked down at his feet for a few seconds, then he took a deep breath and spoke. "Two detectives just came by to bring the latest news, Rose. It's not good." His eyes shifted back down, unable to face the pain he knew would register in Rose's face.

"But…but what kind of news, Mike? Is Tracey hurt? Is she in a hospital? We need to leave right away and bring her home, so I can stay with her until she is completely healed."

"Tracey is not going to heal, Rose. Her body was found early this morning in a park in North Carolina." There, he had said it. Rose just sat there, with her mouth open, unable to speak and just shaking her head. When she at last recovered her voice, it sounded like the voice of a child. "No…no, they are wrong. Tracey is fine, they have the wrong girl. I just know it! It's not my baby."

Mike kneeled in front of her, and took her face into his shaking hands. "Rose, I hope to God you're right, but according to the detectives, it is almost certain that the woman they found is Tracey. They will need dental records and a positive identification, but everything else seems to match."

Rose stood up but she could barely move. "No…it's not possible. I will talk to them. They need to find the parents of this poor girl. They can't afford to waste their time like this."

"Rose…the description of the girl matches Tracey's photo. Let's go talk to them."

When Rose looked into Mike's eyes again, the certainty of her denial wavered slightly, but she brushed off the unwelcome sensation and walked with him to meet the detectives sitting in the living room.

One of the two men, a tall, slim individual in his late fifties, stood up the moment they entered. He had small hazel eyes set deep in his thin face, and his dark hair was streaked with veins of silver throughout. The other man was younger, maybe in his mid-thirties, sporting cropped sandy blond hair and a thin moustache. He wasn't as tall as the other detective, but he appeared more muscular. As if on cue, the second man stood up also, and for a moment Rose hoped they would just disappear and leave her in the comfort of her illusion.

"Mrs. Howard, I am Detective Wilson, and this is my partner, Detective Wheeler." The older man extended his hand, but Rose didn't shake it. "Please sit down, Mrs. Howard."

Rose sat on the leather sofa and took a deep breath. "As I was telling my husband, Detective, I think there is a mistake. This young girl is not our daughter, I am sure of it."

Detective Wilson nodded, well aware of the sense of denial and shock parents experience when told their children were gone forever. "Preliminary identification suggests that the young woman found by Raleigh police early today is your daughter, Ma'am. Of course, we will need to order dental records and we will need you or your husband to identify the body."

"I know how you can tell it is not my daughter, Detective. Tracey has a small Tinker Bell tattoo on her lower abdomen. Does your girl have that?" Rose's tone was nearly defiant.

"I am not sure, Mrs. Howard. The body was just taken to the medical examiner's office. The autopsy will take place later today or tomorrow. I'm afraid I don't have many details, but it would be advisable for someone to travel over there and identify the body."

Mike broke into the conversation. "I can leave tonight if I can find an available flight, or tomorrow morning at the latest."

The detective nodded. "Thank you, Mr. Howard. I will arrange for someone to pick you up at the airport as soon as we have the details of your flight."

As the detectives walked toward the front door, they didn't see the small girl sitting on one of the stairs, and nobody heard her when she whispered. "I knew you were right, Lily. Mom should have listened."

#

The chicken *cacciatora* simmering on the stove sent out a heavenly aroma, and Kathy inhaled deeply while she poured a glass of wine. Tom had called while she was in the shower; she was a little disappointed when she listened to the message he left and heard that he would be late for dinner. She had moved forward with dinner preparations anyway, knowing that, after a horrific day on the job, a good dinner was the best healing tonic for him; even if he got home late, all of

Tom's worries would disappear the moment he tasted the succulent bird. Unlike Tom's ex-wife, Kathy didn't usually mind his working hours; in fact, she treasured having some time alone, and she figured that the daily separations only made every moment they spent together feel more special. Tonight she felt differently, however, and craved human companionship. She hoped that Caroline would call as promised, but knowing her daughter and being familiar with her spontaneous—and sometimes slightly erratic—ways, Kathy wasn't holding her breath. Caroline was a lovely young lady, but it was typical for her to overlap her plans and forget things; Kathy was so accustomed to this side of her that she no longer took her missed phone calls personally.

She took the chicken off the burner and brought her glass of wine to the living room. When she turned the TV on, the channel was set on News 14, so she left it on and almost absently listened to the weather forecast. Intense heat for the next several days...Kathy had a feeling this summer would be a long one. The next segment was about the woman found at Durant Park, so she turned up the volume and listened carefully.

According to the reporter, the police were not releasing much information pending a criminal investigation; there was speculation that the woman had been attacked by a stranger while she was jogging, so women were warned against walking alone, especially after dusk. The footage showed the entrance to the park on Perry Creek Road, and yellow tape could be seen in the distance. Several law enforcement officers were moving around the area, but they were too far away for Kathy to determine if Tom was among them. The next segment was about rebels making headway in Libya, and Kathy decided to turn off the set—not because she didn't care about the people of Libya, but simply because she had heard enough bad news today, and needed to clear her head instead.

She picked up a novel from Lillian Jackson Brown's series and tried to focus on the adventures of Koko, an extremely intelligent Siamese cat who helped his human, James Quilleran, solve several mysteries. This series was one of Kathy's favorites, even if she didn't own a cat and was more of a dog person. She quickly became so absorbed in the story that she felt she could almost reach out and touch Koko's silky fur. When she heard a loud noise in the hallway she jumped and looked around, unsure whether she had really heard it, or if her mind had made it up as a consequence of being so absorbed in a mystery novel. She decided to go check anyway, and put her wine glass down on the coffee table next to the book. As she turned the corner, she saw her personal camera on the floor and instantly panicked. How could it have fallen? She picked it up and examined every part of it; to her relief, it appeared to have suffered no damage. She took a few photos around the house to make sure the camera still worked and, satisfied that it wasn't broken, she placed it gently on the table near the door and headed back to the living room to continue reading.

Tom walked in a few minutes later. "Hey, Sweetheart! I'm home!"

Kathy put the book down and met Tom in the hallway where she kissed him, wrapping her arms around his waist in a welcoming hug. "I hope you are hungry. Some chicken *cacciatora* is waiting for you in the kitchen."

"Mmm-mmm…my favorite. You definitely know how to turn a bad day into a great evening."

Kathy smiled. "I have wine, too. Chilled Pinot Grigio."

Tom looked up toward the ceiling and brought his hands together as he smiled. "Thank you God, for giving me a woman who understands me and knows how to cook chicken *cacciatora*. And if the blessings weren't enough, she can also pick a good wine."

Kathy laughed. "You silly man! But that is exactly why I love you so. Let's go eat."

They walked into the kitchen together, and Kathy turned on the burner to warm up the chicken, while she placed a small baguette on a cookie sheet and tucked it into the oven. She poured Tom a glass of wine and got a new glass for herself, since she had left her other one in the living room. "So, anything new on the girl?"

Tom took a sip of wine before he answered. "Her name is Tracey Newman. The medical examiner still needs to confirm through dental records, but she looks exactly like a young woman who was reported missing last week. Aside from a gunshot wound, the body was intact, so it was easy to recognize. She was originally from Missouri, and was in Raleigh working as a physician assistant at Wake Memorial. She was twenty-three." Tom took another sip of wine and looked down. "In my job, I see death often, but no matter how many years I have done this, it is still hard to see such a promising young life being snuffed so senselessly and so early."

Kathy touched his hand in a gesture of comfort. "I know, Tom. Death rarely makes sense, but in cases such as this it is impossible for a normal mind to wrap itself around the reasoning behind it. Nothing is more precious than life, and yet people kill every day over money, over lovers, over meaningless disputes. I have thought about this young woman on and off all day; I have thought of her, and of her family; I have tried to put myself in her mother's shoes, and even that was almost too painful to bear. Has the family been notified?"

"Yes. This afternoon, and they are not taking it well. We are flying them in to identify the body. They are going to be devastated, especially her mother. From what I've heard, she is still deeply in denial. We got the name of the family dentist in St. Louis, and Tracey's stepfather has already requested release of the records to us. Hopefully, we will have them in the morning."

Tracey...what a lovely name... Kathy's mind was trying to process the information Tom had made available, and she became quiet for a moment. Then, before Tom could ask anything, she stood up, went to fetch two plates from the cupboard, and filled them with steaming chicken *cacciatora*. She refilled their glasses and took the bread out of the oven, then carried everything to the table. They ate in silence for the most part, only making small talk about meaningless and mundane matters that didn't touch either of them personally.

After their dinner, they washed dishes together, and then headed to bed. Kathy brought her novel along, but she couldn't concentrate on the words, so she turned off her reading light and lay still in the darkness of the room, careful not to wake Tom. *Tracey, who did this to you? I wish you could tell me.*

Another sound echoed in the silence of the hallway,

and Kathy jumped. Tom stirred but didn't wake up, so Kathy got up and went to check. When she turned on the light in the hallway, her camera was on the floor again. How could this be? Her mind raced in a million directions to seek a logical answer—maybe Tom had accidentally bumped it when he put down his keys? But if so, why did it wait so long to fall? She picked it up carefully and looked at it, wishing in her heart that the device could talk. She examined the camera again, and as had happened earlier, nothing seemed to be wrong with it. She put it down—this time against the wall and behind her handbag and sunglasses—and walked back slowly toward the bedroom, still wondering what could have caused the camera to fall. A sudden flash of light through the window made her gasp, but no thunder followed it—heat lightning, probably. She lay in bed and pulled the covers up to her chin, needing the comfort of something soft and warm. *Tracey didn't have anything soft and warm to comfort her before falling into eternal sleep...*

Chapter 4

Rose Howard held her daughter's hand while her husband checked their luggage at one of the kiosks in Lambert International Airport. The airport was still showing signs of damage from the tornado that had slammed through the structure just a couple of weeks before, and even if most of the damage was concentrated in Concourse C, the whole terminal buzzed with technicians and other personnel busy getting things back to normal. After they were checked in, they cleared security in Concourse A and, as they waited in line, Rose looked at every face in the crowd, expecting to see Tracey among the multitude of people rushing to catch their flights. But there was no Tracey. Rose felt disappointed, but didn't dare to voice her feelings to Mike, who was already worried enough. Mike was wrong, they were all wrong. Rose couldn't wait to confirm that the girl they had found wasn't her daughter. Mike had begged her to remain home with Alexis, but Rose had refused. There was no time for Alexis to go to Mike's mother, so they all decided to travel together; if anything, because they needed to feel the closeness of family.

"Would you like a cup of coffee, Sweetheart?" Mike's voice was full of concern.

"No, thank you. I had a cup before we left home. Alexis might like some hot chocolate, though." Rose loved Mike, but right now she couldn't stand the way he was hovering over her, so she was glad when Alexis nodded her head excitedly at the prospect of hot chocolate.

The two of them walked away together, and Rose watched them slowly blend in with the crowd until they disappeared from sight. She was a bit worried about Alexis, and felt guilty about her own reaction the day before. Alexis hadn't said a word after that, and she barely picked at her food when she was called down to dinner. Phantom Lily—as Rose and Mike had come to call the imaginary friend over the years—was not mentioned again, but Rose knew Alexis still believed it was really a girl and that she could talk to it.

The weather today was overcast, and the wind was blowing fiercely. Rose hoped it would cause no flight delays. So far, their flight was still on schedule, so she wedged her soft carry-on bag between her head and the wall and closed her eyes. She must have dozed off, because when Mike and Alexis came back from getting hot chocolate, it was already time to board.

She walked the ramp with resolve, her mind telling her that this trip would clear up all the mistakes and Tracey would come home, while her heart whispered an entirely different truth: When she allowed herself to listen to that inner voice she felt queasy.

In spite of the wind, the plane took off smoothly; in no time at all they were above the Gateway Arch, right before clouds got in the way, and Rose felt as if she and her family were floating through a limbo. Musing briefly about Dante's description of traveling from hell to limbo, and then to Paradise, it struck Rose that her own journey seemed to be moving backwards.

"Mom, how long will it take us to get there?" The sound of Alexis's voice was a welcome distraction.

"About an hour and thirty minutes, Sweetie. It's not too far."

Alexis was satisfied with the answer and she settled into her seat with a magazine.

"What is the name of the detective who's meeting us at the airport?" Rose asked Mike who lay against the seat with his eyes closed.

"Lieutenant Lackey, I think. I have it in my organizer. I assume they already made hotel reservations for us," Mike replied, closing his eyes again. Rose wondered if his eyes were just tired from watching her relentlessly. That thought made her smile.

"Strange name, Lackey. I wonder where his family came from." Rose interjected.

"Yeah, it sounds Irish, or Scottish maybe." Mike smiled at her, obviously relieved by her willingness to engage in small talk.

They went through the rest of the trip without

talking much, each of them pretending to be busy with something—crosswords and a kid's magazine featuring Justin Bieber—so they wouldn't need to dwell on what was waiting for them once they got off the plane in North Carolina.

#

Tom left for work before Kathy even got out of bed. When she woke up and went to the kitchen to get coffee, she saw the note he had left for her on the table. *I will call later and explain, but could you meet me at the station at ten?* She glanced at the digital clock on the stove and saw that it was only a little after seven. She had plenty of time to have coffee and to go by the studio, so she lazily reached out for the coffee pot and inhaled deeply. The seductive aroma of coffee snaked its way through her nostrils and reached her brain. The love affair between Kathy and coffee was one that had begun when she was only a teenager, and as years passed, the bond had tightened even more, if that was possible. She watched as the steaming brown liquid flowed effortlessly from the pot to the cup, and she silently thanked the unknown person who initially had the brilliant idea to roast beans, grind them and turn them into a beverage. The first sip was always monumental in her day, and she couldn't imagine starting her mornings without it. After two cups and a shower, she tried to call Tom before she left the house. As always, she got his answering machine, so she picked up her keys, camera and mobile phone and headed out the door. She hadn't even started the engine when the phone rang.

"Hey Sweetie, good morning." Even after all the years together, Tom's voice had the power to turn an average day into a good one.

"Good morning to you. I didn't even hear you leave this morning."

"It was super early. I needed to come in for a while, to make sure everything was in place before Tracey's parents get here."

"What time are they flying in?"

"Just after noon. And this leads me to ask…would you go with me?"

Kathy was a little surprised by Tom's request. "To pick them up, you mean? Why?"

"I have to go meet Doctor Greer as soon as I drop them off. I wondered if maybe you could hang out with them for a while and see that they are settled in. Given that you have a degree in psychology, maybe you can even suggest ways to cope with what they are going through. I know you have chosen to pursue a different career, but these people are probably in great need of a few good words."

Kathy was a little taken aback. In all the years they had been together, Tom had never mentioned her education as a clinical psychologist, and she wondered why this case was different. Regardless, she agreed. "Sure. Do you want me to meet you somewhere? In the message, you mentioned meeting at the station."

"Actually, the airport or the hotel would be great. That way I can go as soon as I introduce them to you."

"Which hotel is it?"

"The Ramada Inn on Capital. Do you know where it is?"

"Yes. What time do you want me to meet you?"

"I called the airport, and they confirmed the flight is going to be on time. It will take us about 30 minutes to drive back from the airport, so do you want to meet us around one, at the restaurant adjacent to the hotel?"

"It sounds great. I will see you there."

"Thank you, Honey. I love you."

"I love you, too."

Kathy clicked the end button on her phone and placed it on the passenger seat before she looked at her watch—9:30. There was time to go by her studio and work on the bridal portraits she had abandoned yesterday. When she arrived at the studio, she immediately sat at her desk and started her computer, working for the next hour and a half with no distraction. When she was finally happy with the results, she hit "Save," and was about to turn off the system when her eyes rested for a moment on her camera. It was so strange how the camera had fallen from the table last night! Not just once, but twice—how could something like that happen? She decided to upload the photos she shot around the house to her computer, to make sure the machine wasn't damaged. Connecting the camera to the

USB connector, she waited until the images appeared on the screen. At first glance they appeared fuzzy, so Kathy swallowed a spontaneous word her mother would not have been proud of, and clicked on one of the images to better understand what the problem was. The picture enlarged to cover most of the screen, and it showed the table in the hallway, but it appeared to be superimposed with a filmy, white splash of light. Had the flash gone off? She hadn't noticed it when she shot the photo, but now she couldn't be sure. She clicked on the other photos; the same sheer image also showed up in front of the couch, the sink in the guest bathroom, different areas of the kitchen, and the staircase. What could it be? Could it be possible that the flash was activated when she took all the photos and she didn't notice? Maybe the camera was damaged after all.

She sent the images to the laser printer to look at them more closely. After they were printed, she took them to her desk and arranged them side by side under the light. Now that she could look at all of them in sequence, she noticed something very strange: The foggy image over the items she had photographed was the same in all the pictures: same size, same shape, same optical illusion suggesting that what was staring at her from those photos was a woman screaming to get her attention. In one of the photos, the woman appeared to be pointing to a necklace laid on the bathroom counter.

#

Having never met Tracey's parents, and not knowing what to expect about their appearance, Tom had prepared a sign with their name written with a broad-pointed black marker. When he saw a middle-aged man about six feet tall, with sandy brown hair and dark brown eyes look in his direction, he immediately walked toward him. Detective Wheeler in St. Louis had indicated Mr. Howard was traveling with his wife Rose —Tracey Newman's mother—but he hadn't mentioned anything about a child coming along. He looked at Mrs. Howard, appreciating her quiet, simple beauty. Sporting mid-length blond hair and an attractive face even without make-up, Rose Howard was a very attractive woman and, as he focused on her face, he noticed that her resemblance to Tracey was breathtaking. The little girl traveling with them was very small, and Tom assumed she was only seven or eight years old. She had long blond hair, neatly combed into a pony tail. Her large blue eyes appeared sad and her shoulders slouched as she walked, as if she were carrying too big a burden for someone so young.

"Mr. Howard? I am Lieutenant Lackey."

Mike Howard extended his hand and flashed a warm smile at Tom. Although he didn't know for sure, Tom believed Mr. Howard to be a salesman.

"Thank you for meeting us, Lieutenant. This is my wife, Rose, Tracey's mother," he said using his right hand to introduce the woman standing by his side. "And this is our daughter, Alexis."

Tom nodded toward Mrs. Howard. "Ma'am, thank you for coming." Then he turned toward Alexis, and smiled kindly, offering a hand for her to shake. "Hi, Alexis, it is very nice to meet you." Alexis smiled back but didn't say a word.

They walked through the terminal without speaking much, moving mechanically through the motions of retrieving their luggage and using the bathroom before leaving the terminal. When they reached Tom's unmarked car, Tom opened the back door for Rose and Alexis, and he asked Mike Howard if he wanted to sit in the passenger seat.

Tom loaded their luggage in the trunk of the car, and soon they were on their way to the hotel. The silence in the car was almost palpable, as nobody could think of anything that should be said. There was a lot Rose wanted to know, but ignorance felt—right now—better than any truth she was afraid she might hear. Mike sat silently in front, mostly pretending he was staring at the view outside the window; Alexis just lay back against the seat, her eyes cast downward toward her hands, which were clasped on her lap. After a 20-minute ride on Interstate 40, they hopped onto the Beltline and, within minutes, they exited onto Capital Boulevard. Traffic was horrific—Capital Boulevard had been described by at least one member of the Raleigh 2030 Planning Commission as an example of a poorly-planned traffic corridor—and Mike wondered if the area was always this congested. It was lunchtime after all, and many people were taking their breaks.

The hotel appeared nice enough from the road; Mike was relieved they were finally here. He hoped Rose was correct in assuming that the body found wasn't Tracey's, though he didn't really put too much faith in that possibility. But, if it was Tracey, they could at least bring her home with them and give her a proper burial.

Tom pulled his car directly in front of the main entrance, cut the engine, and walked around to the trunk for the Howards' luggage. He and Mike rolled the bags in, while Rose and Alexis followed behind. Kathy walked in just as the desk clerk was handing them their keys. She knew she was early for their appointment, but since she was done with errands and she saw Tom's car when she drove by, she figured it wouldn't hurt to meet him in the lobby instead of the restaurant. She smiled and waited for Tom to introduce her.

"Mr. and Mrs. Howard, this is Kathy Spencer. She will make sure that all your needs are met. I have to leave in the next few minutes to attend to some police business, but Ms. Spencer can assist you and maybe take you to lunch. We are scheduled to meet with the Medical Examiner at his office at 4 p.m. and, if it is okay with you, I will come and pick you up at 3:15. There is a little paperwork we need to take care of, but it can wait until after you're settled in."

Mike and Rose Howard nodded in unison. Kathy shook their hands and smiled at Alexis. "Hi, what's your name?"

The little girl raised her eyes to look at her, and responded timidly. "Alexis," she said, but her voice was barely a whisper.

"You must excuse her, Ms. Spencer. She is quite shy, and I think she is a bit tired from the trip."

Kathy smiled wider. "Oh, I understand. It's perfectly okay and certainly to be expected. My major was in child psychology."

Rose looked at Kathy with renewed interest, and her eyes focused on Kathy's face as if she had just now realized Kathy was standing in front of them. "How interesting, Ms. Spencer. Children are amazing."

"They are indeed. I don't practice psychology—I am a photographer, but I really enjoyed working with children during the years of my training."

"I am sorry to interrupt, but I really need to run," Tom said softly. "Mr. and Mrs. Howard, I will see you in two hours, and Kathy…thank you."

"Don't mention it." Kathy smiled as Tom left. "Well, it's just us. Would you like to freshen up first, or would you like for me to show you where you can eat lunch?"

"The front desk can probably store our luggage. Would you like to join us for lunch, Ms. Spencer?"

Kathy thought for a moment. She didn't want to intrude, yet there was something about the dead young woman that profoundly called to her; maybe talking to her family could shed some light on why she felt so touched by this case. "Sure, I would love to."

After securing the luggage in the storage area, they walked outside. At this time of day, the heat was at its highest and very intense. Capital Boulevard was congested with cars slowly streaming past in both directions, and the muffled reverberation of a hundred engines was only briefly punctuated by the siren of a fire engine in the distance.

"There are many restaurants around here; what is your preference?"

"Anything, really," Mike Howard replied. Mrs. Howard confirmed with a nod of her head. Alexis was quiet and kept her eyes down. Kathy smiled at her. "What would you like to eat, Alexis? We have an Applebee's within walking distance. I hear they have fantastic chicken tenders and french fries."

Alexis looked up from her shoes and her lips formed a tiny smile. Kathy's heart went out to her—this was so hard for a child so young to process, and Alexis was probably very confused and scared. Feeling included was something she definitely needed right now, even if all she got to do was to choose the lunch venue. Mr. Howard picked up on it immediately. "Well, you love chicken tenders and french fries, don't you, Alexis? It sounds like the perfect restaurant." Alexis nodded softly and smiled at Kathy again. Mrs. Howard's eyes locked with Kathy's for a moment, and Kathy was sure she detected a silent "thank you" in them.

The four of them walked next door to the restaurant and were seated almost immediately. The food was hot and delicious, and—if only for a brief moment—it provided a sense of normalcy in a day that felt, for the most part, surreal.

True to what Mr. Howard said, Alexis cleared her plate in record time. With a full belly, her voice appeared to have surfaced again, and she started talking non-stop about her school in St. Louis, and about the spelling bee she had won just two weeks before.

"It sounds like you are a good student, Alexis. Do you like school?"

Alexis twisted her little nose to one side and appeared to be weighing the question. "Yes, I guess so. It's fun sometimes. Sometimes it is boring."

Everyone at the table chuckled, and the sound of laughter was like a healing balm for everyone, Kathy included. Her heart ached for this family, and she wished she could do something to alleviate their pain. She knew Rose Howard was doing her best to keep up a brave front, and she was sure a part of her was in firm denial. Mr. Howard's eyes were infused with sadness and worry, and he often looked out of the window near their booth in an almost-reflexive way that, to Kathy's observant eye, telegraphed his anxiety.

"You mentioned that you are a photographer, Ms. Spencer. What made you want to pursue this type of career if you had a degree in psychology?" Mrs. Howard asked.

Kathy thought for a moment before she replied. "I think I have always been intrigued by expressions. There is something magical about a person's eyes, and the way they convey so much about their feelings and personality. I have a passion for capturing different expressions. I specialize in portraits—weddings, school photos, ceremonies of different kinds."

"I love to take pictures!" Alexis volunteered. Her enthusiastic response warmed Kathy's heart.

"It's true." Mrs. Howard confirmed, with a fond look at the child. "Alexis takes pictures of everything. Thank goodness for digital cameras—we couldn't afford to buy or develop all the film she would use up, without them!"

"Well, Alexis," Kathy offered, "Maybe you can come and visit my studio before you go back home. You can try different pieces of equipment and see which one you are more comfortable with."

Alexis' eyes widened in surprise. "Really?! Would you let me use your camera?" Her head jerked from one parent to the next. "Mom and Dad, please…please, please…can we go?"

After her sulking mood of the past few days, Rose and Mike Howard felt like they had just witnessed a small miracle unfold. "If it is okay with Ms. Spencer, I don't see why not." Mr. Howard smiled kindly at his daughter.

"Mr. and Mrs. Howard, if you wish, Alexis can stay with me at the studio this afternoon, while you go with the police."

Rose and Mike Howard exchanged looks and thought for a moment. Mr. Howard spoke for both of them. "Alexis has already been exposed to enough, Ms. Spencer; I was worried about taking her with us this afternoon. We would be extremely grateful if you could show her your studio."

Kathy smiled. "That's wonderful. I will let you rest for a while after we leave the restaurant. I have an errand to run, but I will be back around three to pick

Alexis up. Of course, Lieutenant Lackey has my contact information already, but I will be happy to give you my mobile phone number before you go, in case you want to talk to Alexis while she is with me."

They made small conversation and ate a little. Mrs. Howard, still in denial, ate more than her husband, who barely picked at his plate of blackened tuna and steamed vegetables. There were many questions Kathy wanted to ask, but the tension was so high that she held back. She didn't want to say anything that might break the thread of balance she felt certain Rose Howard was clinging to at the moment. After they were finished, Kathy walked them back to their hotel and left. When she got in her car she started the engine, and her eyes fell on the folder filled with the strange photos she had developed earlier. *Is it you in those pictures, Tracey? What were you trying to tell me?*

In her heart, Kathy knew that something incredible was getting ready to happen.

Chapter 5

"Mrs. Howard, we are ready." The young woman dressed in blue surgical attire smiled softly when she made her announcement. She appeared to be about thirty years old, with blond hair tied in a short ponytail and green eyes framed by long lashes. She barely made a sound as she walked toward Rose, Mike and Tom, who were sitting in the waiting area, and Rose wondered if the unnerving quietness of her steps was connected to her extremely petite size, or to self-training—working in a place such as this, where every tiny sound echoed against the white-washed walls and the hard floors, one had to feel a bit self-conscious about making any noise.

Rose felt dizzy when she stood up, so she closed her

eyes and touched the edge of the seat to restore her balance. A voice screamed inside of her head, telling her that within minutes her world would crumble, but Rose silenced it quickly; she felt relieved when a sudden rush of adrenaline released in her bloodstream and stiffened her spine. She locked eyes with the young woman—Jacqueline Worth, her name tag said—and walked resolutely toward the door the woman was holding open for her. "Very well, let's go."

"Rose, I can go in your place. Why don't you wait here?" Mike called out, but Rose ignored his desperate attempt to shield her from trauma and continued to walk.

She followed Ms. Worth down a starkly white hallway, completely oblivious to the fact that Tom was following behind and, as they walked, they passed another employee pushing an empty gurney. Like Ms. Worth, he was very young—too young, almost, to work in a place like this, where one came face to face with death every day. They stopped by a closed door to the right, and Ms. Worth knocked softly.

"Come in." The voice from inside sounded older

and throaty. *An older man...*

When they entered, Rose saw a gurney pushed against the wall, only a few feet away from a large window covered by white blinds. On the gurney was a white sheet lined with blue at the edges and the shape of a human body beneath the sheet captured Rose's gaze and her breath, momentarily. She suddenly felt her hands shake; her breathing became labored. Ms. Worth laid a small hand over her arm, to ground her and make her feel less alone, and she gently helped Rose walk closer to the gurney. Rose wanted to close her eyes and scream, as the reality of what was happening hit her square in the chest and she felt her heart break in a thousand sharp pieces.

"Mrs. Howard, would you like to sit down?" The older gentleman who spoke had hair and a beard as white as the pristine world that surrounded him.

Rose shook her head and bit her lower lip. "No, I'm okay. Thank you." She attempted to smile, but her face felt riveted to the silhouette under the sheet. She saw the man nod almost imperceptibly to the young woman; after what felt like hours, Ms. Worth's tiny hands gripped the edges of the sheet and lowered it to expose the face of the young woman laying lifeless on the cold metal gurney. The face of her Tracey. Seeing the blond hair tidily arrayed…noticing the pasty white color of her daughter's once peach-toned complexion…something in Rose's head shut off. Her mind desperately tried to erase the image her eyes transmitted and, when it was unable to do so, Rose felt a sudden rush of heat flowing to her cheeks. Then everything went dark.

Rose didn't know where she was when she regained consciousness. All she heard was Mike's voice speaking softly to her, against the background of a loud buzzing that seemed to surround the entire room. "Rose, I'm here, Sweetheart. I'm here." Mike brought her limp hand to his lips and kissed it gently, and when Rose looked into his eyes, she saw a reflection of her own pain. She briefly glanced at Tom, who stood a respectful distance away against the wall and said nothing; then she turned away and closed her eyes, thankful for the numbness that had taken her heart hostage. The illusion she had clung to for the last few days had shattered in a matter of seconds. The detectives were right: The dead young woman was Tracey.

When the white-haired man she had noticed earlier came into the room, Rose turned toward him, her expression telling the old doctor and the Lieutenant what they were waiting to know. Although Mike had volunteered to ID the body when he was informed his wife had fainted, Dr. Greer's reply indicated he saw no reason to inflict that type of pain on both parents. While Dr. Greer obviously didn't know that Mike was not Tracey's natural father, Mike chose not to press the issue.

"I'm sorry, Mrs. Howard. Losing a child is devastating. I will have a nurse come in and take your blood pressure before you go, but I have to ask you to sign these papers for me, to confirm that you positively identify the body as being your daughter's." Dr. Greer's voice was much more subdued and respectful than what Rose first heard when Ms. Worth had knocked on the door.

Rose didn't answer, but Mike nodded and took the papers. Dr. Greer exited the room quietly and Tom followed him outside. The nurse must have been right behind the door, for when the doctor left, she arrived within seconds. Her hair was a warm caramel color, pulled back into a soft bun from which a few rebellious curls had escaped. Unlike Ms. Worth—who looked as if she could stand a few extra meals—this nurse was plump and motherly, and Rose wondered if Dr. Greer reserved her for moments such as this, when someone's world had entirely collapsed.

"Doctor Greer sent me to take your blood pressure, Mrs. Howard." The nurse said with a soft, melodious voice as she placed two fingers on the inside of Rose's wrist to gauge her pulse, as well.

"He told us you were coming." Mike said before moving out of the way to let the nurse through.

After measuring Rose's blood pressure, the nurse looked at her face. "Well, you are still weak, and your pulse is a little low, but your blood pressure is not too bad—115 over 75—so I think it will be okay for you to go when you are ready." She smiled at Rose and was about to walk out the door, when she stopped and turned around. She sat on the chair Mike had occupied until a few moments before, and took Rose's hand into her own, while she stroke Rose's hair with the other. "I lost my little girl too, a few years ago. I know how you are feeling."

Her words were the magic touch that rescued Rose from the icy prison which had sprung up around her heart the moment she saw Tracey laying on the gurney and, as Rose looked into her eyes, she saw that the woman was sincere. Their common loss was a bond stronger than death itself. Rose squeezed her hand, almost throwing herself into the arms of the woman sitting by her side. She rested her head on the woman's ample bosom and sobbed. The woman's arms wrapped around Rose as unchecked tears ran down her cheeks. After a few moments the tears subsided, and Rose pulled back to look at her. "Thank you…I know that you understand completely."

The woman smiled, one of her plump hands quickly wiping her own face as she stood up. "Yes, and I can tell you that it will be a long journey for you. The pain will dull over time, but your daughter will never leave your heart. You will crave to hear the sound of her voice when you need comfort, and when you need to hear it, it will be there, forever recorded somewhere deep inside of you. To this day, if I close my eyes, I can hear my Lisa talking to me. If you have any other children, focus on them, and be grateful for the time you are given with them, no matter how long it is. Your pain might push you to focus on the time you no longer have to spend with your daughter, but I advise you to focus on the time you had with her, because that was a gift to you from God. Some souls are so pure that they only agree to come here for a short while with the distinct purpose to teach us something, and any of us who had them in our lives are very fortunate." With that, the woman walked toward the door, and with one last smile, she was gone. Rose regretted not asking what her name was.

#

Kathy watched Alexis with pride, as the girl ran her delicate fingers over the camera while her eyes reflected her excitement at being able to handle such a sophisticated piece of equipment.

"Wow! This is so nice..." Alexis said while she kept

her eyes fixed on the camera.

Kathy smiled and placed her hand over Alexis' tiny one. "Alexis, how are you feeling, honey?"

Alexis seemed surprised at the question. "I am okay. I just don't understand some things."

"That's a lot to process. Would you like to talk about it?"

Alexis was quiet for a moment, her mind assessing the question, then she looked at Kathy, and her eyes filled with tears. "I'm going to miss Tracey. My mom says Tracey's still alive, but I know she is dead. Lily said…" She stopped abruptly, and bit on her lower lip. Her eyes darted up and down the room as if she was trying to make sure nobody could have heard.

"Lily?" Kathy asked softly, "Is she a friend of yours?"

Alexis thought for a moment, her small hands kneading the top of the camera she was holding; it was obvious that she was making a decision at that very moment.

"Yes," she said as she nodded her head and averted her eyes. "Lily is my friend."

"That's great. Do you and Lily go to school together?"

"Sometimes." Alexis answered evasively.

Kathy was a bit confused but tried hard not to show it. "Only sometimes?" She could sense Alexis' discomfort, and almost let the matter go, when Alexis spoke.

"My mom and dad say Lily doesn't exist, but she does!"

Kathy caught on immediately. "Do your parents call Lily your imaginary friend?"

Alexis's eyes opened wide. "Yes! But she is not imaginary. I can really see her. Has anything like that ever happened to you?"

"No, unfortunately not. But, my sister had one—Jenny—and she talked to her all the time. I used to be jealous of her, because if my sister played with Jenny, I didn't have a playmate."

"Did your sister tell you Jenny was real?"

Kathy smiled. "Yes, many times. And our parents never believed her."

"Same with my parents. They think I made Lily up.

I told my mom what Lily said the other day, and she got really mad at me."

Kathy wanted to know more. "How old is Lily?"

"Hmm…I never asked her exactly, but I think she is about twelve."

"What type of games do you play with her?"

"Anything we come up with together. Sometimes she decides, and other times I do. She likes to play Hide and Go Seek, and another game called Charades. It's a word game, you know. Lily says she used to play it all the time. I like to play computer games, but she says she can't play those."

"I know Charades—my sister and I played sometimes, too. It's an old game which goes back as far as Civil War times." Kathy said animatedly.

"Wow! Really?"

"Yes, a lot of the popular games kids play today originated in the past." Kathy paused for a moment. "So," she then asked, "what did Lily say that made your mom so mad?"

Alexis remained briefly silent, her small hand touching her left cheek. When she spoke, she shook her head softly. "Lily said that Tracey is not coming back, that she's dead."

Kathy arched her eyebrows. "I can see how something so devastating would upset your mom; she is probably still clinging to the hope of finding your sister alive. Did you ask Lily how she knows?"

Alexis shrugged her shoulders. "When I ask her questions, sometimes she just runs off laughing and asks to play. You know, one time Lily helped me find a bracelet I thought I had lost. She told me to look at the bottom of my old toy basket and there it was! Do you think she hid it there herself, just to mess with me?"

Kathy remembered reading several case studies discussing imaginary friends, but she couldn't recall any of them describing similar experiences. "I'm not sure, Alexis. Does Lily ever tell you anything about her life?"

"No, not really. I once asked her why she dresses funny, and she didn't really understand what I was talking about. I thought maybe her family is Amish or something. She always wears these weird dresses and she doesn't know what an MP3 player is. At first I thought she was a bit strange, but she is nice and I like to talk to her."

"That's interesting," Kathy replied. "Maybe her mom sews her clothes."

"Yeah, maybe." Alexis replied, and then her attention reverted back to the camera. "What kind of camera is it?"

"It's a Canon EOS7D. Do you like it?"

'Oh yes! How many megapixels?"

"Eighteen. It's a very versatile camera. And a very expensive one, at that. I usually leave this one at the studio, and only carry the other one with me wherever I go."

Alexis was intrigued. "You mean you have more than one camera you use?"

"Yes. I use this one for portraits and other professional shots, and I carry a smaller Canon for personal use. See? That one over there on my desk. It is a Canon Powershot. It only has nine megapixels, but it is a very reliable camera."

Alexis carefully handed the larger camera back to Kathy and hopped off the couch, heading toward Kathy's desk.

"I like this one," She said as she extended a hand to touch the small camera. "It's more like something I would use. I would worry about messing up the other one. Does it take good pictures?"

Kathy joined her at the desk." Yes, it really does for a small camera. And it is durable, too. It dropped off the table twice last night, and it still functions. I took some photos around the house with it, to make sure it wasn't damaged, and it seemed to work well. The only problem is that the photos seem to have too much light...all of them came out a little strange."

Alexis arched her eyebrow and looked at Kathy. "What do you mean by strange?"

"I'm not sure. I don't think I've ever seen anything like that. They all show an extra shot of light superimposed over the items I was shooting."

"That's wild," Alexis said with as much professional demeanor as she could muster. "Can I see them?"

Kathy shrugged. "I don't see why not. Let me get them for you; I even printed them out." She opened her briefcase and took out a manila folder. She pulled out the pictures, and laid them side by side in front of

Alexis. "See what I'm saying? They all have the same light. I thought maybe the camera was damaged, but I tried taking a few more photos with it, and they came out fine. So, I have no clue what happened to these shots." She turned on the lamp over the pictures to make it easier for Alexis to see them.

Alexis didn't say anything at first. Her eyes darted back and forth from one photo to the next, and her chin began to quiver.

Kathy noticed immediately that something wasn't right. "What's wrong, Alexis? Are you okay?"

Alexis continued to shake her head, and by now tears were running freely down her cheeks. Her hands were shaking as she ran a finger over the images, and she swallowed audibly several times.

"For God's sake, Alexis, what's wrong? You're scaring me!"

Alexis turned to look at Kathy, and her words came out in a pained whisper. "This isn't light, Miss Kathy... this is my sister, Tracey."

#

When Tom got home, Kathy was sitting at the small desk in the kitchen looking at the photos she had shot the night before. She was so taken by her task that she didn't even hear him come in. He stood at the doorway and watched her for a moment—he loved the look on her face when she was completely absorbed by something she was working on. Kathy picked up one shot and looked at it under the light; then she placed it beside the others and seemed to be studying them as a whole. Suddenly she stopped and turned around. "Hey, I didn't know you were home. How long have you been there in the shadows?" She said smiling; then she stood up and pushed her chair against the desk.

Tom walked toward her and wrapped his arms around her waist. "Just a couple of minutes. I love to watch you while you are working. You look like a sexy librarian with those reading glasses on."

Kathy laughed. "A sexy librarian? I like that!"

"So, what's for dinner?"

"Hmm...I'm not sure yet. I just got here not too long ago myself—I had to drop Alexis off at the hotel, remember?"

Tom nodded. "Yes. I so appreciate you chipping in. The family is very distressed. I can only imagine how hard it will be to break the news to their younger daughter."

Kathy tried her best to sound casual, though she knew there really wasn't a way to say what she was going to say and not sound insane. "Alexis already knew, Tom."

Tom shook his head sadly. "Children can be very intuitive, unfortunately. Alexis must have heard some of the conversations between her parents and the detectives who went to their home."

"No, Tom. You're not hearing me…I mean that Alexis really knew. She has a friend she talks to, and her friend told her about Tracey." As she uttered those words, Kathy realized how strange they sounded, even to herself.

"I'm not following you, Kathy. What friend? Should the police know about this?"

"No, no…it's a different type of friend. What you would call an imaginary friend."

Tom raised his eyebrows and his eyes got wider. "An imaginary friend? And this imaginary friend told Alexis about her sister? Of course she did—I assume it is a 'she,' right?—isn't that what imaginary friends do? Kids make them up to feel less alone. That's why they are called 'imaginary.'"

"That's correct, Tom, but I don't think it is the case with Alexis. I really believe Lily is a spirit rather than a figment of her imagination."

Tom looked at Kathy as if she had suddenly grown three heads. "A spirit?! You can't be serious, Kathy. Tell me you don't really believe that."

Kathy weighed her words for a moment. She wanted to tell Tom about the photos, and she already knew that he wasn't going to be very receptive if she pushed the "spirit" issue too far, so she decided to be diplomatic. "I'm not sure, Tom. Alexis was reticent to talk; it was like she was scared I wasn't going to believe her. But, some of the things she said are so unusual for a child to make up that I think they came from someone else."

Tom's curiosity was piqued, but he asked cautiously, "What sort of things?"

"Well," Kathy answered, "for one thing, this Lily wears strange clothes for a modern child, and she won't touch a computer; she doesn't even know what an MP3 player is."

"That's it?" Tom sounded a little surprised. "What kind of imaginary friend did you expect her to create? A gang member?" As soon as the words escaped his lips, Tom noticed that his tone was more irritated than he ever meant for it to be. "I'm sorry, Kathy…it has been a very long, exhausting day. I really appreciate the fact that you were willing to help, and I am sure it was good for Alexis to have someone to talk to, but we are dealing with a child who just lost her big sister—some strange things are going to come out of her mouth."

From his words and tone, Kathy knew that this wasn't a good time to expand the conversation, so she decided to focus on dinner and to leave the really spooky stuff for later, hoping that a full stomach and a backrub would make Tom more receptive. "You're right, Tom. It has been a long day for all of us. Why don't you go change while I whip up something for dinner?" She tried her best to smile nonchalantly.

Tom smiled. "It sounds like a very good plan. I'll be back in a minute." With that, he left the room and Kathy opened cabinets to find something fast and easy to prepare. She found a box of Macaroni and Cheese in the pantry, so she put a pot of water to boil on the stove and some dinner rolls in the oven. She was too tired to enjoy a glass of wine and knew it would quickly put her to sleep, but she also needed Tom to relax enough to hear what she had to say, so she poured two glasses and brought them to the table. By the time Tom came back to the kitchen, everything was ready. They ate quietly for the most part, but Kathy's heart skipped a beat when Tom asked her if she was working on something new.

"No, not particularly. I'm working on a wedding package, but I am down to the last few touches. The bride is gorgeous—she doesn't need too much help to look breathtaking."

"Is that what you were working on when I came in? You were completely taken by those pictures…it almost looked as if you were holding your breath."

This is the perfect time... Kathy toyed with the idea of showing the photos to Tom, but how could she convey what she wanted to say without sounding like she had completely lost her mind? The story of Alexis's imaginary friend had already created friction earlier, and the last thing Kathy wanted to do was to make Tom wonder about her sanity. "Do you have any recent photos of Tracey, Tom?"

Given that Kathy was a photographer who specialized in portraits made the request sound legitimate.

"Yes...I have one on my computer. Why?"

"Just wondering. Would you like another glass of wine?"

"No, thank you. I am so tired that if I drink more than one glass tonight, you will need to carry me to bed."

Kathy smiled coyly. "That's not a bad idea, then. Have another glass." She winked suggestively.

Tom grinned, and he stretched on the chair with satisfaction, thinking that this evening was getting better and better by the minute.

#

Alexis sat on her hotel bed, mentally recalling all that had happened throughout the day. She and her parents had adjoining rooms and the door was ajar; she was trying to be extra quiet in order to not disturb her mother, who was already resting when Kathy dropped Alexis off. Her father had gone out to get some tea for her mother about 30 minutes earlier, and no sound came from her parents' room. According to her father, Rose had taken a sedative when they first got back to the hotel, and she was still asleep. Alexis thought it was a little odd for her mother to take medication to help her sleep so early in the day, but when she saw her father's swollen, red eyes, she didn't have the heart to ask any questions. She already knew Tracey was gone, but her parents hung on to the illusion of bringing her home alive, and their world had crumbled under their feet when they found out it was never going to be. So she sat on her bed and mindlessly looked at a word search magazine her mother had bought her for the trip, but she couldn't focus on finding any of the words.

She didn't know how much time had gone by when she heard a sound and realized her father was back. She tiptoed to the door between the rooms and saw her father quietly placing the cup full of steaming tea on the small table near the window. When he heard the door move, he turned around and smiled at Alexis. "You're awake."

"Yes, Daddy. Is Mom okay?"

Mike put a finger in front of his lips to signal to Alexis that she should let her mother sleep, then he walked toward the separating door and into her room. He closed the door and sat at the edge of her bed. "Mom is going to be okay. What about you, Alexis? Are you okay?" He raised a hand to ruffle her hair, and Alexis rested her face on it. "I'm fine. I already knew, Daddy... you know that. You and Mom think that Lily is not real, and that I've made her up, but I swear, I haven't. Lily told me Tracey was dead before those police men even came to the house."

Mike sighed heavily. "Look, Alexis, we've talked

about Lily before, and even Doctor Taylor explained to you that she is not real—she seems real to you, but she is not."

Alexis didn't say a word, so Mike stood up and kissed the top of her head. "Try to get some sleep, Alexis. Mom is going to need both of us tomorrow."

Alexis nodded and lay her head on the pillow, but as her father got ready to step through the door to go back into his own room, she said: "Do you remember the lighter you lost last month, Daddy? The one that belonged to Granddaddy?"

"Of course I remember. What about it?"

"It's in the tool drawer in the garage."

Mike raised his brow. "How do you know that? Did you see it there?"

"No. Lily told me to tell you it's there. You put it there when that salesman came up our driveway to sell you lawn treatments and you forgot about it."

Mike smiled. "Okay, Alexis. Tell Lily thank you and try to get some sleep."

He turned off the light on his way out and closed the door quietly behind him.

\#

"Goodnight, Kathy." Tom stretched his legs on the clean sheets and hugged his pillow. Their lovemaking had not lasted long tonight, but both of them were happy and relaxed.

"Goodnight, Tom. I love you."

Tom turned off the night light and wrapped his arm around Kathy. Kathy lay there awake, her mind shooting in a million directions. She had tried to find a way to tell Tom about the photos, but the right moment hadn't come along. Sensing that something was wrong, Tom hugged her more tightly, but Kathy couldn't shut down.

"Are you okay, Kathy?"

"I'm fine…" she murmured.

"I know you are not fine. What is it?" Tom nudged her gently.

"Do you really want to know, Tom?" The light was off, but she could see that Tom's eyes were open and looking at her intently.

"If it is not about ghost friends, yes."

Kathy sighed before she spoke. "It's not about ghost friends, Tom…it's about ghosts, period."

"What do you mean? Have you seen a ghost?" Tom said jokingly.

"Yes." Kathy didn't know how else to say it.

"You are kidding, right?" Tom wasn't sure if this was a question or a wish spoken out loud.

"I am not kidding, Tom. Let me show you something." She quickly got out of bed and went to the kitchen to fetch the photos she had taken the night before. When she returned to their room, Tom saw she was holding something and, since she had mentioned having something to show him, he turned on the night light and fluffed up his pillow before raising himself over his elbow.

"Here. Look at these." She handed him the snapshots, one at a time.

Tom looked at them carefully. "I can't really see anything. They appear to be taken around our house, but they are unfocused."

"That's what I thought too, at first. Since the camera fell on the floor—twice—I took a few shots to make sure it wasn't broken. All the photos show the same image superimposed on them. I thought maybe the flash went off, but it couldn't have happened to all of them without me knowing it."

"Okay…so, where are you going with this?"

"Look at the pictures, Tom, and look at the image. It is exactly the same shape and density on all of them."

Tom looked closer, and Kathy moved the night light to shine right over the photos Tom was holding. "What does it make you think of?"

Tom was quiet and, for a fleeting moment, Kathy saw a shadow of awareness flash briefly in his eyes. "What do you see, Tom?"

Tom looked away for a split second, then he turned to meet Kathy's scrutinizing gaze. "If I didn't know better, I would say I am looking at Tracey Newman."

Chapter 6

Tom took a sip of ginger ale from the can he had purchased when he stopped to fuel his car and grimaced. Cutting down on coffee was the greatest sacrifice he had to make in the name of health, but Dr. Valensky didn't exactly leave it as an option. High blood pressure had already forced him to quit smoking, and now he had to give up yet another pleasure—not entirely, since he would never agree to it, but he was down to no more than two cups a day. There were days when Tom wanted to shoot Dr. Valensky the bird and go on a coffee binge. Somehow, getting up in the morning and knowing he could only have one cup made getting out of bed even harder, and most days he developed a dull headache around mid-day, probably from caffeine withdrawal.

Today the headache was here ahead of schedule, and that alone was enough to irritate Tom to no end. He tried not to think about it, as he turned right on Louisburg Road and headed toward Perry Creek. The sky was overcast and the temperature was a bit cooler, so he cracked his window and looked for the apartment complex where Tracey Newman had lived. When he arrived, he pulled his unmarked car into one of the parking spots in front of the building and went up to the second level. A dead plant was standing guard beside the door, and Tom wondered if it died before or after Tracey. He almost expected to find no one there when he knocked, but the door opened to show an attractive brunette clad in gym shorts and a sport bra, carrying a white T-shirt over her right shoulder. Her hair was pulled into a ponytail and she wore a baseball cap. Under the visor, Tom noticed that her eyes were red and slightly swollen. One of them looked faintly bruised.

"Can I help you?"

"Are you Shannon Brinkley?" Tom asked in a soft

but direct tone.

"Yes, that's me, how can I help you?"

"Ms. Brinkley, I am Lieutenant Tom Lackey, from the Raleigh Police Department. May I speak with you for a moment?"

Shannon Brinkley took one step back and turned to look behind before she spoke. "Of course, Lieutenant. Please come in."

Tom followed her to the living room and sat down on a loveseat. "How long has it been since you've seen Tracey Newman, Ms. Brinkley?"

Shannon paused to think before she replied. "A little over a week, I think; maybe two weeks. She didn't show up for work and the hospital called here looking for her. At first I thought maybe she had gone somewhere with Brad, but he doesn't seem to know where she is either."

"Brad?"

"Her boyfriend. They dated on and off. I sort of had the impression they were on the mend lately, so I thought they might have gone off on a romantic trip and she lost track of time. When she still didn't come home the next few days I began to worry and called different friends. Nobody had seen her, so I called her parents to let them know."

"Was it typical for Ms. Newman to leave unexpectedly and without notifying anyone?"

"Not typical, but she could be impulsive at times. She really liked Brad, and I think she would have done anything to get back with him, even if he was seeing someone else."

"Do you know why she and her boyfriend were fighting?"

Shannon hesitated. "Look, I don't want to get anyone in trouble. Maybe it would be best if you talk to him directly."

Tom nodded. "Do you know how to get in touch with him, Ms. Brinkley?"

"Yes. I will write down his name and contact information." She stood up and went to her computer desk in the far right corner of the room, to find a pen and a sheet of paper. She scribbled down the phone number and handed it to Tom. "Here you go. You can probably find him at work by this time of the morning; I wrote down his work number—he works at a warehouse somewhere in South Raleigh. I also wrote down his mobile number."

Tom took the note and tucked it into a jacket pocket. "Thank you, Ms. Brinkley. You have been most helpful. Listen, can you think of anyone who would have wanted to harm Ms. Newman?"

"Harm her? No, certainly not. Tracey was the kindest person I knew."

"How was your relationship with her?"

"My relationship with her?" Shannon opened her eyes in surprise. "We were very close, Lieutenant. We roomed together for the last two years and we were very compatible. Do you have any idea of her whereabouts yet?"

Tom nodded. "Unfortunately, we have discovered her body not too far from here. Her name hasn't been disclosed to the press because her family only recently identified her. I'm sorry."

Shannon sat on the larger couch. Pain registered on her face. "Her *body*? You found her dead?"

"I'm afraid so, Ms. Brinkley."

"But…what happened? I mean, how did she die?"

"I am not at liberty to discuss details with anyone who's not part of her immediate family. I apologize."

"We were not blood related, but we were like sisters."

"I understand, Ms. Brinkley, but unfortunately, I can't disclose any information on the case. Her parents are in town, if you would like to talk to them. They are staying at the Ramada Inn on Capital Boulevard."

Shannon nodded, her tears held back by a dam of disbelief. "But who would have wanted to kill her? She was a kind soul."

Tom didn't reply, though he noticed that the young woman consistently talked about her friend in the past tense even before he told her about the body being found, and used the word "killed" even if she had no way of knowing how Tracey died.

"I need to take a look at Ms. Newman's room, if it is possible."

Shannon stood up and walked toward the hallway as if in a daze. "Follow me, Lieutenant."

She led Tom to a room on the left side and opened the door. Tracey's private world opened up in front of his eyes. He stepped through the doorway and saw the bed had been neatly made up before Tracey left her room for the last time. Even though the walls were painted white—standard for rental apartments—they were adorned with small, Kinkaid cottage prints and paintings of Victorian children playing in flowery gardens. The bed spread also had a flowery motif and her small desk was tidy. The drawers of the desk contained a few office supplies and a blank notebook. A large bookshelf filled with textbooks and romance novels covered one of the walls in its entirety. When Tom opened the closet, he found a half-full laundry basket on the floor, with Tracey's clothing neatly hung above. Everything in Tracey's room was meticulously organized and clean, clearly indicating her life as being orderly and well planned—hardly someone likely to run off on a wild weekend with a boyfriend and blowing off work on a whim, without so much as a phone call. Nothing seemed to be out of place. Still scanning the closet, Tom noticed a box filled with letters. He picked it up and browsed through its contents. Most of the letters were written in an uneven hand and bore no return address. Some of the others were written by her mother; some by a man in Missouri who shared Tracey's last name.

"Who is Frank Newman?" Tom asked Shannon, who was standing by the doorway.

"That's her father. Frank and Rose divorced when Tracey was about ten years old."

It never occurred to Tom that the heartbroken man he had met the previous afternoon was not Tracey's biological father.

"Is he still in St. Louis?"

"Yes, as far as I know. Tracey didn't have a close relationship with him, but they talked from time to time."

Tom made a mental note to call the department in St. Louis and request that someone go to notify the father. It was possible that—as distressed as she was— Rose Rose Howard wasn't going to call him right away, and Frank Newman had the right to know his daughter was no longer living. He opened one of the letters without a return address and found a name at the bottom of the text: Jack. "Who's Jack?"

Shannon blew out a lungful of air and rolled her eyes. "Jack Little. That's Tracey's previous boyfriend."

"Do you mind if I take this box?"

Shannon shook her head. "No. It's okay, I guess."

"Shannon!" A deep woman's voice echoed from the other side of the hallway. Shannon jumped nervously when her name was called. Tom looked at her questioningly.

"That's my friend, Mary. Sorry...she works night shift, and she must have just woken up. Would you excuse me for a moment?"

"Of course."

Shannon slipped into the other bedroom of the apartment and, although Tom tried his best to hear the conversation between the two women, the door she had pulled closed behind her after entering the room muffled most of the sound. He looked around Tracey's room a little longer, but finding nothing else of immediate interest, he headed back toward the living room. He was just about to sit down when Shannon walked into the room. "I apologize. Mary stays here sometimes. She is experiencing some financial difficulties and I am trying to help her out."

Tom nodded. "I understand completely. Does Mary —I'm sorry, I didn't catch her last name—did she know Tracey?"

Shannon hesitated, her eyes darting toward the hallway. As Tom followed her gaze, his eyes fell upon a whole lot of woman walking toward them. Mary Whatever-Her-Last-Name-Might-Be could have been a linebacker on a men's football team. She sported cropped, prematurely graying hair, exposing all too clearly a face that didn't match her gender. Her cheekbones were chiseled and her eyes were small and dark brown; her pencil-thin lips accentuated the harsh look that fit perfectly with her large frame. At a good six feet of height, Mary appeared to have more muscle mass than Tom did. She was dressed in cut-off denim shorts that didn't flatter her legs at all, and a faded red T-shirt of unknown brand. "I overheard you while I was walking out of my room, Lieutenant. Yes, I knew Tracey. It's very unfortunate—her death, I mean."

"How long have you known Ms. Newman, Ms…?"

"Townsend. Mary Townsend. Not too long. Tracey

was already Shannon's roommate when we started seeing each other."

Tom saw Shannon blush a deep shade of crimson, but he pretended not to notice the younger woman's discomfort. "Where do you live, Ms. Townsend?"

Mary plopped on the couch without much etiquette. "I live here now. Shannon is helping me through a rough spot."

"I see." Tom replied and saw the two women looking at each other. He pulled two business cards out of his pocket and handed one to each of them. "If you remember anything else, please call me at any of the numbers on the card." He stood up and headed toward the front entrance. Shannon followed him to open the door. "Thank you for coming by, Lieutenant."

Tom nodded. "Duty, Ms. Brinkley. I am sorry for your loss."

Shannon bit on her lower lip and swallowed audibly. Tears welled in her eyes. "Thank you. I have her mother's mobile number. I think I will call...and maybe I will go by and see her parents today."

Tom went outside and, when he was sliding into in

his car, realized he had not obtained any contact information for the linebacker. He thought about returning to the apartment to ask, but he was in a rush to talk to Brad Johnson; he also needed to make a few phone calls, to locate Frank Newman and the mysterious Jack Little. As he drove off, mentally running through his to-do list, he never noticed that someone was watching him.

#

Brad Johnson pulled the last box out of the truck and ran a hand over his short blond hair while he waited for Darryl Stedman to come help him carry the load into the warehouse. A buzzing sound from his back pocket alerted him to a text message, so he looked at his phone and saw that the message was from Shannon.

"Call me. It's important." Brad looked at the time, glad that his lunch break was only about an hour away. He hoped to be done with these boxes before then— nothing like carrying heavy boxes on a full stomach. He needed to text Shannon back, but as soon as he started

typing, Darryl—an African American man of about 45 with a happy smile and a sunny disposition—came outside, and Brad returned his phone to his pocket. He and Darryl worked relentlessly for the next half-hour, during which time his phone buzzed at least six times. What could possibly be so pressing that it couldn't wait? If he really wanted to, he could reply—but part of him didn't want to know what Shannon had to say. He suspected she wanted to talk about Tracey, and right now really wasn't the time. He was ready to leave and go to lunch, when he heard his name on the speaker: "Brad Johnson, line one!"

Assuming that it was his supervisor checking on the status of the order, he walked to the wall phone and pressed the first button. "Brad Johnson."

"What the hell is wrong with you? Why aren't you answering my messages?" Shannon's voice came through as a hiss.

"I'm working, Shannon. It's been a busy morning. And why are you calling me at work? You know my boss doesn't like personal calls, unless there is an emergency."

Shannon's voice sounded frantic. "This *is* an emergency, you idiot! A detective with RPD came by earlier. They found Tracey's body."

Brad closed his eyes and swallowed hard. His throat suddenly felt constricted; he was struggling to breathe. His legs felt weak, too, and for a moment he had to lean against the wall to steady himself.

"When?"

"He didn't say, but he questioned me…and Mary."

"What did you say?"

"Nothing. What could I say?"

"Are you sure?"

"Of course I am sure!

"When did they find her?"

"He didn't say, exactly. A few days ago, I think. Her family is here in Raleigh. I gave the detective your mobile phone number and your work number."

"Why on earth would you do that?"

"He asked. He was going to find out sooner or later, anyway. I have to go. Call me after you talk to him."

"Yeah…I will." Brad hung up without even saying goodbye. He couldn't believe his name had come up—

what would happen if they found out? He returned the handset to the wall and headed inside to clock out for lunch. When he got to his car, he laid his head back against the seat and took a deep breath. He had a lot at stake. He needed to come up with a plan, or he would have no choice but to face the consequences of his actions.

#

Tom was eating lunch when the phone rang. Before going to visit Brad Johnson at work, he wanted to make some calls to locate Tracey's father, and he needed to find out more about Jack Little. He had picked up a burger and fries on his way to the office and, although he wanted to make the calls before lunch, the enticing aroma wafting from the bag was more than he could resist. He heard the phone just as his teeth sank into the gooey goodness, and a litany of profanities exploded in his head; for a moment he thought of not answering. After all, nobody had seen him come in, and he could pretend he was still out. He would have gladly sold his soul to the devil for a mere ten minutes to just sit back and enjoy his lunch, but it wasn't meant to be. He picked up the phone and growled his last name into it. "Lackey!"

His tone didn't bother Parker, whose attitude on a good day was far worse than anything Tom could ever deliver.

"Lackey, it's Parker. I just got the report from the lab. The shoeprint found in the cabin is of a man's work boot. The print in the cabin was too smeared to really get a clear name of the brand, but our tech believes that the boots could be Redwing steel toes, size nine and a half or ten. The other print we found in the woods near the body is consistent with the same type of footwear. We found another set of prints—aside from Tracey's— right where the body was found, but they could belong to someone else not related to the killing: maybe another jogger who went through there earlier in the day. There is no evidence suggesting that Tracey was attacked by more than one person."

"So our guy is a blue collar. That narrows down the list a bit, possibly. Probably not one of the doctors she was working with—those boots are for heavy-duty work."

Parker agreed. "Yeah. Definitely."

"I found out that Tracey's biological father is not the guy who came with her mother. I guess her parents were divorced. I also found out the name of her latest boyfriend, and the name of another guy she used to see. Can you run a check on these two men? I need to go see Brad Johnson, the current—more or less—boyfriend, before he gets out of work. I'm not sure what time his shift ends."

"I'll run the checks and call you if I find out anything important."

"Good. I'll count on it, thanks." Before Parker could reply, Tom hung up and inhaled the fries that were already getting cold.

As he drove through downtown, Tom thought about Shannon and her girlfriend. They surely were a strange couple. Did they know anything? Shannon seemed to be aware of several things Tom was sure he hadn't mentioned, yet she appeared genuinely heartbroken when told about her friend's demise. She seemed anxious around her linebacker lover, and Tom wondered if the relationship was abusive—after all, hadn't one of Shannon's eyes appeared bruised?

Absorbed as he was in his thoughts, Tom drove automatically, his familiarity with the city serving as a GPS even if he wasn't paying particular attention to the road. He turned right on Maywood, slowing as he looked for the *Caldwell & Sons* warehouse on the left. The building appeared worn out, its large, barred windows and unevenly-colored bricks giving Tom the sensation that he was headed toward an old prison or an abandoned orphanage. He pulled into an unmarked spot on the gravel lot. The air was oppressively humid today, and he looked forward to stepping inside. A pretty blonde greeted him when he entered; Tom couldn't help but notice the contrast between this lovely young person and the older woman who hovered over her shoulder.

"Good afternoon. May I help you?" The young woman smiled politely as she addressed Tom. The older woman looked in his direction, but after one glance, her eyes returned to the documents she was perusing. *Beauty and the beast...*

"Yes, thanks," Tom said, flashing a smile and his identification. "I am Lieutenant Lackey, with the Raleigh Police department. Is Bradley Johnson in, by any chance?"

The sound of Tom's words jerked the older woman's head up from the papers she was clutching. She appeared suddenly interested, but said nothing; rather, she fixed her small brown eyes on Tom and stretched her long, thin neck to look at his badge. The younger woman—an innocent-seeming creature around 25 years of age, with soft hazel eyes and doll-like features—glimpsed quickly at Tom's badge and picked up the phone. "I think he should be back from lunch by now. Let me call his department."

Tom waited while the woman dialed an internal extension, and scoped out the area while she was on the phone. The room looked much warmer and more up-to-date than the exterior of the building, and Tom's eyes fell on a ficus plant near the window which appeared to be well taken care of—surely by the young maiden, since he suspected the old hag would turn the green leaves to stone with just one look. The furniture was traditional without looking stuffy; the large window let in enough light to make the place appear bright and cheerful.

"Yes…okay, Terence. I will tell him." The soft, almost childlike voice of the receptionist brought him back to the moment. The young woman hung up the phone and made eye contact. "I'm sorry, Lieutenant. I just spoke with Brad's supervisor, and he informed me that Brad left a short while ago—stomach upset."

"Too bad. Well, thank you for your help, anyway." Tom said as he took a card from the pocket of his jacket and placed it on the woman's desk. "I can reach him at home, but should you see him before I do, please let him know I am looking for him, and that he can try me at any of the numbers listed on this card. I just need to ask him a few questions."

The young woman picked up the card, transferring it to a small tray on her desk. "I certainly will. Have a wonderful day."

Shortly after Tom left, the young blonde—Shirley was her name—stood up from her chair and stretched.

"Goodness! I feel completely stiff. Yvonne, would you mind the phones for a second while I use the restroom?"

The older woman nodded without smiling or looking in her direction, but as soon as Shirley entered the hallway leading to the ladies' room, she went quickly to Shirley's desk and picked up the card. Securing it inside a pocket, Yvonne returned to her desk and put on a good show of working on payroll. She needed to talk to the Lieutenant before Brad did. It was time for that son-of-a-bitch to pay his dues.

Chapter 7

Rose Howard's hands shook as she accepted the tissue her husband—noticing her distress—passed to her. She dried her eyes quickly and took a deep breath, while she tried to regain enough strength to talk without bursting into tears. She had slept through most of the past 48 hours, her sedative-induced dreams a puzzle of disjointed images produced by her mind in an attempt to make sense of everything that happened. A cup of coffee Mike Howard brought upstairs earlier sat untouched on the table near the window, and a print of blooming sage on the wall right above it seemed far too peaceful in a room where the air felt impregnated with agony and finality.

"I am sorry to disturb you, Mrs. Howard," Tom said gently to the woman who appeared to have aged fifteen years in the course of two days, "we routinely conduct questioning at the station, but your husband mentioned that you didn't feel up to going out, so I took the liberty of dropping by."

Rose nodded, her eyes fixed toward the window. Her husband came to her rescue and spoke for her. "Thank you Lieutenant. We really appreciate you coming by. My wife is very weak and it is very nice of you to take the time to accommodate us. What can we help you with?"

Tom sat on the chair by the desk and pulled a note from the inside pocket of his jacket. "Has Tracey ever mentioned a man by the name of Jack Little?"

Rose gasped and her husband immediately reached out to touch her shoulder in support.

"Was it Jack?" Rose's eyes widened as she waited for a response from Tom. Her cheeks, which had been ghostly white until a few seconds before were now on fire, and her voice burst out in a shriek. "Did he kill her?! Tracey was scared of him."

"How long was he acquainted with Tracey, Mrs. Howard? Have you ever met him?"

"Tracey met him at the hospital. He was one of the people who landscape the grounds there. We met him twice while visiting. He was obsessed with Tracey, and when she broke up the relationship he went crazy. He started following her, and he regularly parked near her apartment to watch her come and go. There was something wrong with him, Lieutenant. I wouldn't doubt that he could do something horrible…like… like…" Rose couldn't finish the sentence. Tears streamed down her face and wet the collar of her gray shirt. For a few moments, her sobs were the only audible sound in the room.

"We don't know if Mr. Little is responsible, Mrs. Howard. We found some letters he sent to Tracey which she kept in a box in her closet, so we consider him a person of interest but so far no evidence has connected him to the case."

Rose looked down. Her hope of nailing her daughter's killer was murdered in its infancy by the words of the Lieutenant.

"Do you know where we could find him, Mrs. Howard?"

"I don't know, Lieutenant. I know that when she broke up with him, Tracey deleted his number from her phone, but his e-mail address might still be in her computer. Tracey mentioned that he e-mailed her all the time, even after she asked him to stop. She would block his address and he would create a new one."

"Can you give me a description of Mr. Little?"

Rose closed her eyes for a moment, as she focused on a mental snapshot of the man. "Short, maybe five-seven or five-eight, dark hair and a tattoo of a dragon on his neck."

Tom scribbled the description on his notepad and created an entry to remind himself about Tracey's computer. "Did you ever talk to him, Mrs. Howard?"

"Yes, on more than one occasion. I met him in person the two times we were visiting, and I spoke with him over the phone a few times before he and Tracey stopped seeing each other. If he was over her apartment, he always answered the phone because he was afraid some other man would call and try to talk to Tracey."

Tom kept his expression impassive as he listened.

Rose continued. "He was jealous of everything. Tracey couldn't even talk to a male friend if she ran into one at the grocery store, or Jack would lose it. He got mad once because some young guy at a cash register smiled at her. He accused her of flirting with him, and ranted all the way back home. His sick jealousy was the main reason why she felt she had to break the relationship with him – he scared her."

"I see. How did he treat Tracey when you were there? Did he seem attentive?"

Rose laughed bitterly. "Attentive? That's not the right word to describe his behavior toward Tracey, Lieutenant. The correct term is overwhelming. He kept an arm around her at all times when people were in the room; as if he wanted everyone to know she was his property."

"Do you know if he is still working at the hospital?"

"I'm not sure. I guess you can check with the administrators there. I don't think he was employed by the hospital; he worked for a landscaping contractor."

"Good enough. I will check with the hospital."

Rose leaned back and closed her eyes. Her husband took her hand into his and caressed it. "I think my wife is tired, Lieutenant. If you would like to talk further, maybe we can go downstairs in the lobby while she rests."

"That's not necessary, Mr. Howard. This is enough for now." Tom stood up to leave and Mike Howard saw him to the door.

"By the way, Lieutenant, please give my regards to Ms. Spencer. She has really been a life saver – Alexis loves talking to her. She has been kind enough to call and check on us."

Tom arched his eyebrow in surprise – Kathy didn't tell him about her continued contact with the family. "I sure will, Mr. Howard. She really is a great person, and I am glad she and Alexis hit it off."

"They did. Alexis was very withdrawn when we first arrived, and she seems more relaxed now, in spite of the storm that hit our family."

Tom nodded and smiled. Maybe Kathy was right in encouraging the little girl to talk. As his mind wandered to the discussion they had the night before about Alexis' imaginary friend, he immediately thought of the photos Kathy showed him before he went to sleep. He was suddenly curious to know if Kathy had shown the photos to Alexis. He left the room and took the elevator down to the lobby. Tracey's face, screaming from the photos, was stuck in his mind as he walked to his car. The sound of his mobile phone shattered the mental image and he answered by the third ring. The voice on the line sounded raspy and labored, but the words it produced hit Tom in the chest.

"I am sorry to bother you, Lieutenant Lackey, but I think you should know who killed Tracey Newman."

#

Shannon Brinkley knew she was in trouble. She suspected it from the moment she ran into an old school friend at the mall and hugged her in front of Mary. Mary's face darkened a few shades when Taylor Martini almost collided with Shannon, instantly squealed and threw her arms around her old girlfriend. When Taylor suggested they eat a late lunch together Shannon tried to refuse, but Taylor wouldn't take no for an answer. She grabbed Shannon by the hand and led her to the food court, all the while talking non-stop and behaving as if Mary wasn't even there. Mary didn't appreciate being excluded, especially when the person cutting her out of the circle was a drop-dead gorgeous brunette from Shannon's past. The chemistry between Shannon and Taylor Martini was almost palpable to her, and it made Mary sick to her stomach. She pushed her plate away as if it were covered with slugs and sat in the inside corner of the booth quietly seething. She answered if someone asked her a question – and in fairness to her, Shannon tried to include her into the conversation several times – but for the most part she felt like an intrusion in a party for two.

The moment Mary and Shannon got in the car – after Taylor Martini profusely hugged her old friend and made her promise to stay in touch – Mary exploded. Shannon was driving since Mary's truck was in the shop, and Mary screamed at her the whole way home. Shannon was scared. It wouldn't be the first time Mary hit her, and Shannon was petrified; she wanted to say something to defuse the situation, but fear kept her tongue tied. When they pulled into the parking lot in front of the apartment building, Mary got out first, and said she was going for a walk. Shannon ran upstairs, her heart beating wildly, and for a moment she considered locking Mary outside. But of course, doing that would anger Mary even more, and from previous experience Shannon knew better than to do something like that – Mary would retaliate.

She opened the door and walked inside. The living room was dark and cool, and Shannon passed it without turning on the light, as she headed to the kitchen to get a glass of water. Her throat was parched and she felt dizzy. The fingers of her right hand went instinctively to her eye, and they touched the bruise Mary had given her just the other day. She couldn't go on like this any more…something had to change.

Her mind shot in a million directions as she desperately tried to come up with a plan fast enough to save her from another beating, but unfortunately it didn't come up with one quickly enough. When the front door slammed, Shannon felt her insides twist and her heart beat so fast she thought it would explode.

"So, did you call your girlfriend while I was gone? I saw her giving you her number. Do you think I'm blind?" Mary's voice thundered in the silence of the room and echoed inside Shannon's head until her ears rang.

"No, of course I didn't. Taylor is only someone I went to school with. There was never anything between us."

"Oh, really?" Mary walked quickly toward Shannon until she was only a few inches away from her. "Is that why the two of you couldn't take your eyes off each other?"

Shannon started to weep. "It's not true, Mary. We were just happy to catch up. That's all…"

Mary snickered as if she found Shannon's words so ridiculous they were amusing. She got close enough that Shannon could feel her hot breath on her face. Mary's smile suddenly turned hard and bitter and her eyes flashed an anger Shannon had never seen before. *It's going to get worse every time…she is going to kill me.*

"That's all? That's all you can say for yourself? You

stupid little slut!" Mary's eyes became small dark slits and her voice came out as a hiss. She grabbed Shannon by the shoulders and dug her fingers into her skin.

"Mary, you're hurting me! Let me go!"

Mary released her grip. "I'm hurting you? Really? This is nothing, Sweetheart. The good stuff is yet to come." She ran her hand over Shannon's head, closed it around her untied hair, and yanked hard. Shannon screamed and started sobbing. "Please don't hurt me... you know I only love you, Mary. I've never loved anyone like you, not even Tracey..." The moment she uttered those words, Shannon was sure she had dug her own grave. Mary dragged her by her hair to the living room and ripped off her shirt before she threw her on the couch. "Show me then. Show me you love me more than you loved Tracey."

Shannon continued to cry as Mary pulled off her pants and her head disappeared between her legs. She felt a wave of nausea wash over her. She didn't want to be there, but by now she was so trapped she didn't know where to turn. She should have listened when Tracey told her to kick Mary out once for all.

#

Tom dialed Parker's mobile phone number and tapped his fingers against the steering wheel of his car while he waited for his partner to pick up. When Parker got on the line, his voice was as unhappy as always, but Tom ignored it.

"Parker, have you found anything about Jack Little?"

"Not yet. Lots of people with the same name, but their ages don't check."

"Tracey Newman's mother believes Jack Little harassed her via e-mail. We need to get her computer. Do you think we can get Judge Harris to sign a warrant by tonight?"

Parker huffed. "That old goat has probably already gone home, but I will call and check."

"Thank you. Also, I just got a call from a woman who claims to know Tracey's killer."

Parker whistled. "Yeah? Who is she?"

"I'm not sure. She wouldn't give me her name. She said she doesn't want to get involved but she knows the killer. She called me from a payphone."

"Seriously? I didn't think people even used payphones any more. So, how are you going to get in touch with her?"

"She said she is going to call me back tonight at nine. I guess I will have to wait for her phone call."

"Strange bird, that one is. Sounds like she watches too many police shows. Probably just a weirdo."

Tom laughed. "Yeah, maybe you are right, but we can't afford to take anything for granted."

Parker's voice sounded more cheerful now. "I agree. No chances. I'm going to call Harris right now. Wish me luck."

"Good luck, Parker. Call me as soon as you know something. I am going to call Brad Johnson and see if I can talk to him.

"Ten four."

Tom clicked the red button on his phone to end the call, and immediately dialed the number Shannon gave him for Brad, but he got his answering machine, so he left a message. He decided to go back to Tracey's apartment – warrant or not, Shannon Brinkley seemed agreeable to letting him in without too many formalities. He drove north on Capital Boulevard and damned himself for not taking a different route when he got stuck in traffic near the intersection with Sumner Boulevard. The nearby mall was considered a blessing by many who purchased homes in the area, but it was a curse for anyone trying to drive through there during rush-hour traffic. He finally made it through the next two intersections and sped until he got to Perry Creek Road. He turned right and drove quickly to the apartment complex, and he parked his car in one of the spaces farther away from the building – he certainly didn't want to occupy one of the spots assigned to the residents who were probably, by now, ready to go home after a long day. If anything, growing up in a small town taught him good manners; and, he thought smiling, what the town didn't teach him, his mother surely did. Mrs. Lackey had no tolerance for poor manners or lack of consideration toward others. He went up the stairs two steps at a time and knocked on the door. No answer, even though the lights were on inside. He knocked again and waited, his ear close to the door to see if he could detect any sounds coming from within. He heard someone weeping softly, so he knocked once more. "Police! Please open the door!"

He stood by the closed door, uncertain of what he should do. He couldn't just barge in, and yet his instincts told him he needed to do just that. He was ready to knock again, when the door opened. The sight of Shannon Brinkley made him suck in his breath. Her hair was disheveled and she had on a powder blue robe stained by the blood that ran profusely from her cut and swollen bottom lip. Her eyes were red from crying and the fear in her eyes was intense enough to make Tom shiver. "Ms. Brinkley…what happened?"

The gentleness in Tom's tone crumbled Shannon's resolve to keep quiet and she collapsed against his chest sobbing. Tom held her up and walked her toward the living room where he helped her sit on the couch. Torn clothes were abandoned on the floor beside it. When he noticed that Shannon's eyes darted from side to side of the room and back to the open front door, Tom went quickly to close and lock it, then he returned to the couch and sat beside Shannon.

"Tell me what happened, Shannon. Who did this?"

Shannon continued to cry as if she didn't hear him, but before he could ask again, she raised her eyes and looked into his face to see if she could trust him. Her voice was as small as the voice of a wounded child. "It was Mary. She got jealous because I ran into a friend from school, and she accused me of liking her."

"Has she ever done this before?"

Shannon nodded, and she pulled down the shoulder of her robe to expose a large scar. "I got this when she threw me into the kitchen table one night. I hit the corner and I had to go to the hospital to get stitches. That night she was mad because I told her that Tracey didn't want her to stick around as much as she did."

A light flickered in Tom's mind. "Tracey didn't get along with her?"

Shannon laughed bitterly. "Who could get along with her, Lieutenant? She is mean and hateful, and she doesn't think twice about using violence to get her way."

"Shannon, do you think it is possible that Mary harmed Tracey? She obviously felt Tracey was an obstacle in her relationship with you."

Shannon licked her bottom lip and grimaced when she tasted iron from the fresh blood that continued to seep from the wound. "I've wondered about that too, Lieutenant. Mary hated Tracey. She was sure there was something going on between the two of us, and she went through my things constantly, looking for evidence. When she didn't find anything she got even angrier and accused me of hiding things from her."

Tom paused to think for a moment. Everything was moving too fast for him to properly process the possibilities.

"Shannon, could I take Tracey's computer? I know I should have a search warrant, and my partner is working on it, but could I take the computer in to be analyzed? Your cooperation would save us a huge chunk of time."

Shannon nodded. "I don't see why not."

Before he got up from the couch to go to Tracey's room, he asked: "Where is Mary now?"

"She went to work. She has a lot of debt she is

trying to pay off, so she is working graveyard shift because it pays more. She took my car because hers is in the shop."

"Do you want to go ahead and press charges, Shannon?"

Shannon shook her head. "No. It's going to be okay now. After the pressure has been released she is good for several days."

Tom didn't insist. From previous experience with victims of domestic abuse, he was well aware that pressing charges unless the abused victims were fully ready to go all the way with the process was a dangerous thing to do; even more dangerous than staying. Years ago, when he was still a uniformed officer, he was called in to a domestic disturbance; the woman who opened the door insisted that a mug had fallen from the cupboard and hit her. Of course he knew she was lying, so he convinced her to press charges. The next day she dropped the charges, and went back home to her husband. She was found dead in her home a week later, and two young children were left without a mother or father.

He walked down the hallway to Tracey's room and found her laptop inside a case on her desk. He picked it up and went back to the living room where Shannon was still sitting on the couch with her eyes open and staring at something only she could see – most likely, she was replaying the whole episode with Mary in her mind. He coughed softly to alert her of his presence in the room, and then walked to the front door. "I'll be on my way, Shannon, but if you change your mind, call me." He scribbled his home and mobile numbers on a business card and handed it to her. Shannon took the card and placed it in the pocket of her robe. She didn't say anything. She opened the door and watched him walk down the breezeway to the stairs, then she quietly closed the door.

Tom got in his car and put the computer bag on the passenger seat. As he drove off, he looked toward the window of Shannon Brinkley's place, and saw the lights going out. It wasn't the first time Mary hit her, and Mary hated Tracey. Could Mary have killed Tracey in a fit of jealousy? She could have been angry enough to follow her when she went jogging and confronted her in the woods. The puzzle was far from being complete, but as he drove off in the night, Tom hoped the pieces would soon begin to fall into place.

#

By the time Kathy drove home it was already dark. After spending the afternoon with Alexis, her mind was filled with information that was screaming to be processed and filed. She and Alexis had a special bond, which the little girl's family didn't seem to mind. Kathy believed Alexis and her story of Lily. Although she never had an imaginary friend herself, her sister swore up and down her own "friend" told her things she couldn't have known otherwise. The day her sister told her about the secret things Kathy had written in her diary about Billy McRae, Kathy ran to check her diary, sure that her sister had broken into the lock; but the diary was sealed and in exactly the same place where she had left it, so she knew her sister wasn't lying. From that day on – even if her studies later on taught her differently – Kathy believed that imaginary friends were spirits that would connect with a few gifted people. And how could she not believe in ghosts? The thought of Tracey's face in the photos made her shiver.

#

When his mobile phone rang, Tom was just getting ready to pull into his driveway after stopping by the lab to drop off the computer. He looked at the clock in the car – nine o'clock sharp. He clicked the green button on his phone and answered. "Lieutenant Lackey."

The same raspy voice from the afternoon filled the line. "Lieutenant, I told you I was going to call you."

"Yes, I was expecting you. So, what did you want to discuss?"

"Brad Johnson killed Tracey, Lieutenant. He was afraid she would tell hospital administrators that she was stealing drugs for him. If news of that came out, he would have probably lost his job, and he couldn't afford that right now."

Tom arched his eyebrows. "Are you sure of this? How do you know?"

"I know. Go talk to the hospital people, and they will tell you there was an ongoing investigation. Brad Johnson is a junkie, Lieutenant, and Tracey was his dealer. When they broke up she threatened to tell, and he had to silence her."

Tom made a mental note to go by the hospital the next day, and he hoped to get more information from the person on the phone. The voice sounded feminine, but it was so muffled he couldn't be sure. "Listen, can you tell me what kind of drugs Tracey was getting for him?"

The line went dead. Tom had one more clue to follow and one more truth to uncover.

Chapter 8

Tom walked through the sliding doors of the main hospital entrance and went straight to the reception desk. The area looked more like the lobby of a luxury hotel than a hospital – well-cared-for plants had leaves so green and moist they appeared to be freshly stroked by the brush of an artist, and the sitting area featured appealing and comfortable couches that would have been perfect in a country club. The classy designer decorations, tastefully spread around the room, clashed with the blue signs on the walls directing people to different wards. Instinctively, Tom breathed through his mouth – after being hospitalized several times as a child because of his asthma, he abhorred the smell of antiseptic that was characteristic of hospitals. This place, however, emanated the buttery sweet scent of gardenia.

"May I help you, Sir?" The woman at the reception desk – a volunteer, according to her name tag -- appeared to be in her mid-forties, with honey-hued short hair and warm brown eyes. Her lips were plump and barely tinged by a touch of lip gloss the color of apricot, set in a perfectly oval face.

"Yes," Tom said, discretely showing her his police badge, "I would like to talk to someone in administration. I spoke with Your Chief of Hospital Police, Mr. Barrett, on my way here, and he mentioned he would be out this afternoon; he said it is okay for me to speak directly to Mr. Russet.

"Of course, Sir. One moment, please." She picked up her phone and dialed an internal number. After talking for less than thirty seconds, she placed the phone back down and looked at Tom with kind eyes. "Mr. Russet asked me to send you to his office. Let me give you a map." She traced the route on the map with a yellow highlighter and handed it to Tom. "Here you go,

Sir. Follow the directions on the map; Mr. Russet's office will be on your right."

The map guided Tom through several corridors until he arrived near a small cluster of offices. He scanned the name tags beside the open doors until he found the right one. He knocked lightly and waited for the man sitting at the desk to raise his head and acknowledge he was there. Mr. Russet looked up and waved Tom in.

"I am Donald Russet. The receptionist said you needed to talk to someone in administration. How can I help you?"

Tom walked in and sat in one of the two chairs across from Mr. Russet.

"I am Lieutenant Lackey, with the Raleigh Police Department. I am investigating the death of Ms. Tracey Newman."

The man shook his head and not one of the few hairs left on it moved, trapped in place by an unforgiving overdose of hair spray. Reading glasses were lowered toward the tip of his nose as he focused on Tom, and his long, thin fingers came together as if in prayer. "That's terrible news about Ms. Newman,

Lieutenant. The hospital is deeply sorry for her untimely departure."

"I understand there is some sort of internal investigation going on, centered on Ms. Newman taking possession of medications that were property of the hospital."

"Yes. Ms. Newman was unfortunately caught in the act of filling her bag with several doses of Xanax and Lendormin. Both are benzodiazepines."

"Benzodiazepines?"

"Yes. They are medications similar to barbiturates. Sedatives."

"I see. Did the hospital press charges, Mr. Russet?"

"No. We decided it would be best to keep the matter as discreet as possible to avoid any unflattering publicity, but of course we were going to dismiss Ms. Newman as a result of the investigation."

"I understand. Did you tell Ms. Newman that she was going to be fired?"

"Not immediately, Lieutenant. Initially Ms. Newman was suspended from her duties at the hospital."

Tom arched his eyebrows in surprise. "She was? Are you certain of that?"

"Of course. I talked to her myself."

"The woman who reported her missing said that the hospital called after Ms. Newman missed two days of work."

"That's unlikely, Sir. Ms. Newman never came back after she was told she was suspended."

"Do you remember the exact date of your conversation with her?"

"No, but I can look it up." Mr. Russet stood up from his chair and walked to a file cabinet. He pulled out a beige folder which he brought back to the desk.

"Here it is. April 21. We spoke at three o' clock in the afternoon. She left the premises right after that, I believe."

Tom nodded and tried to work the timeline in his head. Tracey left the hospital probably around three-thirty or four, and nobody saw her, or her car, at the park during the afternoon hours. In fact, the park caretaker who was on duty that day was sure that no car was left in the parking lot by the time he left. Strangely, her car was in the parking lot the next day, although the park personnel didn't think it was important enough to call the police at the time. So, if Tracey left the hospital around four at the latest, where did she go from that time until after five o' clock? There was no activity on her credit cards and she didn't make or receive calls. He needed to talk to Shannon again, and find out if she had gone back home to change before going to the park to jog.

"How long do you think she was here for, Mr. Russet? Fifteen...thirty minutes? An hour?"

"Oh, less than that, Lieutenant. We spoke several times during the course of the investigation, so that afternoon we only met for a few moments for her to find out what we had decided. She was probably here for about ten minutes."

"So you would assume that she left the hospital around three-fifteen?"

Mr. Russet nodded somberly. "Yes. I would say that three-fifteen is correct."

"Another question, Mr. Russet...do you know a man by the name of Jack Little?"

"I'm afraid I don't. Who is he?"

"From what I've gathered so far, he does, or did, landscaping work for the hospital."

Mr. Russet raised his head knowingly. "Oh yes. We contract a landscaping service – he must work for them. Why do you ask?"

"I have reason to believe he knew Ms. Newman."

"I see. Well, he was not directly employed by the hospital."

Mr. Russet stood up, sending a subtle signal that he was ready to wrap up the conversation. As annoying as Tom found his behavior, he got up and handed him one of his business cards. "Thank you for your time, Sir. You've been of great help."

"Don't mention it. I'm glad I could be of service. I would really appreciate it if your department didn't mention Ms. Newman being involved in an internal investigation. The last thing we want to do is to undermine the integrity of our personnel and the good name of our hospital. I am sure you understand, Lieutenant, that it would be a sour pill for our patients to swallow."

"I can't guarantee that, Mr. Russet. Unfortunately, the press has a way of digging out the most guarded pieces of information." With that, Tom left the office and headed out to the parking lot. He wondered if Shannon knew about her friend stealing medications, so he resolved to go back by the apartment a bit later in the day. Right now, his focus was on Brad Johnson and on the skeleton he was probably determined to keep in his closet.

#

Kathy sat at her desk staring at the photos she took at her house. She tried to magnify the images to see if she could make sense of them, and understand once for all if the foggy apparitions were the product of a faulty flash or a ghostly visit. After looking at them for so long, her eyes were burning and the mystery was still unsolved. Could it be possible? Could it be that Tracey came back to give someone a message?

It was all too much to process, and the sharp waves of pain she felt in the crown of her head were a sure sign that a migraine was on the way. She stood up and stretched, her eyes immediately focusing on the empty coffee pot near her desk. She decided to brew enough for one cup – just a treat to offset the stress she was under – and walked to the window to check on the weather while the coffee was brewing.

Dark storm clouds were blowing menacingly from the west, carried by an unfriendly wind that bent the newly planted trees across the street almost to the ground. The rain hadn't started yet, but from the look of things, it wouldn't be long before it did. The gloom of the day added to her mood, and she felt unmotivated to do anything, even if she had several projects waiting to be worked on.

A steamy, snorting sound coming from across the room announced that coffee was ready, and Kathy walked toward her small coffee station with nostrils open wide, eager to capture every whiff of the bewitching aroma that was quickly spreading through the entire room. She poured a cup and took it back to her desk, and before she could get sucked into the images of Tracey again, she quickly exited the program and clicked instead on a series of portraits that needed a few touch ups. She went through each photo and jotted down the numbers and respective adjustments on a notebook beside her computer, and she was almost done when someone knocked on the door.

She opened to find an acne-ridden teenager standing timidly by the door, his shaggy blond hair strategically covering his forehead where the pimples were probably at their worst. His ill-fitting uniform gave away his reason to be there.

"Oh yes, you're here to pick up the packages, right? They are over there by my desk. I already talked to Wanda at the shop and she told me she would address them for me since I ran out of shipping forms."

"No problem, Ms. Spencer. Wanda told me to just pick up the packages and to get the list of names along with the codes."

The phone rang from the other side of the studio.

"Would you excuse me one second, please? I will be right back." Kathy said as she hurried to pick up.

When she heard the voice of the bride's mother on the other end of the line her heart sank – this was going to be a long conversation. "It's wonderful to hear from you, Mrs. Downey. Belinda's portraits are beautiful! I can't wait for you to see them."

She tried several times to shorten the conversation, but the woman's constant vomiting of new words and new issues made it impossible. "Mrs. Downey, would you excuse me for a moment? I have someone here to pick up some packages." Mrs. Downey continued to talk as if she never heard Kathy's request, so Kathy muted the phone and yelled across the divider to the young boy who was waiting by the door. "Hey! Can you please go ahead and take the packages? I'm afraid I am going to be on the phone for a while. The list is right beside my computer."

The boy yelled back. "No problem, Ms. Spencer, I will take care of it."

Kathy clicked off the mute button and almost laughed when she heard Mrs. Downey still talking – the poor woman never realized the sound was turned off for a blessed few seconds. It took a while to finalize all the details and to get the overwhelmed mother off the phone, and Kathy wondered how stressed *she* would be if preparing for her own daughter's wedding.

She went back to her desk, and wasn't happy to discover that her perfect, hot cup of coffee was now lukewarm and not as inviting as it was before the delivery boy and the phone got in the way of a well-deserved break. She drank it anyway, welcoming the smooth, sultry liquid as would a baby eager to find her mother's breast. She placed her mug on the coaster near the picture frame containing a photo of herself and Tom vacationing in Boone, NC, and got ready to go back to work on the list of adjustments, even if her head was now pounding. She grabbed a couple of pills from her desk drawer and downed them with another cup of coffee before she looked for the notebook with the notes she had taken earlier.

The list was gone! It was on top of her note pad before all the commotion took place and now it was gone. What could possibly have happened to it?!

It didn't take long to solve the mystery – as Kathy looked around her desk, the list she had prepared to go with the packages was still where she had left it. The kid had taken the wrong list! She burst into spontaneous laughter the moment she thought of the puzzled face Wanda at the shop probably made when the boy presented her with a list of photo adjustments. That child really needed a haircut; not only was his hair long enough to cover his pimples, it was also long enough to cover his eyes and suck away his better judgment. How did the little shit not see that the list he took had nothing to do with shipping? On top of it all, he had to literally rip it off the notepad!

The thought of starting anew was depressing, and she was tempted to postpone the project until the next day, but the deadline for those photos was quickly approaching, and no matter how many other things were absorbing her attention at the moment, her professionalism would not let her call off a due date.

By now, the storm was right over the studio. Powerful flashes of lightning were almost simultaneous with the thunder explosions that followed them. The sky was very dark, and Kathy switched on the desk light. As the lamp reflected directly on the notepad, she saw that the first page was indented in several places, and her heart jumped with excitement when she realized that everything she had written on the page the boy had taken was reproduced on the page underneath it. All she had to do was to lightly color that page with a pencil to bring up the notes she jotted down earlier. Electrified by this discovery, she opened the drawer of her desk to pull out a new pencil and started feverishly shading the page with grey: as an unexpected miracle, the words and codes she had previously written became visible.

She worked relentlessly for the rest of the day; touching a nose here and a wrinkle there, until everyone in the portraits looked perfect.

Suddenly, she heard her stomach growl, and realized she had never really eaten anything all day, so she shut off the computer and grabbed her purse before heading out the door. By the time she got to her car, the storm had passed and the sky was completely clear. Yellow droplets of pollen-laden rain were stuck to the windshield, so she ran the wipers to clear it. The wipers smeared the droplets and made it completely impossible to see, but after running for a few seconds, visibility started improving. A few more strokes and the water and pollen were gone, leaving behind only the paw prints of her neighbor's cat – Peter the cat seemed to have claimed Kathy's car as his latest spot of choice for naps.

She was getting ready to enter the freeway when something clicked in her mind, something so barely tangible and yet so potentially powerful that it almost made her lose control of the steering wheel when she brought one hand instinctively to her mouth. *The indentation and the paw prints...no matter how faint, a print of what was there is still present, even if not readily noticed...*

Tracey's eyes...could Tracey's eyes have recorded a print of the image that was last imposed on the retina? Even if the image was gone, maybe it retained a print somewhere. Her mind shot in a million directions, too excited to focus solely on a few possibilities. She didn't know enough about the human eye to determine the ratio of probability, but she knew the right person to ask: Dr. Greer himself. It was time for Kathy to pay a visit to the good old doctor and ask him some technical questions. If the print was recorded somewhere, then all she had to do was to take a few photos of the part of the eye where the print was left and see if it could be lifted.

She was so excited by the time she got home that she almost forgot to prepare dinner, but thankfully Tom called to let her know he was on his way home. She started a pot of spaghetti and let the pasta cook while she changed into something a bit more comfortable. When she went back to stir the spaghetti, she thought of all the things that happened: The camera falling, the images of the screaming woman, and now the delivery boy picking up the wrong list. Her imagination escaped from the no-nonsense grip of her rational left brain, and wandered to unexplored territories. Maybe Tracey just wanted to get her attention to the camera, and making it fall off the table – not once but twice – was her way to guide Kathy to a develop a new perception of things. Tracey was dead, but her spirit was still lingering around to help Tom and his team bring the person responsible to justice. Now it was a matter of figuring out what type of technology she could use, and it was definitely necessary, at this point, to talk to Dr. Greer. She promised herself she would call him in the next few days.

#

On the other side of town, Alexis Howard was finally alone. She was sure that, with her parents being gone for a few hours, Lily would stop by to see her. When her mother suggested looking for a baby-sitter, Alexis insisted she was a big girl, quite capable of staying alone for a short while, and she promised to keep the door locked. In the end, her parents relented, and they left to make arrangements to fly Tracey's body home. She missed Lily, and she missed the privacy of her own room at home – being in a hotel room was cool for a couple of days, but the threat of the adjoining door being flung open at any time was gradually getting on her nerves. She lay on the bed and closed her eyes, waiting for Lily. She took a few deep breaths and tried to relax as much as possible, knowing it was the best way to call upon her best friend.

Suddenly, she felt a soft breeze passing by, and goose bumps covered her entire body. Lily always announced her arrival that way.

"Lily, where are you?" She said opening her eyes and scanning the room. "I can't see you."

"I am right here." Lily's voice was small and she giggled, delighted to play hide-and-go-seek. "Look to your left."

Alexis looked but still couldn't see her. "Lily, please come out. We don't have much time to play, since I don't know when Mom and Dad will be back. I need to talk to you."

"Okay." Lily was suddenly beside the bed and she ran her hand on the soft cover. "I like this! It is pretty. It has flowers all over it, and flowers are my favorite."

Alexis was smiling too, now. Her relief at seeing her friend spread over her face like a blanket of lights. She patted a spot on the bed, inviting Lily to sit down. Lily smiled and adjusted her dress to sit.

"Aren't you hot with that dress on? It looks heavy." Alexis asked, pointing a finger at her friend's wool dress.

"No. I don't really get bothered by temperature changes. Anyway, what did you want to talk about?"

Alexis sighed before she spoke. "Well...it's about

my sister Tracey. Is she okay?"

"Of course she is. It took a while for her to believe she was dead, but she finally caught on. She was upset because of her baby."

Alexis arched her left brow and crunched her little nose. "Baby? Tracey didn't have a baby."

"No, but she was going to."

"Are you sure? How come Mom and Dad didn't say anything about it? Tracey wasn't even married."

Lily smiled, a light of knowing flashing in her eyes. "They didn't know. They still don't know. But Tracey was going to have a baby if she lived. You don't have to be married to have a baby, silly."

"You don't?"

"No. People usually get married first, but you can have a baby out of wedlock."

"But so, who is the daddy?"

Lily laughed. There were many things Alexis was too young to know, but Lily knew that her friend was intelligent enough to understand if she explained it in easy words. "Well, when a man and a woman fall in love, they sometimes love to be together. And they can have a baby that way."

Alexis nodded, awed by the wisdom of her young friend who seemed to know everything.

"But who's the daddy of Tracey's baby?"

"He's a tall man who's already a daddy to other children."

Alexis's eyes widened and her mouth opened in surprise. "Really?! Where are the other children?"

"At home with their mommy. They don't know about Tracey's baby."

"WOW! Wait until I tell Mom and Dad … "

"You can't!" Lily's tone changed from soft to angry. "If you tell them they will think you're crazy and they will give you medications, and I will never be able to come and see you again."

Alexis gasped. She couldn't bear the thought of losing Lily. She had just lost a sister; she certainly didn't want to lose her best friend. "I'm sorry. I won't say anything, Lily. Please don't be mad at me."

"Okay. But let's not talk about this any more right now. As you said, your mom and dad will be back soon, and we barely have any time left to play. What should we do?"

"I guess we could play hide-and-go-seek again. This room is full of places we can use to hide."

A giggle was back in Lily's voice. "Okay. You count and I'll hide."

Alexis closed her eyes and counted until ten. When she opened her eyes again, Lily was gone.

#

Donald Russet dabbed at his perspiring forehead with a white handkerchief while he waited for files on his computer to be permanently deleted. He made a mistake when he decided to open an Excel file on his work computer to keep track of his expenses. The file contained too many entries that could be traced back to the times he and Tracey went out together. He didn't think of it at first, of course, but now that a formal investigation into Tracey's death was underway, he had to get rid of any and all evidence tying her to him. Helen wouldn't have it, and if she found out he was having an affair, she would leave with the children, and he couldn't imagine living without them.

His mind wandered back to the day when he first met Tracey. From the moment she entered his office, he was awestruck: As the light filtering in from the window shone upon her golden hair, Donald thought he had just seen an angel. Tracey was kind and beautiful; she was young and ambitious; and more than anything, Tracey was passionate. When Tracey spoke of her love for animals, and her career in the medical field, her cherub eyes sparkled, and Donald found himself lost in their blue depths. And Tracey seemed to be responsive to his advances too, most likely because, after her own father skipped town when she was younger, she was still searching for a father figure. Donald was more than happy being her father, and her friend, and her lover. He was hurt when he found out she was still occasionally seeing Brad Johnson, the boyfriend she frequented on and off before starting her liaison with Don, and he knew she was stealing medications for him. If he could have his way, Don would have loved to get rid of Brad and to set up Tracey in a small apartment of her own, where he could go and see her at his convenience. But

Tracey wanted more. She wasn't satisfied with a small apartment and wanted to live at Donald's big house. When he mentioned that his wife and children were there, she smiled and innocently said: "Well, that's not too hard to fix, is it? All we have to do is tell your wife the truth. When she realizes we are in love, she will be okay with stepping aside. After all, neither of you have been happy together for a long time. Right? Right. Don and Helen didn't spark wild fires, but they had a partnership, and Don wasn't willing to lose everything he had for Tracey. That's why he thought of "catching her" while she stuffed her bag with medications. Maybe if she left the hospital, and he promised to not notify the authorities, she would back off. Of course, she agreed; the last thing Tracey wanted to do was to lose the job she had fought so hard to have. It wasn't until the last night when she came by after Don called her to inform her of his decision to let her go, that everything flipped upside down. Tracey stormed into the office, and accused him of using her for his own pleasure. Her last words to him were coated in ice, as she looked at him and told him she was going to see his wife, to share something interesting with her. He couldn't let that happen: He had too much to lose.

A gentle knock on the door of his office startled him and transported his mind back to the present. Ginger, the accountant, stood at the door with a smile pasted on her plump face. "We are ready for the monthly meeting, Don. Are you coming?"

Don looked at his computer screen, and he smiled when he saw a notification informing him that the chosen files were permanently removed from his computer. "I'm on my way, Ginger. We have a lot to discuss this month." He stood up and walked resolutely toward the small woman waiting for him. He closed the door to his office and headed down the hallway to the boardroom.

Chapter 9

Tom walked up to his desk hoping to balance the files he was carrying while he held on for dear life to the forbidden cup of coffee he purchased on his way to the station. He dropped the files and logged into his computer, then took a sip of coffee while he waited for the files to start up. He drank half the cup before he saw Dr. Greer's report in the inbox he kept on his desk, so he put down the cup and opened the envelope.

Cause of death, as he already suspected, was a gunshot wound to the chest. The bullet tore through the muscles and perforated one of the main arteries, causing massive internal bleeding and almost instant death.

As he scrolled down the document, Tom's breath

caught in his lungs. *Death of the embryo is estimated as occurring no longer than an hour after the death of the mother.*

Embryo?! What embryo? Was Tracey pregnant?

Tom grabbed the phone and dialed Dr. Greer. He was relieved when the receptionist answered and sent his call through.

"Hello? Dr. Greer here." Dr Greer's voice could hardly be mistaken – he sounded like a baritone with laryngitis on the best of days.

"Doc, it's Lackey. I just saw your report – Tracey was pregnant?"

"I'm afraid so, Lackey. The embryo was only about fourteen weeks old, so we didn't know until we stumbled into it during the autopsy."

Tom closed his eyes and exhaled. "Dear God… whoever killed Tracey killed two people…"

"Yes. That's mighty sad. Two young lives snuffed senselessly like that. Do you have other questions for me, Lackey?"

"No…this is it. Thank you, Doc."

Tom hung up the phone and opened Tracey's photo

on his computer. His heart hurt when he looked at her; so young, so beautiful, and now she was gone. So was her baby. How could Tom find a way to break the news to Tracey's parents? He decided to talk to Kathy first, and to see if she could provide a few key strategies to sensibly deliver this new horrible update. But first he had to go find Brad Johnson, and get some answers. He looked at his watch – nine o' clock in the morning. Brad was surely at work by now. Tom picked up his car keys and his sunglasses and headed out to the parking lot. With the temperature already in the mid-eighties at such an early hour, there was no doubt in Tom's mind that Raleigh was in for a scorcher of a day.

He drove to the warehouse and parked in the gravel lot. When he stepped through the main door, the same two women he had seen before were sitting at their desks, and the younger one – Shirley, he remembered – greeted him warmly.

"Good morning Lieutenant. How are you?"

"I'm fine, thank you; I hope you are. I'm here to see Brad Johnson."

"He is in the warehouse. Would you like me to call

him?"

"Yes, please."

He waited for a few moments, and he was surprised when Brad Johnson walked through the door. He expected someone burlier and rougher than the college kid who stood just a few feet away. He had short blond hair and his skin was lightly tanned; he was over six feet tall and quite handsome, even in overalls. He hardly looked like a drug addict, but Tom knew that there were many types of drugs out there, and many types of users.

"Can I help you?"

"Hello, Mr. Johnson," Tom said amicably while extending his hand. "Yes, I would like to ask you some questions."

"I am working right now."

"It's okay, Bradley. You can take your lunch right now." The voice of the older woman sounded like nails scratching a chalkboard. *That voice—where had he heard it before...?*

Brad nodded, shooting a nasty glance toward the woman sitting at her desk. She responded with a satisfied grin and toyed with the silver charm hanging from the necklace she wore around her neck. The charm moved to expose a large mole on her chest that almost made Brad gag.

"Okay. I'll take my lunch now. Where would you like to talk, Lieutenant?"

"What about my car?" Tom replied quickly. "You can bring your lunch if you want."

Brad shook his head and followed Tom outside. "I'm not hungry, thank you."

They walked out, but as Tom turned around he saw a smile creeping up on the old woman's lips. The moment she saw him looking at her, the smile morphed into a scowl and she buried her head in the papers in front of her.

Tom and Brad Johnson stepped outside and walked silently to the car. Tom started the engine to get some cool air into the vehicle and pulled out his notebook from his pocket.

"Mr. Johnson, I need to ask you a few questions about Ms. Newman."

Brad simply nodded, but he fidgeted in his seat.

"How long have you known Tracey Newman?"

"I don't know. About a year…a year and a half, maybe."

"Was there a romantic involvement between you and Ms. Newman?"

Brad hesitated.

"Were you involved with Ms. Newman?" Tom repeated the question.

"Yes. We were seeing each other from time to time."

"From time to time? Do you mean that you weren't a couple?"

"We were, but we were an open couple. Both of us could date other people."

"Were you dating other people, Mr. Johnson? While you were seeing Ms. Newman, I mean."

"No. I wasn't. I was seeing someone when I first met Tracey, but it wasn't serious."

"Do you use drugs, Mr. Johnson?"

Brad was suddenly nervous, and he shook his head without responding.

"Do you use drugs, Mr. Johnson?"

"No. I don't."

"Are you sure, Sir? Would you be willing to undergo a drug test?"

"Is this about me or about Tracey, Lieutenant? Unless I am being charged with something, I would prefer to keep my life private."

Tom raised his hands, palms facing Brad Johnson. "Of course, Mr. Johnson. But you see, my questions are perfectly justified, since we received a phone call informing us that you killed Ms. Newman because she provided drugs to you."

"Why would I want to kill her if she was my dealer?"

"Hmmm…good question. Let's see…could it be that you were afraid she would tell people at your place of employment? I understand the company has a very strict drug policy. Or maybe she refused to continue her dirty deed? Did you know that Ms. Newman was pregnant, Mr. Johnson?"

Brad's eyes almost exploded from his face. "What? Tracey was pregnant?"

"That's what I said. She was a little over three months along."

Brad whistled. "I wonder if she got pregnant from the guy she worked for."

Tom was surprised. "What guy?"

"His name was Don, I think. He is married, too."

"Is he a doctor at the hospital?"

"No. I think he is one of the administrators."

"Have you ever seen him, Mr. Johnson?"

"No, but Tracey seemed to be really taken by him. I know she wanted him to leave his wife for her."

Tom scribbled the name 'Don' on his notepad, immediately thinking of Donald Russet, the man he met at the hospital. "Do you know anything about him?"

"No, I'm afraid not."

"Okay, Mr. Johnson. I am still waiting for an answer to my question."

"What question was that?"

"Would you be willing to take a drug test? Someone seems to think that Tracey was stealing pills for you, and that you killed her to stop her from saying anything."

Brad shook his head, and a sad look descended on his face. "I wouldn't hurt Tracey, Lieutenant. We weren't exclusive as a couple, but I loved her as a friend. Look, I have used drugs in the past – I still do occasionally – and Tracey helped me get them sometimes, but even if I lost my job because someone found out, it would still be no motivation to kill her. No job is worth someone's life."

Tom looked at Brad's face attentively and his gut feeling was that the young man was being sincere. "Tell me Brad…I can call you Brad, right?"

"Of course."

"Why does the old woman you work with not like you? I noticed she smirked when you walked outside with me." He didn't want to tell Brad that he was pretty sure she was also the same person who called him the night before accusing Brad of killing Tracey.

"I'm not sure. She's never liked me very much, since I started working here. I tried to be nice to her, but it didn't make any difference. I think she is just one of those people who doesn't like anybody and enjoys seeing others suffering. A bitter old hag, if you pardon my French."

Tom made a mental note to interview the woman.

Of course, he couldn't prove she was the person who called, since the call was placed from a public phone, but he could maybe fib a little and squeeze some information from her. He was about to wrap things up with Brad when his mobile phone rang.

"Lackey."

"Lackey, it's Parker. Tracey's buddy, Shannon Brinkley, tried to commit suicide. She is at Memorial right now – they are trying to revive her. I'm in the waiting area right now."

"Shit, Parker! I will be there as soon as possible. Don't leave before I get there."

He clicked the off button of his phone and turned toward Brad. "I need to go right now. Police business. I will be in touch soon. Meanwhile, if you can think of anything, call me. Here is my card." He handed Brad one of his business cards and as soon as the young man got out of the car he turned on his lights and siren and sped down the road. Why would Shannon try to commit suicide? Was she just overwhelmed because of her violent girlfriend, or was there more to her decision? The case was getting more and more confusing by the day. With so many characters in the picture -- each of them with a different motive to kill Tracey – Tom wondered for a moment if the killer would ever be brought to justice.

#

When Tom arrived at the hospital, Shannon had been revived and admitted to ICU. Parker met him at the main entrance and led him through the maze of different departments until they reached the critical care unit. A nurse tried to stop them at the entrance to Shannon's room, but one quick look at their badges made her recoil like a snake being threatened with a rake.

Shannon was almost unrecognizable under all the tubing, and Tom felt a weight on his heart when he noticed the light bruise still on her eye and an additional large bruise on her shoulder near the scar she showed him the other night – when she dropped the sleeve of her robe to expose the scar, that bruise wasn't there. He instantly felt a surge of anger rise from the pit of his stomach, and he cursed under his breath. The goddamn linebacker hit her again. Tom would have loved to be alone in a room with that woman for a few minutes, and his intentions were far from romantic.

Shannon's skin looked gray, and even her dark hair appeared to have lost its luster; it hung as limp and heavy around her shoulders as an ill-fitting frame set around a tragic picture.

"What happened?" He asked Parker who stood by the entrance to the room.

Parker shook his head. "It's still fuzzy. Her roommate found her collapsed in the bathroom by the bathtub. The docs are thinking overdose, but they are still waiting for the toxicology report before they can confirm."

"By 'roommate' you mean Mary Townsend?" His tone was suddenly harsh.

"Yes, big football-player-looking thing. She said she got home from work and found Shannon in the bathroom of their apartment."

"Mary Townsend is Shannon Brinkley's lover. Abusive lover, I should say. The poor girl fighting for her life in that bed has enough bruises to prove it, including a new one she didn't have a few nights ago. Do you think she had anything to do with Shannon's alleged 'suicide'?"

Parker paused to consider the possibility. "Well, she seemed pretty tore up, but I guess anything is possible. We did find a suicide note, though."

"Oh yeah? What did it say?"

"That's where it gets tricky, Lackey. In her note, Shannon asked Tracey for forgiveness and she said she couldn't live with that burden."

"What burden?"

"She didn't say. Could she have killed Tracey?"

That possibility never occurred to Tom before, but of course, as Parker mentioned a few moments ago, anything was potentially viable. "Why would Shannon have killed her though? What could her motive be?"

Parker shook his head. "Beats me. You never know what type of skeletons people have in their closets."

"No kidding. I talked to Brad Johnson today—the guy Tracey dated on and off—and he told me that Tracey was having an affair with a married man at the hospital where she worked. Since we know she was pregnant, and he certainly didn't want that bit of happy news to leak to his wife, that makes him a person of interest. Brad Johnson is a junkie, and Tracey was feeding him pills from the hospital; he surely didn't want to lose his job at the warehouse if that came out, since they have a strict no-drug policy. Mary Townsend hated Tracey because she suspected that Tracey and Shannon had a tryst and knew that Tracey had asked Shannon to get rid of her. And let's not forget the stalker Tracey was doing her best to avoid. All these people had perfectly good reasons to want Tracey Newman dead."

"Damn! From the picture Tracey looks like an angel." Parker said after he processed the list of Tracey's enemies.

"And maybe she was. We don't know. Maybe all these people were simply taking advantage of her. Shannon Brinkley was the person who knew her best, and could have shed some light on the whole murky bottom, but she is currently on a respirator and unable to talk."

"Shouldn't we interview Ms. Townsend? Maybe she knows something."

"Yeah, and we also need to let Tracey's parents know they lost more than just a daughter – they also lost a grandchild."

Parker 's eyes darkened with sadness. "Do you want to tell her family yourself, or do you want me to?"

"It's okay. I'll do it after I ask Kathy some advice on how to approach a grieving family to deliver even more bad news. Her degree in psychology is coming very handy."

"Good thinking, Lackey. We'll get to the bottom of this." In an unprecedented gesture, parker patted Tom's back as a sign of encouragement.

"Yeah...I know we will. It's just that with so many paths to walk it is easy to miss something along the way. Where is the Townsend woman now?"

"I think she mentioned she was heading back home to shower and change."

"Good. I will catch her there if I hurry."

"Do you want me to come along?"

"Suit yourself. Nothing much we can do here."

They headed out toward their respective cars. Tom waited at the exit from the parking lot for Parker to catch up, and as soon as he saw his car coming, he sped toward the beltline heading to Tracey's apartment. Mary Townsend was responsible for injuring Shannon before; did she try to kill her this time? Maybe she found out that Shannon told on her and her anger escalated. Or could it be that Shannon had discovered something that had to do with Tracey's death and the killer tried to silence her? Or, even worse, could Shannon have killed her best friend and was now unable to live with the guilt? Many questions, and not enough answers; many tiles and no connecting pieces. As he drove along, something else floated to the edge of his consciousness: When Brad had exited his car yesterday Tom noticed he was wearing Redwing steel-toed boots! Shannon knew Brad, and he probably had regular access to the apartment. Tom hoped to find the killer before any more innocent lives were taken.

#

Tracey was running through the forest. She turned around several times to see if the man was catching up to her, and she tripped on a root hidden under a bed of leaves. The man was getting closer – she could hear his labored breathing and his footsteps approaching. He was going to kill her. By now, Tracey had no doubt of it. She tripped on one more root, and her ankle was cut by a line of thorns near the ground, but she ignored the pain and continued running. Someone else called her name – a woman's voice -- but the voice was too far for her to make out whom it belonged to. She saw something through the trees, and focused on what appeared to be a light shining through the foliage, but the man was upon her now. When he got close enough, he leaped and landed on top of her, slamming her to the ground. As Tracey fell, her baby slid out from inside of her and lay on the ground, the tiny face barely formed contorted in a silent scream. The baby died a few moments later, a tiny hand touching his mother's lifeless body as he left this world before he had the chance to even enter it.

Alexis sat on the bed and screamed, unable to slow down her breathing or the pounding of her heart. Tears had soaked her pillow and she felt like throwing up. By the time her parents ran to her room, she was dry-heaving.

"Alexis! What's wrong?!" Her father ran to the bed and turned on the lamp on the bedside table, while her mother, awakened from a drug-induced sleep, stumbled to the door uncertain of what was happening.

"Tracey! It was Tracey! She was running through the woods, Daddy, and a man was chasing her. Then a woman came for her, but Tracey never made it. The man caught her before her friend reached her, and Tracey had her baby right there on the forest ground. The baby died, too."

Mike Howard wrapped his arm around his daughter's shoulders and drew her toward his chest. He held her for a few moments without saying anything, hoping that physical contact could help her snap out of her nightmare more effectively.

Alexis smelled the familiar spicy scent of her father's cologne, and she inhaled deeply as she sought comfort in his embrace. The feeling of security that washed over her vacuumed away the debris left behind by her terrible dream.

"It was a nightmare, Alexis. Tracey didn't have a

baby, and no friend found her. She was found by someone else a few days later."

"No, that's not true! Lily said…" She bit her lip when she realized that she had broken her promise to Lily.

Her father looked at her sternly, but a deep love was apparent in his eyes. "Alexis, you really need to make an effort not to mention Lily around your mother. You know it upsets her terribly, and right now she is upset enough."

This was her chance to make it right and still be true to Lily's wishes. "You're right, Daddy. I will try harder."

Her father smiled and kissed her forehead. "Do you want me to leave the light on?"

"Yes, please, Daddy."

He stood up and headed toward his room, but he stopped to blow her a kiss before he disappeared through the adjoining door to join his wife who had already gone back to bed.

Alexis lay on her bed, her body tired but her mind on high alert. She was sure she had heard a woman's voice, but her mom and dad would never believe her.

Only Lily believed her. And Kathy. With a promise to herself to call Kathy the next day, she closed her eyes and went back to sleep.

#

Kathy couldn't believe that she was still at the studio at eleven at night, but since she had work to finish, and Tom had called earlier to say he was going to be home late, this was the perfect evening to catch up.

She was still working on the final touches for a family package, when she heard a strange sound which at first impression sounded like a book falling on the ground. When she went to investigate she found one of the old photo albums had fallen from the bookshelf and landed on the floor. During its descent, it opened to a page that was particularly dear to her heart – it was a collection of photos that were taken when Caroline was six years old. The photos were alternated with selected drawings Caroline had created at school, including a Mother's Day card that particularly touched her soul. The card, in child-like handwriting said: *I love you*

Mommy, because you will never abandon me. Kathy remembered that in those days Caroline was particularly shaken when she heard of the tragedy that had befallen her best friend – her friend's mom went to the grocery store one day, and she never returned home; months later, she sent a brief note to let everyone know she was happy and healthy, and with the love of her life. For several days, Caroline had been Kathy's shadow, but knowing the reason behind her daughter's 'sticky' behavior, Kathy took the opportunity to hug Caroline even more often than usual.

She touched the card gently with one finger, then closed the album and replaced it on the shelf. She wondered what made it fall, but her attention was quickly rerouted to the work she still had to finish. She stayed on task for another hour, until her eyes started to burn. She shut down her computer and quickly grabbed her purse and camera before she turned off the lights and went out the door. She sat in her car for a moment and pinched the bridge of her nose before she started the engine, but when she glimpsed the window of the studio as she backed out of her parking spot she saw the light coming back on. It flickered once and then it went out again. She didn't have the strength to go back upstairs to check on things, and she wondered if she was just seeing things, so she drove off and promised herself she would investigate the strange occurrence in the morning. Inside the studio, the photo album was once again on the ground.

Chapter 10

Kathy hung up the phone and sat on the couch to think. It was only a few minutes past eight o' clock in the morning when Alexis called to tell her about the dream she had last night, and from her hushed tone Kathy was sure Alexis was trying to hide the phone call from her parents. She didn't like that at all – as a parent and as a psychologist she knew that it wasn't good to encourage children to hide things from their parents, and yet, when it came to Alexis, Kathy also knew that her parents were unable to lend the type of ear their daughter needed.

The dream was scary – a nightmare, in fact. Alexis told her that she didn't rest well at all after that, and even with the lights on, she was afraid to fall back to sleep because she was worried about going back to the same dream. Kathy was well aware of the fact that dreams allow people to process information, and she found it a bit strange that Alexis dreamt of her sister having a baby, until Alexis said that her friend Lily mentioned something about Tracey being pregnant; Alexis also told Kathy that 'the daddy was a man who was already a daddy to other children' – Lily told her so.

Poor child! All these emotions running through her mind and nobody she could talk to about them…

The sound of the front door opening made her jolt, and she turned her head automatically to see who it was.

"Hey Honey! It's me! I forgot some files I brought home to read."

"I'm in the living room!"

Tom poked his head into the room and smiled. "Are you taking an early morning nap? I thought you usually get ready around this time – aren't you going to the studio today?"

"Yeah…I will in a minute." That was all she said. She knew how Tom reacted to her telling him about

Alexis's friend Lily the first time, and she didn't want to spoil the day so early on.

"Are you okay? You're not sick, are you?"

"Oh no, I am taking a few minutes to relax and have a cup of coffee."

Tom went to sit on the couch directly across from the loveseat she sat on. "These have been a crazy few days – everything has happened. Oh, by the way, thank you for checking on the Howards from time to time. They really seem to appreciate all you're doing to help Alexis through this crisis."

"It's my pleasure, really. Alexis is a wonderful child, and she likes photography."

"Yes, she is wonderful, but I think her parents are a little worried about her."

"Oh? What are they worried about?"

"Her imaginary friend, for one thing. Mr. Howard told me this morning that Alexis had a nightmare last night.

Kathy hesitated for a moment, then she decided to come clean. "Yes. Alexis called and told me about it just a short while ago. Did Mr. Howard tell you what the nightmare was about?"

"No...not specifically. He only said Alexis had a nightmare about Tracey dying, and he is concerned because she seems to be more withdrawn than usual."

"It's normal, Tom. Even more than adults, children need time to absorb the impact, and sometimes they need time for their minds to find a place and a reason for everything."

Tom smiled. "Thank you, Doctor. Your training is really helping a lot, and I cannot tell you how much I appreciate your concern. I didn't know you were still in contact with the family."

"I wasn't planning on it, but Mrs. Howard is so distraught that she is unable to be there for Alexis right now and Mr. Howard asked if I would talk with her from time to time, since – quoting his words – I understand young minds. I couldn't refuse, and to be honest, I really like Alexis – she reminds me of myself when I was her age."

"Well, no matter what the reason, I am sure the Howards are very grateful, and so am I. Knowing that someone else is there for them makes me feel better about things. And, I need professional advice from you as well."

"Something relating to photography?"

"Hmmmm….no. I would like for you to suggest the best way to tell someone something horrible when their world is already turned upside down. How can I say something in a sensible way, so that it will cause the least amount of stress?"

Kathy thought for a moment. "It would depend on the situation, I guess. What's happening?"

"Tracey was pregnant. Three and a half months along. Dr. Greer found the baby when he performed the autopsy. He was actually surprised her body didn't try to purge it on its own, but it is probably because she was found not too long after her death. How do I tell her parents that they lost not just one child, but a grandchild also?"

Kathy was frozen on the spot. Her mouth opened and closed several times, but no sound came out. Her mind replayed every word Alexis told her no more than thirty minutes before, screaming to make sense of something impossible. When her voice came back, she looked at Tom with a puzzled look on her face, her hands wrapped around the coffee mug as if physically touching something could help her feel more grounded.

"When did you find this out?"

"What? About Tracey being pregnant? I found out yesterday. Why?"

"And you haven't told her parents yet?"

Tom noticed Kathy's nervousness and watched her as she squeezed her fingers around the mug until her knuckles turned white. "No…that's why I am asking you to help me find the right words."

Kathy stood up from the couch and walked to the window; she pretended to look at something outside, in faint hope that a few extra seconds of thinking could give her the answers she so desperately needed.

"Kathy, what's wrong?"

Kathy turned toward him, and took a deep breath. "I told you Alexis called me earlier, Tom, remember?"

"Yes. What does it have to do with me telling Tracey's parents that she was pregnant?"

Kathy walked back to the coffee table and smacked the coffee mug on the table so hard Tom thought it would break. "It has everything to do with it, Tom! In Alexis's dream Tracey was pregnant. She was running from a man, and the man caught up with her. When she died, her baby came out of her, and it died. She also said that a woman's voice was calling Tracey, and that Tracey was running toward a light."

She stopped a moment, to allow her words to sink. Tom just sat there, his face impossible to read.

"What are you saying, Kathy?"

"Dammit, Tom! You've always been a sensible man! I know your job forces you to be rational and to categorize everything, but you have to admit there is something strange about the way Alexis knows things."

Tom nodded. "You're right, Kathy, but not all that she said matches the truth. There was no one else in the woods when Tracey died – certainly not a woman she knew."

Kathy threw her arms up in the air. "But how do you know that, Tom? How can you be sure?"

"Because we could only find one set of prints at the scene, Kathy. In truth, we found foot prints at the cabin where we believe Tracey was hiding, and also near the murder scene, but we think they belong to the same person. Same pair of steel-toed boots."

"Are you sure they are the same?"

"The brand matches. The size of the foot print in the cabin is impossible to determine because it appears smeared, and we couldn't find other footprints in the cabin that are clear enough to test, but the ones we found in the woods appear to be a size ten. A man size ten – hardly the size and make of shoe a woman would wear. Other footprints at the scene don't appear as fresh and could have been left by anyone walking in the area before the crime took place."

"But how do you explain the fact that Alexis *knew* of the baby?"

"Tracey called home a few days before she died. Maybe she told her sister about it."

Kathy shook her head. "She's just a little girl, Tom. Why would Tracey tell her and not her mother?"

Tom was running out of explanations, and his frustration bled into his words. "I don't know, Kathy! But I think that chasing ghosts is not going to help us catch the killer any sooner. If we focus on something so absurd, we are going to lose track of the real evidence. I would appreciate it if you could just stop with these crazy ideas!"

Kathy looked at him as if she had never seen him before; in this light, she never had. Her voice lowered to an icy whisper. "Are you calling me crazy, Tom? Is that it?"

Tom slammed his fist into the arm of the chair he was sitting on and stood up.

"I'm sorry Kathy, I didn't mean to imply that. It's just that things are complicated enough without spooks and dreams. I have to go and tell this family there is another family member to bury, and frankly, I don't know where to start. Tracey's mother is a shadow of the woman I met when she first arrived, and there is only so much more her husband can bear without going mental."

Kathy swallowed bitter tears, and for a moment she cursed herself for allowing Tom's words to hit her at the core. Her heart broke for Alexis, as she knew the little girl was trapped bearing a gift—and a burden—that was too much for her to carry alone, but frustration at the fact that Tom would not listen to reason made the blood boil in her veins. "How can you be so stubborn, Tom? Why can't you just listen to her? Just once. Give her a chance to say what she knows."

Tom walked to the table near the door and retrieved his car keys along with a small pile of files from the chair close to the table. "Not a chance, Kathy. This is a child who's suffered a great loss, and you are asking me to put her through questioning. And how do you think her parents would feel about that? Huh? There are strict regulations prohibiting officers from interrogating children, Kathy, and I am not going to lose my job just because all of a sudden you decide to play psychic. Honestly, I am surprised that you would go on with this charade, and now I am beginning to understand why you chose to be a photographer instead of a psychologist: Your imagination gets the best of you."

With that, he was gone. He slammed the door behind him, leaving Kathy in the hallway staring at the closed door, and feeling hot tears fill her eyes. Like all couples, they had argued in the past, but never over something like this and, as far as she could remember, never so harshly. She couldn't think of another time when Tom slammed the door or threw a poison dart at her integrity. The fact that he thought less of her now made her heart hurt, yet she couldn't give up. She owed it to Alexis and, she thought closing her eyes, she owed it to Tracey.

#

Tom knocked on the door and waited for Mary Townsend to open it. He was still frustrated from his exchange with Kathy, so he hoped that the Townsend woman was at least going to be cordial. He wasn't worried so much about her hostility as he was worried about his own reaction if she said something that pissed him off. Tom was usually proud of his calm demeanor and, thanks to his mother, he had a healthy respect for women, but Mary Townsend didn't fit his image of a woman, and he felt that all boundaries were off. He despised men who abused women, and felt no differently about women abusing women: Only a sick coward would harm another person to feel in complete control. He felt his hands closing into fists as an image of Shannon's bruised face and shoulder flashed through his mind, so he took a deep breath and exhaled loudly.

"Can I help you?" Mary Townsend's voice didn't sound happy when she opened the door, but then again, Tom never expected her to be pleasant. This Mary didn't have a little lamb – she was the wolf who ate the little lamb. She stood in the middle of the open entrance with one hand on the door handle and one hand on the door frame, sending a less-than-subtle signal that he wasn't welcome inside.

"I stopped by yesterday but you were not home. I have a few questions to ask you about Shannon Brinkley. You are the person who found her, right?"

"I was at work yesterday. And I was sleeping just now. How long is this going to take?"

"Not too long Ma'am. May I come in?" Tom accentuated the word 'ma'am,' sure in his heart that Mary Townsend didn't appreciate being addressed as a lady. Just getting under her skin felt like a small victory right now.

Mary moved away from the door but her face

continued to reflect her annoyance. "Sure. Come in and make yourself at home. Do you want a beer?"

A beer?! At this time of morning?

"No, thank you Ma'am. I can't drink while I am working."

"Your loss." Mary walked to the kitchen to grab a bottle of beer for herself and joined Tom back in the living room. "So, what do you want to talk about?"

"The police report shows that you came home around seven o'clock in the evening and found Shannon Brinkley collapsed on the bathroom floor."

"If you already know that, what do you want to know from me, Lieutenant?"

"In the original report you said that you were coming home from work, but you work night shift."

"That's correct, but someone called in sick and I was asked to switch shifts."

"What did you think when you first found Shannon, Ms. Townsend?"

"I thought she had slipped on the wet floor and maybe bumped her head."

"And instead?"

"Instead I found an empty box of pills and I knew she had tried to kill herself."

What sort of pills were they?"

"I think they were over-the-counter sleeping aids."

Did Ms. Brinkley have trouble sleeping at times? Did she typically take sleeping pills?"

"Sometimes, when she was working nights and had to sleep during the day."

"I see. Can you think of a reason why Ms. Brinkley would want to die?"

Mary Townsend laughed bitterly. "After finding her note, I have wondered if Shannon was the person who killed Tracey, and if she did, it is possible that she might have felt guilty afterwards."

"Is there anything else aside from the note that would give you reason to think Ms. Brinkley is guilty of murdering her friend?"

"She took my car that night, and she brought it back with mud in the undercarriage and a dent in the fender. I took her car to go to work, so I didn't find out until the next day when she came back and said that she got lost and ended up on a country road. Of course I knew she was lying and we got into an argument."

"So why didn't you report that to the police?"

Mary shrugged her shoulders. "I don't like cops. They're trouble."

"I understand, Ms. Townsend, but do you know that withholding information during an investigation is a crime?"

"Don't play that game with me, Sherlock. You are not going to intimidate me so easily. I didn't do anything wrong and I am helping you right now. Take it or leave it."

Tom decided to change the line of questioning. "What did you do when you realized she had tried to kill herself?"

"I called 9-1-1."

"Do you mind if I take a look at Ms. Brinkley's room?"

"Actually I do, Lieutenant. Shannon's room is also my room, and I need to go back to sleep. Unless you have a search warrant, I am kindly asking you to leave."

"Very well," Tom said standing up, "I will need you to come to the police station for an affidavit. We will need to record what you just told me. We will also need to analyze your car for possible evidence."

"Shannon left a suicide note. I think what she wrote speaks for itself."

"Why would Shannon want to kill Tracey, Ms. Townsend?"

"Because Tracey stole something that was very important to Shannon, Lieutenant."

"Really? What was that?"

"Her reputation."

"How so?"

"Shannon grew up in a very strict religious family who would not accept her gay lifestyle. Tracey went to Shannon's family and told them of her relationship with me."

"Why would Tracey do that?"

"Because Tracey didn't like me, and she would have done anything to get me out of the picture, even if it meant that Shannon would lose everyone she loves."

"Why do you think Tracey didn't like you, Ms. Townsend?"

"Because the man Tracey claims was stalking her is

my brother."

#

No word from Tom. This had never happened before. Not that they fought often, but anytime they argued over something, Tom was usually ready to kiss and make up within the hour. Something was different this time, and Kathy couldn't help feeling anguished, knowing all too well that lack of communication was the beginning of the end for most relationships. She tried to call him at the police station several times and was directed to his voice mail, so she tried his mobile phone but got no answer there either – was he just busy, or was he still so mad that he couldn't talk to her? The mere thought of losing Tom was eviscerating, and Kathy felt lost.

She heard the phone ring and jumped – the caller ID displayed 'unknown name, unknown number' on the screen, so it probably wasn't Tom, but she picked it up any way.

"Hello?"

Static was all she could hear on the other end of the line.

"Hello…who is this?"

No answer. Kathy felt the hair on her arms sticking up, her first thought that Tom was maybe in trouble somewhere and he couldn't talk. Panic overtook her. "Tom, is that you? Please say something!"

She heard a click, and the line went dead. She dialed star-sixty-nine to call back, but since the call was anonymous it could not be traced or redialed. She waited for the phone to ring again, and every fiber of her being was on alert. What would she do if something happened to Tom? She couldn't bear the thought; she stood up and furiously paced the room to get rid of the excess energy in her body. She couldn't stand feeling this way, so she called the station again. The information desk picked up by the third ring.

"Hello, this is Kathy Spencer. Is Tom Lackey in?"

"I'm sorry Ms. Spencer, he left early this morning and he hasn't returned yet. Would you like me to connect you to his voice mail?"

"No, thank you. May I speak to Sergeant Parker?"

"I'm sorry, he is out also."

"Did they leave together?"

"No Ma'am, not that I know of. Each of them took their own cars."

By the time she hung up the phone she was a nervous wreck. Tom typically turned his phone off if he was in the middle of an interview but he regularly turned it back on and returned calls after he was finished. Why didn't he return her calls?

Sitting there was driving her crazy, the ghosts of her failed marriage to Andy coming once again to haunt her. That's how things started falling apart for the two of them…and what if something happened to Tom? How could she live with herself knowing that the last time she saw him she didn't even tell him she loved him?

The moment that thought entered her mind she banished it quickly. What was wrong with her? Tom wasn't Andy, and nothing had happened to him. But then, who had called a little while ago?

She was so taken by her thoughts that she didn't realize another storm was approaching, but when the wind coming in from the open window blew a few magazines off the table in her waiting area, she hurried to close the window and pick up what had fallen. One of the magazines was open facedown on the floor, and when Kathy picked it up, she noticed the title of the article: "Can Abandoned Children Ever Trust Again?"

Her heart skipped a beat – there seemed to be an almost eerie connection to the card inside the photo album that had fallen off the bookshelf the day before... mothers abandoning their children, trust, pain...why had these two similar items fallen within the last twenty-four hours? Was there a link to them? The strange phone call flashed through her mind...*Tracey, was that you calling?* She closed her eyes for a moment and took a cleansing breath. Maybe Tom was right – maybe she was losing her mind.

#

"Jack Little is your brother?"

"Yes, Lieutenant, he is my half-brother."

"Do you know of his whereabouts?"

Mary Townsend shook her head. "Nope. He left

town a couple of weeks ago."

"Did he leave before or after Tracey's murder?"

"Whoa…wait a minute, Sherlock…you don't think Jack did it, do you?"

"Jack Little had a relationship with Tracey Newman, and from what I've heard, it wasn't a loving one."

"Jack loved Tracey, but he couldn't stand the fact that she was running around behind his back. He wouldn't hurt her, I assure you; Jack wouldn't hurt a fly. Maybe you should look at some of the other men she was sleeping with if you don't believe what I am telling you."

"Men? Do you know who they are?"

"Brad Johnson was one. He is a complete loser and a drug addict. Tracey was getting dope for him. She decided to cut him off when she got busted at work, and he didn't like that."

"Who else?"

"Who knows?" Mary hissed under her breath, "Tracey was a slut. There is no telling who else she was sleeping with."

"Do you have any other family in town, Ms. Townsend? Maybe one of your relatives knows where your brother is?"

"No. Jack and I only had each other. Our mother was like Tracey: a cheap whore who slept with everybody. The state removed us from her custody when we were little because she was caught up in some drug affair and went to jail. We lived with her mother for a while, God bless her soul, and we went to foster families after she died."

#

Alexis peeked in her parents' room and sighed in relief when she saw them both deeply asleep. She needed to talk to Lily again, and since she left home, Lily visited less and less. Alexis felt alone. She liked Kathy a lot, but she was worried that her parents were going to become suspicious if she called her too often, so she spent most of her time laying on her bed pretending to read the same magazine she brought along for the trip. No matter how much she loved Justin

Bieber, even his smiling photos weren't enough to make her feel better at this point.

She closed the door separating the two rooms as quietly as she could, and went to lay down on her own bed. As always, she closed her eyes and breathed deeply to still her body. It wasn't long before Lily announced her presence.

"Hi Alexis. Can you play today?"

Alexis's face was sad. "No, I'm afraid not. We can't wake up Mom and Dad, but I was wondering if we can talk for a while. I've missed you, Lily."

Lily smiled. "I have missed you too. It's boring where I am without you. There are no kids to play with. Well…actually there is one little boy, William, but he is too little, and he is always crying for his mother. He is not much fun to be around."

Alexis's eyes widened. "Really? Where is his mom?"

"He doesn't know. He has been looking for her for a while, but he hasn't found her yet. Someone told him she is looking for him too, but they haven't found each other yet."

"That's terrible! Poor kid…and poor mom!"

"Yes, it is pretty sad, but that's how things are sometimes. He thinks his mom abandoned him, and he is angry and upset, and his mom would do anything to connect with him and make him happy."

"But why did they get separated?"

"It's complicated, Alexis. And I am not too sure of the details. People get separated all the time, and the worst thing is that each side blames the other for the separation, when in reality everyone had reasons to behave certain ways."

Alexis looked at Lily with a puzzled look on her face. "I'm not sure I am following you, Lily. What ways?"

"Never mind, it is not important any more. What counts is Tracey. Did your mom and dad make arrangements for her body?"

"Yes. I think we are leaving soon to take her body home."

"Where is it now?"

"I am not sure…I think it is still at the morgue. They don't tell me much – they think I'm too young to understand certain things."

"I'm not surprised. Well, can we play now?"

"We can't, I told you. Mom and Dad are sleeping. They are already furious enough that I continue telling them about you."

"Then stop telling them! And you are as boring as William today. I need to go."

"Wait, Lily! Don't leave!"

Lily didn't answer. Alexis felt a cool breeze pass by her, and suddenly she was alone again. Lily didn't like it too much when they couldn't play.

Chapter 11

"Lackey, I think I hit the jackpot."

"What do you mean, Parker? I'm not in the mood for word games." There were several reasons why Tom was irritated today, one of them being his state of affairs with Kathy. Tom had been through the coals with his first wife and he remembered their arguments – fights, he should call them – all too well. He and Kathy never really argued before, and he didn't know what to do with this turn of events. He respected her point of view, yet he couldn't allow her to cloud his better judgment with stories of ghosts and imaginary friends who lurked in the shadows. The unsettled atmosphere in his relationship, however, was not the only thing that was bothering him: Mary Townsend and her abusive ways bothered him. And, he thought, if Shannon really had killed her best friend, what did that say about his instincts as a detective? The thought that he felt protective over a potential cold-hearted killer made him feel foolish. Had the cute little brunette really played him like that? The letter she left was typed, so it was impossible to determine whether she wrote it herself or if someone else did. His hands squeezed around the steering wheel and he took one deep breath to steady himself.

"Who pissed in your cereal this morning, Lackey? I found Jack Little – I thought you'd be happy to hear."

Tom's attention was piqued. "You did? Where? His sister told me he left town a couple of weeks ago."

"Nope. He is in town, alright. He lives in a rented efficiency near the hospital. The name on the agreement is Joseph Bernardini."

"How the hell did you find him?"

"Small world. I was actually driving behind him yesterday, and his plate was expired, so I pulled him over. The name on his driver's license was Joseph

Bernardini, but the plate was registered under the name of Jack Little. I didn't want to scare him out of town, so I didn't say anything, and made a note of the address listed on the license, which is different than the one used for the vehicle registration. When I mentioned that his plate was expired he said that he was driving a friend's car; I let him go."

"Good work, Parker. Do you want to go see him with me?"

"Sure thing. Are you coming to the station?"

"Yes. I will be there in five minutes, so meet me in the parking lot and I will pick you up."

He hung up from Parker and drove the two blocks that separated him from the station, all the while thinking about the different people involved in the case. When he drove into the parking lot Parker was already waiting outside by the main door, so he pulled up for him to get in the car. Parker had a grin on his face, something that in itself was quite unnerving.

"What are you grinning about, Parker? Something funny?"

"Yeah, actually...I was just thinking about the face

Little is going to make when he sees me again today."

Parker really had a strange sense of humor.

"Well, hopefully he won't get spooked and flee. I would love to be able to ask him a few questions."

"I was just thinking that. What about if I wait in the car and you call me if you need help?"

Along with the odd sense of humor, Parker also had a well-configured mind when it came to strategies. "Let's do that. He doesn't need to feel like we are stalking him. Not yet, at least."

'So you mentioned that his sister told you he left town. How the hell did you find his sister?"

"Mary Townsend is his sister. I wonder if he is as big as she is – we might need reinforcements if he gets despondent."

"Son of a bitch! You're for real? He's her brother?"

"Yes. She dropped the bomb this morning when I went by to see her."

"Damn! This is getting more and more complicated by the minute!"

"Oh wait. You don't know the best part yet: Mary Townsend said that Shannon Brinkley is possibly the killer."

"That little thing in the hospital?"

"Come on, Parker, you know that size doesn't really matter, and friends regularly fuck their buddies. It could be; who knows?"

"Yeah, I guess so. It's just easier to picture the Townsend woman doing it, but I suppose anything could have happened."

They pulled into the parking lot and Parker pointed at the maroon Buick sitting wounded in a spot toward the end of the lot. "Here's the car. He's home."

Tom pulled his car beside the Buick and Parker remained inside. Tom got out and walked to the door of the efficiency that was registered under Joseph Bernardini.

The building was shabby, as was the whole area around it. Across the street were a couple of houses that had probably been fairly pleasant many years before but had fallen victim to age and neglect; old couches seemed to be the choice of outdoor furniture in this part of town, since both houses – and a few others on each side of them – had them on display on the rickety porches. Two youths with sagged pants and fake gold chains stood by the entrance of another home on which the peeling mustard-yellow paint had faded to the shade of spoiled mayonnaise.

Tom knocked on the door but nothing prepared him for the surprise that awaited him the moment the door opened and a short, dark man with a head of close-cut, curly hair and beady black eyes materialized from inside. *He and Mary Townsend might have shared a mother, but their fathers were probably night and day...*

"Mr. Jack Little?"

The man looked at Tom suspiciously and his dark eyes narrowed into charcoal slits. "Who wants him?"

"Lieutenant Tom Lackey, with the Raleigh police department, Sir. Are you Jack Little?"

"I don't go by that name any more. I decided to change life and I am starting on a clean slate."

"That's honorable, Sir, but I was wondering if you could answer a few questions for me."

"What is this about?"

"It's about Tracey Newman, Sir. I understand you and Ms. Newman had a relationship."

"That was a long time ago, Lieutenant. Tracey and I had different goals in life, and I decided to move on."

Tom nodded. "I see. May I come in?"

"Actually, I am on my way to work, Lieutenant. Unless this is urgent, I really need to ask you if we can arrange a phone meeting. Is Tracey okay? Is she in trouble?"

Tom couldn't read his expression – did he really not know Tracey was no longer living?

"I'm afraid Ms. Newman is deceased, Mr. Little. I am touching base with everyone who knew her, trying to understand a bit more about whom she was."

"Tracey is dead?" Tears filled his eyes and quickly ran down Jack Little's cheeks. His legs trembled and he steadied himself against the door frame. "What happened?"

"I was hoping you could tell me that, Mr. Little. Can you think of anyone who would want Tracey Newman dead?"

"Are you saying Tracey was killed by someone?"

Tom didn't respond, but Jack Little found the information he was seeking in Tom's eyes.

"Oh my God…not Tracey…not my sweet girl…" He burst into sobs so intense his whole small body shook with them.

"Can I help you inside, Mr. Little? Maybe you should sit down."

"Tracey didn't deserve this. Whoever did it should die for this."

"Can you think of anyone who might have a reason to harm her?"

"The only two people I can think of are Shannon and maybe that new guy Tracey was seeing."

"Do you mean Shannon Brinkley, Sir?"

"Yes, her roommate. She didn't like Tracey, you know?"

"Why was that, Mr. Little?"

"Because she thought Tracey ruined her reputation, and my sister believed that Shannon also had a thing for this guy Tracey was seeing."

Of course…Mary Townsend saw ghosts of lovers lurking everywhere.

Tom arched his eyebrow. "Which guy? Are you talking about Brad Johnson?"

"Yes, the junkie. They might have been on this together."

"Why would you think that, Mr. Little?"

"Because Tracey had a large insurance policy, and when she was seeing Brad Johnson she made him her beneficiary. After they broke up, she told Shannon she was going to change the policy and make her little sister her beneficiary. Tracey didn't know Shannon liked her boyfriend."

Tom was utterly confused. *Isn't Shannon gay?!*

"Pardon the forward question, Mr. Little, but I was under the impression that Shannon Brinkley is in a relationship with your sister."

"She was – is. Shannon is bisexual."

Tom didn't expect this type of revelation, and he couldn't help noticing that Jack Little was at ease using the past tense when he talked about Shannon, although he just discovered she was no longer of this Earth. "Are you in contact with Shannon Brinkley, Mr. Little?"

"No, I don't like her. Never have."

"So you aren't aware that Shannon Brinkley is at the hospital right now, fighting for her life?"

"No, I didn't know."

"I see. Well, here is my card, Mr. Little. If you can think of anything that might help the investigation, please call me."

The small man took the card and stuffed it in his trousers pocket. "I will, Lieutenant. You must excuse me now, but I really need to go."

"No problem, Mr. Little. Thank you for your time."

Jack Little disappeared behind the chipped, faded door, and Tom walked briskly toward his car. Parker was on the phone when he got in, and he seemed excited about something. He hung up a few seconds later. "I got the records for Jack Little, a/k/a Joseph Bernardini. He is clean, but I also ran records for Mary Townsend, since they are kin. She is no angel -- lots of DUIs and a revoked license."

"Damn it, Parker…there is something missing here. I feel like we are running in circles. Did you know Tracey had a life insurance policy to which Brad Johnson was initially the only beneficiary? According to Little, she decided to amend the policy and nominate her little sister in place of Brad after they broke up."

"What? Seriously? I didn't find any policies. Does her family know?"

"They never mentioned, but I will ask when I go by there a bit later to let them know about the baby."

"Wow! These people can't catch a break, can they?'

"No, I'm afraid not. And the saddest thing for them to find out is that their little girl seemed to have more bones hidden away than Jeffrey Dahmer.

#

It was a bit past six when Tom dropped Parker off at the station, and although Mr. Russet was probably already off work, he decided to go by the hospital anyway. If he couldn't talk to him today, he could at least check on Shannon's condition.

He parked his car and took his time walking to the building, as he felt the need to be out in the sunshine for a while, and gather his thoughts. Even after all these years in law enforcement, Tom was still amazed at what surfaced any time one started digging into someone's past. Apparently good people were still hated by some, and most of them had something to hide. He wondered about the mysterious man Tracey was having an affair with, and he hoped Mr. Russet could shed some light on this.

He walked through the sliding doors and went directly to the information desk.

"Is Mr. Russet still here by any chance?"

The receptionist, a young woman in her mid-thirties with bleached blond hair and a prematurely wrinkled face smiled and picked up the phone. "Let me check for you, Sir. One moment, please."

Tom scanned the room as he waited and he noticed a family of four people – father and three children – sitting together in one corner of the waiting area. The father held a little girl of no more than a couple of years of age, her eyes heavy with sleep, and he kissed her repeatedly on the forehead; two boys less than ten years old were fidgeting in their seats, and Tom smiled as he saw himself mirrored in one of them; when he was about the same age, his own mother had been in a minor automobile wreck, and Tom still remembered how he felt sitting in the waiting room – although he was apprehensive about his mother's wellbeing, he wanted to get up and play but his father wouldn't have it.

"Sir, Mr. Russet is not answering his phone, but I haven't seen him come through yet, so you might want to go by his office and see if he still there. Do you need a map?"

"No, thank you. I know where it is."

He left the desk and turned at the corner by the elevators to get to administration. When he reached Mr. Russet's office he saw the door ajar, but when he peeked inside the man was not at his desk. He was ready to leave when Mr. Russet came down the hallway accompanied by a tall blond clad in a powder blue designer suit and heels that made her tower over Mr. Russet dramatically. When Mr. Russet saw Tom standing by the door, his face dropped one shade of color. He walked resolutely toward the Lieutenant and puffed his chest while the corners of his mouth went automatically up to form a hint of a smile.

"Lieutenant…I was just getting ready to leave for the day. May I help you?"

"Yes, Mr. Russet. I was wondering if I could have a

word with you. It won't take long."

"Certainly. Let's go in my office. Thank you, Erin, I will see you tomorrow." He said as he walked toward the door and quickly dismissed the young woman.

Tom followed him inside and sat on one of the two chairs in front of the desk.

"I'm sure you understand it has been a long day, Lieutenant, and I am quite tired and ready to go back home to my family. I have commitments for the evening."

"I'll be brief – it has come to light that Ms. Newman was involved in a relationship with someone in administration by the name of Don. Any idea who this person might be?"

Mr. Russet's face lost color again before exploding into a shade of bright pink, made even shinier by tiny droplets of perspiration that formed on his upper lip. It was as if the word 'guilty' flashed in neon letters on his forehead. Was Mr. Russet the mysterious man Tracey was seeing?

Donald Russet swallowed audibly and Tom watched him shift uncomfortably in his seat. The man's inner conflict between coming clean and continuing to hide his indiscretion was playing as a silent film on the black screen of his dilated pupils. Tom shifted his approach to a more personal level, and addressed the man by first name, making a statement more than asking a question. "Was it you, Don? Did you have an affair with Tracey? Nobody is judging here, but I have to know who she was seeing."

Don appeared to be on the verge of tears, but he took a deep breath and straightened his spine, though his shoulders were still a bit droopy. "It's not how it was, Lieutenant."

Bingo! Tracey was seeing Don Russet...

"Why don't you explain it in your own words, Don?"

Don Russet loosened his tie and undid the first button on the collar of his immaculate shirt. "Tracey and I were friends, more than anything. I think she saw me as a father figure, and I guess she was the daughter I always wanted – ambitious, driven and kind. Tracey was a very sunny person."

"Were you having a relationship with her, Don?

More than a father-daughter relationship, I mean…"

"Not in the beginning. I simply admired her resolve and her unbridled enthusiasm. Tracey never complained about being worked too hard, and she welcomed every opportunity to learn something new. I wanted to see her succeed and become the professional she had the potential to become."

"When did your relationship change to a more intimate one?"

"It wasn't long, I'm afraid. You see, I haven't seen many fireworks in my personal life the last few years, and I was naturally attracted and intrigued by Tracey's passion for life."

"And Tracey? Was she interested in pursuing a relationship with you as well?"

"Believe me, Lieutenant, I was very surprised too in the beginning. Tracey was so beautiful, and so bright, that I found it hard to believe she was falling for someone like me. We went out to dinner a few times, and things quickly escalated."

"Is your wife at all aware of this relationship?"

"No! Of course not…Helen wouldn't take an extramarital relationship lightly, and I am afraid she would leave me."

Tom decided to throw the ball in Don's court to see if the man would catch it. "Were you aware of Tracey's pregnancy, Don?"

Once again, Don was caught in a conflict and his uncertainty was painfully painted on his drawn face.

"I was, Lieutenant." He said in a defeated voice tinged with shame and hopelessness.

"Were you the father of Tracey's baby, Don?"

"I couldn't be sure. I know she was seeing someone else from time to time."

"Brad Johnson?"

Don Russet nodded silently.

"How did you react when Tracey told you about the pregnancy?"

"I was upset, as you can surely imagine. I had already told Tracey that it was best to interrupt our relationship when it became too demanding and dangerous, and then she came out with this piece of news. She was upset that I was going to let her go, too, but of course I had to follow the rules – she was, after all, caught with her hand in the cookie jar, or in the medicinal cabinet I should say. Exonerating her from her responsibilities could have cost me my job." Don smiled suddenly. "I suppose I shouldn't tell you these things without an attorney present, should I? They will probably come back to bite me, but I am tired of hiding, and I haven't done anything wrong – well, maybe I have done something morally wrong, but certainly nothing illegal." His sincerity was almost disarming, and Tom didn't quite know what to do with it – either the man was caught in the middle of a really bad situation and was only guilty of cheating on his wife, or he was a brilliant player who knew what cards he should throw on the table.

Tom threw the question out there for Don Russet to chew. "Did you kill Tracey Newman, Don?"

There were many emotions playing on Don Russet's face, but they all appeared bathed in honesty. "I didn't kill Tracey. I loved her. God help me, I loved her more than I should have, and it was wrong, but I would never harm her."

"Did Tracey ever confide in you about being scared

of anyone?"

"Yes, she actually did. She was very cautious around some woman named Mary, and she also told me of a guy she used to date, who stalked her."

Tom nodded. "Jack Little. That's the man I asked you about when I first came to see you."

"Yes, Lieutenant, but I never met Mr. Little in person, and in all honesty, I don't personally know all the people we contract to come and work on the grounds – they are provided by an external service. From what Tracey told me, he never tried to harass her while she was at work, or I would have made sure to let his employer know."

"Who do you think killed Tracey?"

"I don't know…nobody deserves to die like that."

"Like what, Don?" Tom asked, well aware that no details of the murder had been released to the press.

"I…I don't know. I meant nobody deserves to be murdered."

"I see. Well, thank you for your time, Mr. Russet, I think it is enough for now." Tom stood up and placed his notebook in the inside pocket of his jacket before he walked to the door.

"Lieutenant?"

"Yes?"

"Can we keep this private? My affair with Tracey, I mean…it would destroy my family and possibly my career."

"I don't know, Mr. Russet. Unfortunately, that's out of my hands."

Don Russet didn't respond, and when Tom turned to look at him before closing the door, all he saw was a broken man.

Chapter 12

Tom's mobile phone rang just as he got ready to walk outside to weed his flower garden. He was certain that most of his colleagues would have picked on him if he told them how he was spending his day off, but he inherited a love for flowers from his mom, and gardening was always a good thing to clear his mind. He had barely gotten on his knees to pull a few clumps of knot grass when he heard the unwelcome ring.

"Lackey here."

"Lackey, it's Parker. I stopped by to check on Shannon Brinkley and I had a run in with the linebacker. The hospital was able to track down a couple of Shannon's relatives and they are here now, but they don't want Mary Townsend around, and she is about to explode."

"Damn, Parker, I was just getting ready to work on my yard."

"You what?"

"Never mind, Parker, I'll be there in a little while. Cool her down for me. And by the way, we need that search warrant for her apartment. Shannon didn't seem to mind us snooping around, but Mary Townsend is not so agreeable."

"Imagine that…"

"Yeah, well, we need that warrant. Can you get on it today?"

"I've been on it -- it should be ready by noon."

"That's great. Let me rinse my hands and I will head your way." He hung up the phone without a final greeting knowing that Parker wouldn't mind.

By the time he arrived at the ICU, Parker had already left and the picture wasn't pretty. Mary Townsend was in one of the waiting rooms and almost charged him when she saw him coming around the corner. "They are not letting me see Shannon! Do something about it or someone is going down!"

Tom rushed to her and brought his finger to his nose urging her to lower her tone. "Stop screaming, you will get yourself kicked out."

"They can't stop me from seeing Shannon! She is my girlfriend!"

Several heads turned in her direction, but Mary Townsend didn't even acknowledge them. Her eyes were smoldering charcoals, ready to grill the next person on her path. Tom grabbed her arm and pulled her to the side. "Shut up, Townsend! I am not kidding – you are going to be banned from even coming on these premises if you keep it up."

"What's the trouble here?" Two security guards approached with their chests puffed out, but they quickly deflated when Tom flashed his police badge.

"It's all good, officers. Ms. Townsend here is a little upset, but I have it under control. Thank you, we will be leaving shortly." He nearly dragged Mary Townsend toward the elevator before she could speak, and he saw the two security guards watching them until they disappeared behind the elevator doors.

"What is wrong with you, Townsend? You know that area is full of critically ill patients. This kind of drama is not allowed up there."

The elevator opened in front of the cafeteria. "Let's go get a cup of coffee and talk." Tom's tone didn't leave any room for arguments, and Mary followed him without saying a word.

They went through the line and got coffee, then they went to sit at one of the booths.

"Look, Mary…is that okay if I call you Mary?"

Mary nodded, then she smiled. "I've been called worse."

"Look, Mary, you already know that Shannon's family is a bit – how can I say it…"

"I know Lieutenant, but I am just going to check on Shannon. No matter how they feel about me, it's not fair that I can't see her."

"Unfortunately those are their wishes, and nobody at the hospital has the authority to deny what they ask. I can't do anything about it, either."

"I know…" Tears spilled out of Mary Townsend's eyes, and Tom looked at her without knowing what to say. "And look, I also wanted to tell you, Lieutenant... please forget all those things I said about Shannon. I don't know if she killed Tracey. All I know is that she resented Tracey and her suicide note sort of confirmed the suspicion in my mind."

Tom nodded. "We have a search warrant, Mary. We have to come in and look around the apartment a bit. My partner is going to be on his way there shortly, and I am meeting him as soon as I leave here. Do you want to go with me? It would make it a lot easier if you let us in willingly."

"Yes...listen...about Shannon's bruises...I know she has told you about our arguments, and I admit that I have a problem with my anger – I have never been able to deal with it too well, but I really love Shannon, and I am committed to getting some help to learn how to handle my emotions better. I know we can work on our relationship and make it work if there are no obstacles in the way."

Tracey was an obstacle in the way...

Tom tried his best to remain impassive, though he did feel a hint of compassion toward this giant of a woman who seemed lost at the moment. "I know, Mary. Anger is a bad beast, but it can be overcome."

Mary nodded, Tom's words having a calming effect on her.

"Mary, is your car back?"

"Yes, why?"

"Because we will need to impound it to have it analyzed. Can you use Shannon's car for the time being?"

"Yeah, I guess, until her family kicks me out of the apartment, at least."

Tom looked at his watch. "It's almost twelve. Parker was picking up the warrant around twelve. Let's head back to your place."

Mary stood up and she suddenly didn't look as tall and as threatening as she had before. "I really never meant to hurt Shannon, Lieutenant, and in case you are wondering, I never hurt Tracey."

#

It was nearly one in the afternoon when Tom, Mary Townsend and Parker met in the parking lot of the apartment. Parker looked a bit surprised to see them arriving together but didn't ask.

"I've got the warrant. We are ready to go in." Mary Townsend glimpsed at the document in his hand and went upstairs to open the door. Tom and Parker followed her in. The apartment was dark and it smelled of stale smoke. Saying that the living room was messy was a huge understatement, and the kitchen counter was covered in dirty dishes.

"Sorry, I am not much of a housekeeper. I didn't expect company."

"We're not running a 'good housekeeping' contest. We're just going to look around a bit."

"Suit yourself." Mary plopped down on the living room couch and turned the TV on.

Tom and Parker opened every drawer, every closet, every box they found in the house, but nothing of interest materialized. When they were about to give up, they noticed a small case under Tracey's mattress, and when they opened it they saw a document neatly folded inside – Tracey's life insurance policy. The only beneficiary was listed as Bradley Ryan Johnson. "Hey, we've got something here!" Parker said excitedly.

Tom went over to take a look but he didn't feel like smiling. Of course, the insurance policy alone wasn't enough to charge Brad Johnson with murder, but it certainly offered new possibilities. Tracey was stealing drugs for him and she stopped after being caught. Of course, if she told someone, his job at *Caldwell & Sons* – a family-run operation with strong moral standards and zero-tolerance for drug use – would have been jeopardized. This fact alone was enough to turn Brad against Tracey, and the possibility of becoming a rich man in the event of her death certainly made it seem even more likely that he would have an interest in seeing the woman dead. Silence and money were surely powerful motives.

Parker's phone rang while he looked through the rest of the box contents, and he picked it up by the second ring. "Parker here."

"Sergeant Parker, this is Jeremy Miller. I have finished analyzing the computer Lackey dropped off a few days ago. There are a few things on the hard drive that you might find interesting. One of them is a photo sent by someone named J. Bernardini just two days before the murder. The photo shows a very creepy table literally covered with photos of Tracey Newman. The message sent along with the photo said: "I will love you even after death do us part."

#

It was nearly five o' clock in the afternoon when Kathy looked at the clock on the wall of her studio. She had been waiting all day for a call of apology from Tom, though she knew that maybe she was the one who should call and apologize – after all, she could understand how it would be hard for him to accept some of the things she felt without compromising all he ever held true and sacred. She was about to pick up the phone when someone knocked on the door. Surprise was the first thing that registered in her mind the moment she saw a distraught Mike Howard standing in front of her, his hair disheveled and his sunken eyes reflecting the anguish that gripped his soul.

"Mr. Howard…what's wrong? Did something happen to Alexis? Or to Mrs. Howard?"

The man just stared at her, tears erupting from his eyes. Until now, Kathy never noticed the toll the events of the past week had taken on him. The lines on his thin face looked deep and exaggerated, scars from a war without winners.

"It's Alexis, Ms. Spencer…"

Kathy felt her heart sink and she tried her best to suffocate the shrieking sound that rose from her throat. "Where *is* Alexis? What happened to her?!"

"She is not talking or eating, and she just stares into space as if she is trying to shut out the world. We have tried different things, but nothing seems to work – she is just too far for us to reach her."

During her training, Kathy studied cases of children suffering from different types of psychosis who gradually lost touch with reality and stopped talking and connecting to the outside world, but she didn't feel Alexis's alienation was due to psychosis. Rather, it was more likely that something had scared her and she was trying to process it.

"Did something happen that might have unsettled Alexis?"

"Yes, I am afraid so. Your...Lieutenant Lackey stopped by for a brief visit to inform us of Tracey's pregnancy, and as soon as he left, Alexis came bursting through the door saying that we had to listen to her, that she already knew Tracey was pregnant because Lily told her. When my wife heard that nonsense, she momentarily lost her better judgment and she lashed out at Alexis, calling her heartless and crazy. This is not normal behavior for my wife, Ms. Spencer, please believe that, but she has been under so much stress lately that something inside of her snapped. As soon as she said those words, she realized the impact they had on Alexis, and she apologized, but Alexis locked herself in her room and would not talk to anyone. The only thing she said before slamming the door was that she wished she could have died instead of Tracey, so at least she could be with her friend Lily."

Kathy wiped the tears that were running unrestrained down her face. "May I see Alexis? Maybe I can talk to her."

Mike Howard smiled. "I was hoping you were going to suggest that, Ms. Spencer. Yes, thank you. Alexis seems to have a special bond with you, so I am hoping that having you near is going to help her unlock the door she has closed against suffering and loss."

'Let's go," Kathy said as she grabbed her purse and car keys, "I will follow you back to the hotel."

She knew how to get there, but waited for Mike to lead the way in his rental car. In fifteen minutes they were pulling up in the parking lot of the hotel. When they got upstairs, they entered Alexis's room through the adjoining room.

"We had to get in her room from the other door earlier, since she locked this one. Thankfully, she didn't think of locking both. When we got inside, we found her like this."

Kathy could have burst into tears the moment she laid eyes on Alexis. She lay on her bed turned toward the window, her eyes fixed on something only she could see and her mouth slightly parted but otherwise motionless. A barely noticeable rivulet of saliva had spilled from her parted lips and had run down her chin. Kathy checked her pulse and felt relieved when she felt a strong beat. She sat on the bed beside her and gently caressed her hand. "Alexis, it's me, Kathy. I know you can hear me."

Alexis didn't move. Mike and Rose Howard walked closer to the bed but Kathy raised her hand to silently stop them from coming any closer.

"Alexis, I know what happened. I know that the Lieutenant confirmed what Lily told you, and it is a lot for you to comprehend. It is okay, Honey. I believe you. I believed you when you called me and told me what Lily said." From the corner of her eye, Kathy saw Alexis's parents exchanging glances. "It is a huge burden for you to carry alone, Alexis; please, let me help you. I can't help you if you won't talk to me. Lily doesn't want to see you like this, *does she...?* And I don't want to see you like this. I know you and Lily are together right now, but being with her is not your place yet. Lily is dead, and she is lonely, but your place is here in this world with your mom and dad, and with your other friends."

"Ms. Spencer," Mike Howard's voice sliced through the air of the room, "may I have a word with you?"

"Of course." Kathy gently let go of Alexis's hand and got up from the bed.

"Would you be so kind as to go downstairs with me?"

Kathy nodded and followed him, and only when she looked into his eyes did she notice an icy layer that wasn't there before. They rode the elevator down in silence, and only when they walked out the main door toward the restaurant, Mike Howard let his frustration burst.

"What do you think you're doing?"

"I'm sorry…I don't think I understand. *You* are the one who came looking for me."

"Yes, I did; because I thought you could actually help Alexis. I didn't expect you to push her deeper into the abyss of insanity."

Kathy felt heat rising quickly to her cheeks. "I *was* helping Alexis! Alexis needs to have someone who believes in her, someone who doesn't think she is crazy. And yes, I do believe her, and do you know why?

Yesterday Alexis called me very early in the morning to tell me about a dream she had, and she explained that she was terrified because Lily told her Tracey was pregnant. Now, Lily, her *imaginary friend* as you call her, told her this before any of us knew of Tracey's pregnancy. How – tell me how, Mr. Howard – could Alexis have just imagined that? I am a rational woman, but I am also open to the possibility that some things cannot be explained. Alexis has a gift, and you and her mother make it sound like a curse!"

Frustration cursed through Kathy's body like an electrical current, and she couldn't fight back the tears that suddenly poured from her eyes. "You have a little girl up there who's beginning to think her parents don't want her because she is crazy. She is shutting out the outside world to stop it from delivering more pain. How can you not see that?"

Mike Howard just stood without saying anything, the expression in his eyes impossible to read.

"Please let me talk to Alexis, Mr. Howard, I know I can get her out of her state."

"How, Ms. Spencer? By feeding her fantasies? Or

are you actually saying that this Lily is a ghost?" Mike Howard's voice was swollen with anger and pain.

"I wish I could show you something, Mr. Howard. I have some photos that I took at my house, and they all show a very eerie image of Tracey's face imposed over the items I was trying to photograph…."

Mike Howard laughed nervously. "Are you hearing yourself, Ms. Spencer? I have had enough of this. My whole family has had enough of this. My wife has gone through all she can take, and I would appreciate it if from this day forward you stay away from us." He turned on his heels and left Kathy standing alone in the parking lot. Her heart ached for Alexis, and in fact, her heart ached for the whole family, but if they didn't allow her to talk to Alexis there was very little she could do. She walked back to her car and wiped her eyes before she started the engine and left to go home. As she drove off, she looked up toward Alexis's room, and when she did, she thought she saw a little girl wearing piggy tails waving goodbye.

#

Alexis had never seen a prettier park. She didn't know where Lily was taking her, but so far she loved the area. There were flowers everywhere, of all shapes and sizes, and in the distance she could hear children squealing excitedly.

"Where are we, Lily?"

"I don't know the name of the place, but it is nice, isn't it? There is a play area over there, right past that hill. Come on, let's go look at it!"

The two girls ran toward the green hill, their hair sparkling like dew in sunshine, and their clothes flowing in the soft breeze that lifted just a few seconds before.

"I have a surprise for you," Lily said, "but I can't tell you what it is yet."

"For me? I love surprises, Lily! You are the best friend anyone could have in the whole wide world."

They ran the short distance to the hill and suddenly Alexis stopped to look around. She spun around herself to take it all in – the puffy white clouds that looked like cosmic cotton candy, the tall, majestic trees that seemed perfect for a book and an apple, and the bright yellow playground with three swings and spiral slides.

"Wow! This place is amazing! But where is everybody?"

When Alexis looked at her friend, she was taken aback by the sad look in her eyes.

"I don't know. I can hear the other children too, but I can never see them."

"Oh Lily...is that why you are always so eager to play?"

Lily smiled. "Yes. This beautiful playground is lonely if I always have to play alone."

"Where are your parents, Lily?"

"I'm not sure. I was told my mother sent me back because she wasn't ready for me. It was hard to accept in the beginning, but I got used to it. That's why I was trying to help William when I saw him looking for his mother. I swear, I tried! It was like he couldn't even hear me – he just kept on walking and crying."

"But who takes care of you now? How do you do things without adults helping you?"

"Oh, adults do help me sometimes. Not *all* the time, but they do when I need them."

"That doesn't sound too bad then...at least you

don't have people telling you that you are crazy."

"Yes, I don't have to worry about that. In fact, I don't have to worry about anything at all. And I have warned you about telling your parents about me. If they give you medicine, the door is going to close, and I won't be able to get through any more to see you."

"I know, Lily. I do my best to keep it all to myself, but sometimes it is really hard. Like, for example, when you told me about Tracey's baby...how could I *not* say something?"

"It's okay, Alexis. Now close your eyes and I will show you your surprise."

Alexis did as her friend asked and when she opened her eyes again, Tracey was standing in front of her, holding a tiny baby. Alexis wanted to jump and hug her, but she was afraid to harm the small creature Tracey was cradling in her arms. "Tracey! Is that really you?"

Tracey smiled. Her hair was no longer just blond but a cascade of gold; her eyes were deep pools of blue Alexis wanted to dive into. "Of course it's me, silly. I am not sure exactly where we are, but I like this place. And I got to meet your friend Lily – we talk a bit from time to time, when I am not too busy taking care of Justin."

Alexis couldn't wipe the grin off her face. "Is Justin the name of your baby?"

"Yes. Do you like it?"

"I do! I am going to be the best aunt ever. He is going to love auntie Alexis."

Lily's soft voice broke into the conversation. "You can't play with the baby, Alexis. In fact, you are not supposed to be here at all – you know that."

"But, I thought you said you wanted me to stay, Lily."

"I do, but Uncle Jessie says you can't stay."

"Who's Uncle Jessie?"

"He is one of the adults I was telling you about. He said that you need to go back and help."

"Help? Who?"

"He didn't say. Uncle Jessie always talks in riddles, it seems. But we can't argue with him."

"Well, okay then…but can I talk to Tracey a little longer?"

Lily thought for a minute. "Okay, Alexis. You can't

stay long, but I guess a little chat with your sister can't hurt anything."

When they turned around, Tracey was gone.

"Oh? She was here just now...where did she go?" Alexis asked.

"I'm not sure, but we can look for her after we play for a while. Come on, let's go."

The two girls ran together toward the playground, and Alexis never heard her mother calling her name.

Chapter 13

Mike Howard glimpsed at his wife sitting in the chair beside him, and for the first time he fully realized the toll this tragedy had taken on her. In the past, Rose Howard always took pride in her appearance, but now her face was free of make-up, her hair appeared dull, and her silk shirt hung loosely on a body that had become too thin in a matter of days. Her eyes were fixed on the doctor in front of her, but Mike wasn't sure if Rose could actually hear him talk. Like Alexis, Rose had withdrawn into herself, and Mike was quickly losing the ability to reach out to her.

"I believe it is best for Alexis to be reintegrated into a more familiar environment." The voice of Dr. Brenner spread through the small office, and Mike was grateful for the distraction – worrying about Rose had become his number one job these days.

"Then I will make arrangements today, Doctor. We were planning on staying in the area for the length of the investigation, but since our daughter's body is ready to be released for burial, we really don't have a reason to stay. We can stay in touch by phone, and if necessary I can fly back here on my own. I believe it will also be good for my wife to go home."

The doctor took a good look at Rose and nodded. "I agree with you. What she has been through is very hard to process in a foreign environment."

Rose didn't respond, but rather sat motionless, her eyes dark and empty. Her hands were clamped over her lap and her face was so still that Dr. Brenner – a man in his late fifties with a receding hairline and a salt-and-pepper beard but still quite attractive in his own distinguished way – felt compelled to look at her repeatedly to see if she had moved at all. Rose Howard's heart was still beating, and blood was still being pumped through her body, but her soul had taken a leave of absence the evening she saw her daughter's body laying lifeless on the gurney.

"What exactly is wrong with Alexis, Doctor?"

"In all honesty, Mr. Howard, I don't know. Like Mrs. Howard, Alexis seems to have found a sanctuary within, and she has shut the door on the outside world. It is a fairly common defense mechanism, but her refusal to eat and drink can be extremely dangerous, especially at such a young age. My advice is for Alexis to be taken back home after she is released from this hospital, to see if getting back to everything that's familiar to her will help her snap back. Of course, I would like to admit her and keep her overnight just to make sure she is getting the fluids and the nourishment she needs. Once you are home, you can talk to her pediatrician and maybe get a few referrals for mental health practitioners in your area."

Mike nodded, but Rose did not budge, her detachment from reality keeping her safe in a cocoon of denial.

"Of course, Doctor. Whatever you think is best for her."

"Is Mrs. Howard eating and drinking?"

"Yes. Not as much as she should, unfortunately, but it is to be expected I suppose."

Doctor Brenner nodded and stood up, extending his hand to shake Mike's as he pushed back his chair. "Very well, then. I will instruct the nurse to get Alexis into a room and to start an intravenous drip. She will also bring you any paperwork you need to fill out."

"Thank you, doctor." Mike shook the other man's hand, glad for the direct contact with a human being.

Doctor Brenner stood by the door of his office to see the Howards out, and felt his heart tighten as he watched Rose leaning on her husband for support.

Mike held Rose's hand as they walked toward the triage area where Alexis was being monitored by a nurse, and he helped her sit on the chair near the bed. "Stay here Sweetheart. Can I get you something to drink? Coffee? Tea?"

Rose just shook her head but didn't speak, and her eyes filled with tears as she focused on Alexis's small body being swallowed by a white sheet on the large bed. She wept softly and reached out for her daughter's hand, then brought the tiny hand to her lips and kissed it tenderly. "Alexis, please come back to me. I can't lose you too."

Mike felt his heart shatter in his chest from the impact of Rose's words, and he swallowed hard to push back his own tears. He placed his hand on Rose's shoulder and squeezed it gently. "She will come back, Rose. You heard Dr. Brenner – being home, surrounded by everything she loves, will help her. I am going to call the funeral home and the Lieutenant right now, and try to arrange everything by tonight. Hopefully they will release Alexis tomorrow and then we will leave as soon as possible. There is nothing for us to do here right now, and our daughter needs to go home."

For the first time since acknowledging Tracey's death, Rose's eyes filled with resolve. The fog that had kept her shielded from absorbing the truth had lifted. She lost one daughter, and she would have to bear the weight of that pain the rest of her life, but right now she needed to pull herself together for Alexis. "Go back to the hotel, Mike, and work on getting us back home. I will stay here with Alexis."

In the last few weeks, Mike had felt completely alone; now, he and Rose were a team again. The relief he felt from Rose's unexpected reaction flooded his body and tears ran freely down his face. He didn't even bother wiping them away and, instead, he hugged his wife and kissed her tenderly on the forehead.

"I'm sorry, Mike."

"What are you sorry for, Love?"

"I'm sorry I let self-pity get in the way. Neither you nor Alexis deserved that. I feel terrible that I got so wrapped up in my own feelings that I forgot how hard things were for the two of you."

"You lost a child, Rose. Nobody can fault you for that."

"You're right, but I have another child, Mike – one who is alive; who's suffering from losing her sister and is surely confused about a lot of things. It is up to me to help her through this."

Mike nodded. "It's up to us, Rose. And I am glad we found out that talking to that woman was only making things worse."

Rose didn't respond.

"Hopefully Dr. Brenner is right," Mike continued, his energy renewed by his wife's response, "and Alexis will shift back to her old self once she is exposed to familiar things in her own environment."

"I'm sure he is right, Mike. We just need to take our little girl back home, and everything will work itself out."

Mike hugged her one more time before he left. He blew a kiss in her direction,   and then he was gone. Rose lay down beside her daughter and wrapped her arms around her small body; it wasn't long before she dozed off. In her dream, two little girls were running through a park, and Tracey was with them, holding a newborn baby. One of the young girls was Alexis, the other one appeared to be a bit older and dressed in outdated clothes. Rose called them, but they ignored her at first, and it wasn't until she ran to them that they all turned around and acknowledged her presence. The girl with her hair pulled into piggy tales locked eyes with her, and Rose froze. She saw the little girl with the piggy tales sitting alone outside a farm house, crying softly. A woman stepped out of the front door, and with a harsh voice told the girl to go inside to help. "You have to pull your weight," she told her, "I can't do it all on my own. The good Lord knows I had enough mouths to feed and enough children to take care of before He took your mother during childbirth." The little girl went inside with the woman, her head bent down as she sadly looked at the worn shoes on her feet. When the door closed, Rose was transported to a different scene, taking place in the woods behind the farmhouse: The girl with the piggy tales was being raped by a soldier. From the uniform, Rose thought he was fighting for the Union, but since history was never her favorite subject, she wasn't too sure. The man forced himself on her, and when she screamed he placed his hand over her mouth -- in a few moments he had stolen her innocence, and now he was stealing her life. As Rose cried for a young life snuffed so senselessly, she was whisked away to yet another place. She saw herself in an operating room, waiting for anesthesia to take effect. She knew that within a few minutes she would be asleep, and the fruit of her relationship with Matthew Lawry would be plucked from her existence. As the blissful feeling of numbness from the sedation took effect, Rose said goodbye to the baby she would never hold. Then everything went black, and when Rose looked again, she was back at the park. Alexis was pulling the little girl's hand, urging her to follow. "Come on, Lily, let's go play!" They ran up the hill together, but suddenly, before they disappeared over the hill, the girl turned around and looked at Rose again with sad eyes. "Do you understand now, Mother?"

With that, they were gone, and Rose was left standing alone, crying for the little girl who never knew the warmth of a loving family.

"Are you okay, Mrs. Howard?" The voice of the nurse filtered through the fibers of her dream, and her hand gently touched Rose's arm to awaken her.

Rose was confused for a moment, her eyes trying to adjust to the reality of the hospital room, while her arms were still wrapped around Alexis.

"Yes…I'm sorry, I must have dozed off."

"Oh, okay…you were crying in your dream, so I just wanted to make sure you are alright."

Rose wiped the tears from her eyes and looked at

Alexis first, and then at the nurse. "I'm fine. I was dreaming of my daughters."

Rose smiled and touched Alexis's hand. "I thought one of them was lost forever; it didn't occur to me that some day she would become Alexis's best friend."

#

"Do you know if the apartment complex offers any additional storage space, Ms. Townsend?"

Mary was already annoyed about the intrusion so early in the day, and dealing with Sergeant Parker was no picnic in the park. For some reason unknown to her at the moment, his presence alone irritated the hell out of her, and she was ready to wrap up the search and go back to bed. "I don't know, Detective. I didn't live here full time until recently, in case you have forgotten."

Parker huffed, and ignored her abrasive tone. "The management office should know. I guess I will have to give them a call."

"You do that. Now, can I go back to bed? I didn't get home until four hours ago, and I wasn't expecting company."

"Where is your car, Ms. Townsend?"

"It is being repaired."

"I see. What was wrong with it?"

"The fender was dented."

"How did that happen?"

"I'm not sure Detective. You should ask Shannon that – she is the one who damaged it."

"Unfortunately Ms. Brinkley is unable to answer my questions at the moment."

"Then I am afraid you are out of luck. I already told your pal Lackey everything I know. Compare notes with him. Now, if you will excuse me…" Mary stood up and headed down the hallway toward the bedroom, leaving Parker alone in the living room.

He left the apartment and headed toward the main office. A pleasant looking woman dressed in a powder blue suit welcomed him with a broad smile which appeared as artificial as the platinum hair cascading over her shoulders. "Good morning, may I help you?" Her southern accent was atrociously thick and syrupy enough to make Parker fear an increase in blood sugar. He flashed his badge and went straight to the point.

"I am Sergeant Parker, with Raleigh Police. As you know, we are investigating the death of Tracey Newman, one of your residents."

"I know! Quite dreadful, isn't it? God bless her little heart – such a nice young lady…"

"Yes, it's a pity. I was wondering if the apartments have additional storage space on the premises."

"Oh yes, of course. Each apartment comes with additional storage. It's a separate building."

"I see. And where is the building?"

"I will go with you, Sergeant. I'll bring the master key."

"Thank you, Ma'am."

Parker grimaced as the tall blonde walked in front of him to lead the way and left behind an invisible cloud of sweet perfume – Jasmine, he thought, and definitely lots of it.

They drove to a building directly behind the one where Tracey Newman lived, and Parker followed as the woman walked toward a unit situated at the far right corner. "Here it is. This is the storage unit assigned to Ms. Newman's apartment." She unlocked the door and stepped back to let Parker in.

The small unit was stuffy and smelled of mold. Parker shifted to breathing through his mouth, something Dr. Greer taught him to do when he went in to assist autopsies. The belongings stored inside were the usual ones people kept in storage units – a pair of hiking boots, a few bags of old clothes that were probably meant for charity, a card table and folding chairs, and a few suitcases. Two cardboard boxes were stuffed in the corner to the left, and Parker peeked into the first one – old notebooks and a discarded tape player were laid over a folded blanket. He moved the box on the top and opened the second one. "Holy shit!" The profanity he inadvertently let out crystallized in the humid air and made the woman in the blue suit gasp. He pulled out the box and laid it on the floor of the unit, then ran to his car. "Don't touch anything!" He yelled to the woman who was almost tipping over on her heels to see what was in the box but had no courage to move from the place where she was standing.

He grabbed a pair of gloves from the box on the passenger seat and called Lackey. "You are not going to believe what I have here."

"I hope something more than I have. I'm at Jack Little's place, and it appears that he has left town. I was going to question him about that e-mail and the photo he sent Tracey."

"Well, get your ass here right away. This is big!"

Lackey knew Parker better than most people at the department, and didn't waste time trying to pry information out of him. "Where are you?"

"Storage unit behind the apartment building where Tracey Newman lived."

"I'm on my way."

Parker ran back to the unit and put his gloves on. "How many keys to the unit are available to residents?"

"One usually, but we can provide additional copies for a fee."

"How many keys did Ms. Newman have?"

"Well, she had two to start with, since her roommate, Ms. Brinkley, paid for an extra one. But, I remember very clearly that about two weeks ago, a friend of Ms. Brinkley's came by the office and said that one of the keys was lost, and she was picking one up for her."

"What did this friend look like? Did you get her name?"

"I certainly did. I was the person who gave it to her. Her name was Mary Townsend."

#

Kathy dialed the number for Dr. Greer's office she found in Tom's old address book. For the longest time he wrote every number in the little booklet, and it was only recently that he transferred phone numbers and addresses into the new phone she got him for Christmas. Kathy had suggested he should throw the little black book away, but Tom had vehemently refused, on the basis that electronics sometimes fail while good old address books never do. Today, Kathy said a small blessing to thank God for Tom being so old-fashioned.

"This is Dr. Greer. I am away from my desk right now, so leave me a message and I will call you back as soon as I can. If you need to talk to someone right away, press 'one' now and you will be connected to the receptionist." Dr Greer's voice on the recording had the promise of a baritone, and Kathy wondered if his voice sounded as deep in person.

"Dr. Greer, my name is Kathy Spencer, and I am Lieutenant Lackey's girlfriend. I have a few medical questions for you, in connection with the case of the young woman who was found at Durant Park. I would really appreciate it if you could call me back. My number is 919-875-1450."

She had barely disconnected when the phone rang, making her jump.

"Hello?"

"Ms. Spencer? This is Frances Downey. Are my daughter's portraits ready?"

"Almost, Mrs. Downey. I've been a little sidetracked the last few days, but I should have them ready by tomorrow for you. What time would you like to come by?"

"The bridal party is going to be the day after tomorrow, Ms. Spencer! We are not going to have enough time!" The panic in the woman's voice was tangible, and Kathy did her best to reassure her, though she could feel her eyes roll toward the back of her head.

"I will make sure they are ready by tonight before I leave, Mrs. Downey. If necessary, I will personally go to set them up in the party room. If you prefer to pick them up instead, they will be available tomorrow morning at, say, ten o' clock?"

"Hmmmph! I will come and pick them up. I will be at the studio at 9:55."

"Of course, Mrs. Downey. I will be here."

She hung up the phone and turned toward the computer. She clicked on the file Mrs. Downey was so distraught about, and several image tiles appeared on the monitor screen. She selected each of them individually and sent them to the printer. When she picked up the prints, something caught her eye: The bride and groom-to-be were smiling gloriously from every shot, and some of the photos featured relatives proudly standing beside the happy girl, but there was no trace of Mrs. Downey! Kathy was sure she had taken pictures of the bride and her mother together – how could one forget doing anything Mrs. Downey was involved in? *Make sure you capture the light filtering through that window, Ms. Spencer…I think the greenery outside will give a sense of freshness to the photos, I'm sure you agree…I should sit, Ms. Spencer, don't you think?*

There was no doubt Kathy had immortalized Mrs. Downey in numerous photos, so where were they now? She found the photos – exactly as she remembered them -- but the young bride was standing alone in them, her bright and hopeful face dominating each shot. Kathy was confused – how could this have happened? And, worst of all, *how* was she going to explain it to the abrasive Mrs. Downey tomorrow morning? Surely Mrs. Downey was going to be furious, and right now she really didn't have the energy to deal with the tantrums of a diva. She scanned the hard drive to see if the original photos were maybe saved in a different folder, but nothing turned out.

She got up from her desk and starting walking in circles around the room – something she subconsciously did any time she was trying to find a solution to something impossible – all the while rehearsing her apology to Mrs. Downey.

*I'm sorry, Mrs. Downey, but your persona magically deleted itself from the photos…*no, too strange. *Mrs. Downey, I must have accidentally deleted you off the photos, but I will be happy to take a few more shots of you and your daughter after the party, free of charge of course*...Hmmmm...this one didn't sound too bad. Kathy made a mental note to rehearse it a few more times to make it sound credible. In reality she had no idea what the hell happened, but she had to come up with something to say. Owning responsibility, she knew, was one of the best ways to appeal to people's compassion.

She went back to the computer and opened the file again – still no pictures of Mrs. Downey. She rebooted the computer and clicked the file again, holding her breath and praying in her own head, but when the file opened, Mrs. Downey was still Missing In Action. She finished printing the shots of the bride alone and placed them on her desk, to insert them in the frames that were waiting in a box by the door.

After she was done, she was satisfied with what she had, but the mystery had yet to be solved. It was like a virtual eraser had hacked her computer and deleted Mrs. Downey from her daughter's existence.

Kathy shut down the computer and grabbed her purse to go out to lunch, just as a storm approached. In the distance, the sound of a baby crying was silenced by an explosive clap of thunder.

#

"I have told you over and over, Lieutenant. I didn't put those boots in the storage unit. I have no idea how they got there." Mary Townsend tried to remain calm, but her tone reflected a frustration that was quickly reaching the boiling point.

The two detectives exchanged a quick glance, and Tom walked across the room to pick up the blood-stained boots that were retrieved in the storage unit. "Look here, Mary, we have a witness saying that you went to pick up a key right around the time that Tracey went missing, and you told Sergeant Parker that you weren't even aware of additional storage being available. Don't you think it is a strange coincidence?"

Mary didn't respond. Instead, she shook her head and looked down. Tom brought the boots right to her, and placed them on the coffee table in front of the couch. The dark blood stains were visible through the clear plastic bag that Parker had put them into for protection.

"Take a look at these boots, Mary. Are they yours?"

"No, they aren't." Mary's voice filtered through gritted teeth.

"How do you think they ended up in the storage unit?"

"I don't have a fuckin' clue, okay? Santa Claus could have put them in there as far as I know! I didn't want to get into a conversation with the other cop because I was tired, and the reason why I went to pick up another key is because Shannon couldn't find her own or Tracey's."

"Do you know anyone who wears boots like these, Mary?"

"Lots of people wear these boots. Why, my brother even has a pair…" the moment those words left her lips, Mary's face dropped a shade of color. The same realization washed over Parker, as the words of the IT technician echoed in his mind: *One of them is a photo sent by someone named J. Bernardini just two days before the murder. The photo displays a very creepy table covered with photos of Tracey Newman. The message sent along with the photo said: "I will love you even after death do us part."*

"Lackey, may I talk to you a minute?"

Tom followed Parker to the other end of the room. "What is it?"

"Remember the weird e-mail that Jack Little sent to Tracey right before she died? Don't you think it is strange that the same man owns a pair of boots like these?"

"It is strange, Parker, but it is only circumstantial evidence. And our guy seems to be out of town. I was there when you called me and his landlord said she hasn't seen him around in a few days. One of the neighbors reported hearing a TV being on, but she is eighty years old and suffering from dementia, so her testimony is shit. We need to get into the apartment, but we're not going to get in there without a warrant, and Judge Harris doesn't dispense those too easily, as you know."

"Well, we need a warrant if someone knows we are

going in. But Sister Mary here might have a key." Parker replied matter-of-factly.

"Mary," Tom asked as he walked back to the couch where Mary Townsend was sitting, "do you happen to have a key to your brother's apartment?"

"Why do you want to know?"

"Listen, Mary," Tom said in his most paternal voice, "between the e-mail he sent Tracey, and these boots here, your brother Jack could be in a lot of trouble. If we get into his place, and we find his boots, then he is off the hook. We're not trying to hurt him, even if you are probably thinking the opposite right now."

Mary thought for a moment, her eyes darting from one side to the other of the room, as if trying to decide between the lesser of two evils.

"If I get you inside Jack's apartment and you find his boots, are you going to leave us both alone?"

"If we don't find any incriminating evidence, you bet."

"Let's do it. Let's go right now."

Parker looked at Tom with a puzzled frown on his face, probably more than a little confused by Mary's will to cooperate. Tom nodded and led the way.

The three of them got into Tom's car and headed south on Capital Boulevard toward the Beltline. They arrived in Jack's neighborhood within fifteen minutes. An old woman with a faded housedress was outside the building watering a potted plant that appeared as worn out as its surroundings, with puke-colored leaves hanging down over the cheap plastic container. When she saw the two men knocking on Jack's door, she stopped watering the plant and addressed them with a smoky voice. "If you is looking for Mr. Bernardini, he be gone."

"Are you the landlord?"

"Yes, Sir, that's me alright. He owe me rent fo' this here month, and he gone like a thief in the night."

Or like a murderer in the night... Tom thought, but those words never formed into a sentence others could hear.

"This is his sister, Mrs...Mrs...what is your name, Ma'am?"

"Mrs. Jenkins. Herriette Jenkins."

Tom hurried to shake her hand. "I am Lieutenant

Lackey, and this is Sergeant Parker, with Raleigh police. We received a missing person report and we are inquiring on the whereabouts of Mr. Bernardini."

Parker walked up. "Wait, I was here a couple of days ago, and the landlord I met was a different person. A man, to be exact."

Mrs. Jenkins pursed her lips for a few seconds, then she said, "You met my boyfriend, William."

"It could be." Parker replied, before retreating behind Tom.

"Is there any way you would allow us in, Mrs. Jenkins? Just to take a look around?"

"You gotta warran'?"

"We just want to take a friendly look. His sister here has a key, but we wanted to make sure it is okay with you first."

"It don't bothe' me none. Just turn off the lights befo' you leave."

"We will, Ma'am. Thank you."

Mrs. Jenkins went back to water the sick plant, while Tom, Parker and Mary walked the rickety steps to the front door. Mary unlocked the door and walked in first; Tom and Parker followed her."

The house was meticulously clean – almost too clean for a man living alone. The blinds were closed and the whirring sound of the window air-conditioning unit echoed against the barren white walls. The living room was sparsely furnished, aside from a couch, an old TV and a small, chipped coffee table. No pictures on the walls, no knick-knacks anywhere, no sign of books or magazines anywhere: The place looked uninhabited. Tom and Parker moved to the small kitchen, where— aside from an ancient stove—the only items were an old avocado green Formica table accompanied by two chairs, and a small refrigerator. The bathroom was no different. A faded blue shower curtain was the only splash of color in an entirely white room. The only thing on the counter suggesting occupancy was a hair brush.

When they walked into the bedroom, both Parker and Tom froze. In front of them was a table covered with small items and photos of Tracey, the frames of which were darkened by the soot from nearby candles. The candles were long extinguished, and a small pool of hardened wax had formed a perfect circle.

"Holy crap! What the fuck is this?!" Parker almost yelled.

Mary came around the corner, and echoed Parker's sentiment. "Oh my God…what is this?"

"This, ladies and gentlemen, is a shrine – a shrine for Tracey, to be exact." Tom explained in an even voice even if he was a little surprised himself by their discovery. He had seen the photo Jack sent Tracey, but in person the table looked different, bigger and certainly creepier. "No offense, Mary, but your brother appears to be a little fucked up in the head."

Mary didn't say anything. She turned away from the table and went to sit on Jack's bed, as tears threatened to erupt and ruin her masculine appearance.

Parker went to open the drawer of the bedside table and found it locked. He pulled a small knife from his pocket and forced the lock to open. He used the tip of the knife to lift a gun from the wooden enclosure. "Well…I'll be damned. Go grab a bag, Lackey. If I am not mistaken a .44 Magnum is exactly the same type of gun that shot Tracey Newman."

Chapter 14

Tom stretched his legs under the desk in his office and wished he could go home. Things between him and Kathy were better but still didn't feel the same. She seemed very disheartened when she got home the night before, but didn't volunteer any information and Tom didn't ask. She went to bed early; Tom was sure he heard her crying from the living room, but he made no attempt to go into the bedroom and see if she was okay. What was wrong with him? Kathy was the best thing that had ever happened to him, and he wasn't even trying to stop himself from screwing up the relationship. He dialed her number at the studio and waited for her to answer.

"Hello"

"Kathy, it's me…"

"Tom…is everything okay?"

"Yes…no…I mean, everything is okay with me, but I don't feel that *we* are okay."

Kathy's heart thumped violently against her chest: Wasn't this how things ended with Andy? *Nothing is wrong with me, Kathy, but we aren't working out any more…*

"I guess we aren't, Tom. Is that all?"

"No, it's not. I wanted to know if you would like to go out to dinner tonight. Parker told me of a nice little restaurant not too far from home. What do you say?"

Relief spread through Kathy's entire body and she felt her knees soften. "I would like that. What time would you like to go?"

"Seven, maybe? I should be out of here by then. I probably won't have time to go home and change, but I can meet you there after I leave the office."

"Seven is great. It will give me time to bring some portraits to a reception hall before we meet."

"Great! And Kathy? I'm sorry…"

273

Kathy felt tears burning behind her eyelids and she swallowed the knot in her throat to keep her voice steady. "I'm sorry too, Tom. The past couple of weeks have been emotionally exhausting."

"Yes, they have, and I really hate that my own work issues have affected our private lives."

"No big deal. And just so you know, I won't be seeing Alexis any more. It was time for me to distance myself from the Howards anyway." Her heart broke as she spoke the words, but she was able to hide the pain from Tom, somehow.

Tom smiled. "Good. I know you are attached to that little girl, but it really is time to let go. And if I am not mistaken, Dr. Greer said they are sending Tracey's body to the funeral home tomorrow, so it can be prepared to travel home for a proper burial."

Alexis is leaving town...

"I hope the family can overcome this tragedy. They will if they stick to one another."

"I am going to call them shortly to let them know that we have a warrant for the arrest of Jack Little."

"The guy who stalked her? Did he kill her?"

"We found the murder weapon at his house, and he left town right before we got there. He sounds pretty guilty to me. We also looked for a pair of steel-toed boots his sister says he owns, but we couldn't find any. Meanwhile, we found a pair of the same boots in Tracey's storage unit, and they were splattered with blood."

"That's a shame. Hopefully Tracey's family will find some peace now, if that's at all possible." Her first thought was of Alexis, and how knowing her sister's killer was going to be apprehended was going to affect her, but she brushed the thought away quickly.

"So, I will see you at seven, right?"

"Yes, where do you want me to meet you?"

"I will be parked in the Perkins lot at about 6:50; then you can follow me to the restaurant if you want."

"Sounds great! I'll see you there."

Tom hung up, feeling a bit better. Parker walked into his office within a few seconds, bearing a handful of papers and a somber face, his usual.

"The warrant is out to all agencies in the nation, so no matter where our friend has gone, we will find him."

"That's great, but I wonder why he would choose to hide the boots at the place where his sister lives. And how did he get a key? According to the Barbie doll at the management office, it was Mary Townsend who went to ask for an extra key."

Parker's face appeared assorted in thought. "Hmm…I've wondered the same thing, but I guess we'll be able to get all those bits of information in place after we get him into custody. I'd better head back over there. We didn't leave anyone in charge, and you are not planning on going back right now, are you?"

"Actually, I was hoping to take the evening off. Things have been a little tense between Kathy and me lately, because of the long hours and all, so I was thinking of taking her out to dinner."

"You do that, Lackey. I'm on my way to Little's house. I will call you if we find anything else."

Tom's phone rang just as Parker was getting ready to leave.

"Lackey, can I help you?"

"Lieutenant, this is Officer Rogers. I am calling from Jack Little's house."

"Yes, Officer Rogers. Parker is on the way. He should be there in less than thirty minutes. Did you find something else?"

"I think so, Sir. We found a receipt for a bus trip to St. Louis, Missouri, in a box filled with photos of Tracey Newman and her family. A lot of the photos are of a young girl that looks like Tracey Newman, Sir."

Alexis…

"I'll call Parker and let him know, Officer. Make sure you secure the area and you don't let anyone in."

Tom hung up the phone and dialed Parker's mobile number. "Parker, one of the uniforms just called. They found a receipt for a bus trip to St. Louis in a box filled with photos of Tracey's family."

"Sonofabitch! I wanna rip his head off with my bare hands!"

"Yeah, me too. Are you sure you don't need me?"

"Nah. Take care of your lady, Lackey. I've got this. I'll call you if anything comes up."

"I'll make sure to have my phone on. Thank you, Parker, you're a pal."

Parker huffed and hung up. Tom looked at his watch – four-thirty in the afternoon – and decided that maybe he should leave now and go buy some flowers for Kathy. He didn't get flowers very often, but he knew she liked them – white roses, especially – and tonight was the perfect occasion to be a little romantic. Maybe he could stop by a jewelry store and get a little trinket for her, too, just to show her how important she is to him. If he hurried, he would even have time to go home and shower before meeting her. He grabbed his car keys and his mobile phone and left the building. Had he stayed a few minutes longer, he would have known that Brad Johnson had been busted selling drugs in a seedy part of town. When the officers searched his car, they found a . 44 Magnum inside the glove compartment. A blood-spattered T-shirt was also hidden inside a grocery bag in the trunk.

#

It was almost four-forty when Kathy looked at the clock in her car, and she hoped to catch Dr. Greer before he left for the day. No matter what she had said to Tom – and no matter how much she wished she could put this case behind her – she couldn't just sit back and do nothing. Dr. Greer had been very helpful when she spoke with him on the phone, and he confirmed what she thought: Images didn't remain on the eye, since the information captured was transferred by the optical nerve to the brain, but although science couldn't prove that a print of the image could remain on the retina or the iris, it didn't disprove it either. One of Kathy's skills was to use different techniques to remove imperfections of any type from photographs, so her goal was to first analyze Tracey's eyes with an Iriscope, and then to take several digital pictures of each eye and enlarge them enough to see if anything aside from the usual was visible. She didn't want to ask Dr. Greer on the phone if he would allow her to take the photos—this was something she really needed to address in person.

By the time she pulled into the parking lot of the medical building that was almost a second home for Dr. Greer – a decade of hearing of his insane working hours from Tom had crystallized this image of the good doctor in her mind – it was only five minutes before five. She almost ran inside and asked the receptionist to announce her. The receptionist asked her to sit in the waiting room and she paged Dr. Greer.

Kathy looked around the room, and wondered how anyone could spend an extended amount of time in this place. It wasn't gloomy or unattractive, and whoever took care of decorating had done a good job masking the lugubrious atmosphere into a more clinical one, but it was still a place where death reigned supreme. She wondered how many bodies Dr. Greer had worked on over the course of his long career, but before she could come up with a tentative answer to that question, a deep velvety voice filled the pockets of silence which, until that point, had been interrupted only by the receptionist typing on her computer.

"Ms. Spencer? I'm Dr. Greer. I understand you want to see me."

Kathy stood up and extended her hand to the doctor. "Yes, Dr. Greer. I have something to ask you, but I didn't think it would go over too well on the phone. Do you have a moment to talk to me?"

"Of course. Would you like to come to my office?"

"I would. Thank you, Doctor."

She followed Dr. Greer through an intricate maze of narrow hallways, and as she walked a step behind him she couldn't help but stare at the pristine white color of his hair; it was almost hypnotizing, and from a rear view it was hard to tell where his hair ended and his lab coat started. Set against the white walls and walking with his hands in his pockets, Dr. Greer was nearly invisible from behind, except for the brown trousers that poked from beneath his coat at knee level.

They entered a small office on the right, and Dr. Greer invited Kathy to sit on one of the chairs in front of his desk while he took his place across from her.

"So, what did you want to talk to me about, Ms. Spencer?"

Kathy scrambled to find the right words that wouldn't get her kicked out the moment they came out. "As I told you on the phone, Doctor, I am a professional photographer and an amateur iridologist."

Dr. Greer nodded but didn't interrupt. Kathy took his silence as a cue to continue talking. "We discussed how images immediately leave the eye when they are transferred to the brain through the optical nerves, but you mentioned that research is inconclusive when it comes to the possibility of images leaving a print of sort on some parts of the eye itself – something very faint, maybe, like a fingerprint."

"We already talked about this on the phone, Ms. Spencer. Is there something else you would like to ask or discuss?"

Kathy swallowed hard. "Yes, Doctor. I am wondering if you would allow me to analyze Tracey Newman's eyes with an iriscope, and if it is possible for me to take a few digital photos."

Silence fell between them for what felt to Kathy like an eternity. She could almost hear the thumping of her heart against the chest cavity, and she wondered if Dr. Greer could hear it too.

"As I previously said, Ms. Spencer, science does not support your theory."

"Yes, but what if there is one chance in a million that I can lift an image? Wouldn't it be worth trying? Look, Dr. Greer, I know that arrangements are being made to transfer Tracey Newman's body tomorrow. This is my only chance to do this. Please, I am begging you to let me try."

"The eyes are one of the first things in the body to deteriorate, Ms. Spencer. I doubt you would be able to get an accurate reading, if you could get anything at all."

Kathy felt the door between Dr. Greer's rejection and his approval cracking slightly, so she quickly slid her foot in the opening to prevent it from closing on her dreams of finding Tracey's killer.

"I understand that, Doctor, and I am prepared for defeat if necessary."

"I am not sure I can help you analyze the retina now. Retina scanning involves a process that could take some time."

"I understand; I have done reasonable research on that. Could I at least look at the iris in both eyes? I have some instruments with me, and it won't take long."

Dr Greer studied Kathy's face for a few seconds before he replied.

"Why is this so important to you, Ms. Spencer?"

Kathy didn't expect this question, and didn't know what to respond. "I'm not sure, Doctor. I have become obsessed with this case, and I feel that if there is one chance that I can help, I am willing to go all the way with it."

"You are interfering with an investigation, Ms. Spencer."

"No, not really. You have the body here and have already conducted an autopsy. I only want to look at the girl's eyes." She was a bit surprised at her own tone, but determined to stand her ground.

"Very well then," Dr. Greer said standing up from the over-stuffed chair he was sitting on, "Do you have time now? My wife is visiting friends tonight, and she won't be home until late."

Kathy was surprised to hear that Dr. Greer was married. In her mind she had painted him as single.

"Absolutely! I'm just going to run to my car to pick up a few things and I will be right back." Right after she spoke, she felt embarrassed by the way her words had come out – she sounded more like a little girl on Christmas morning than a respected professional.

Before Dr. Greer could re-think his agreement, she almost ran out the door to go pick up her things from the trunk of her car.

"Meet me in room C when you get back inside. I'll have the body ready for viewing."

"I will, Dr. Greer! Thank you!"

She passed the receptionist without saying a word to her, and practically ran to her car where she picked up two small cases from the trunk and went back inside. The receptionist was ready to say something when she saw her walking in, but Kathy sped by her desk again and disappeared through the white door before any sounds could escape from the young woman's lips.

She tried to remember the path she had followed earlier with Dr. Greer, but one hallway led to another and in no time she was lost. She felt relief pour through her when she saw a young man clad in green scrubs walking toward her. His dark hair and complexion, along with the colorful attire, were a welcome change from the ethereal appearance of a place entirely bathed in white.

"Excuse me, can you direct me to room C? Dr.

Greer is expecting me there."

The man smiled, and his front teeth showed a small gap which Kathy found unique and attractive.

"Yes, it's right down the hallway on the left. Third door on your right."

"Thank you." She smiled back and hurried to the room where Dr. Greer was waiting for her.

When she walked into the room, Dr. Greer was standing beside a gurney where a body lay covered by a white sheet. One of the pasty white feet protruded from the bottom of the sheet, and the first thing Kathy thought of was to check if the reputed toe tag was indeed attached to the body the way she always saw in movies. She didn't see one, but since the other foot was covered, she couldn't be sure it wasn't there. The room emanated a strange odor – a mixture of rubbing alcohol and formaldehyde. The overhead neon light bathed the entire room, and reflected against the white tiles of a nearby table to lend a sparkle to one of the surgical tools on a tray set right beside it.

"Here is Tracey Newman, Ms. Spencer. I will allow you to take a few photographs of her eyes, but you will need to do it quickly."

Kathy nodded and pulled both the iriscope and her camera from the black leather bag she retrieved from the car.

"I will need to have her eyes propped open for a short while."

"That's going to be the tricky part, but we can try." Dr. Greer picked up two shiny tools that reminded Kathy of pliers, positioning one on the top lid and one on the skin beneath the eye. He pulled gently until the first eye opened and the iris was exposed.

"I'm afraid you won't be able to get much of a reading. As I mentioned earlier, the eyes are one of the first organs to become compromised."

Kathy stared at Tracey's open eye, the pupil beneath the milky layer dilated so dramatically that almost no color was left. She felt a deep shiver originating in the deepest part of her stomach and working its way first up her arms and then down to her shaking hands. She positioned the EyePix Handheld in front of Tracey's eyes, happy to have chosen a portable device instead of the full package which requires one to sit in front of the iriscope. Tracey obviously wouldn't have been able to sit and stare into a camera positioned on a table stand, and Kathy would have had a hard time positioning the camera correctly otherwise. She took several photos with the iriscope and a few with her own camera. She would have loved to take some pictures of the retina also, but she was fairly sure that Dr. Greer would not agree to dissect Tracey's eyes to reach the retina situated at the back of each orb. Keeping her thoughts to herself, she prepared the cameras again to shoot images from the other eye.

When she was finished, she capped the lenses of both cameras, and Dr. Greer gently pulled the lids closed over Tracey's eyes. He examined the eyes closely and walked to the tray near the table to pick up something that looked like needle and thread. "I will have to stitch the lids closed. Unfortunately, skin doesn't retain much elasticity after death."

He skillfully placed a stitch into each lid and in no time at all Tracey appeared to be sleeping peacefully once again.

"So, why did you use two different cameras?"

"One of them is not a simple camera; it's a tool used in iridology."

"I've heard of it, but I'm afraid I don't know much about it."

"Iridology is the study of the iris. It is believed that eyes aren't only the window of the soul, but also terminals for most nerve endings in the body; I guess it follows the same concept as reflexology. Professional iridologists can detect illness in different areas of the body just by looking at a patient's eyes. I took a course in it once; found it fascinating. I started looking around for a bargain on a camera and found one online for only five-hundred dollars."

Dr. Greer whistled. Kathy smiled.

"Yes, I know, it is a small fortune for a tool I very rarely use, but the new ones go for as much as three thousand dollars. The day after I bought it I wondered if I had lost my mind for 'throwing so much money down the toilet', as my husband-at-the-time very colorfully said. I knew the day would come when it would be handy. I never expected to become a professional iridologist, but I toyed with the idea of studying this new field to add an understanding of alternative medicine to my existing medical background."

"So, how does it work?"

"It takes very high resolution photos of the iris. The photos can then be sent to a computer for viewing. I can go into detail if you wish to know the technicalities."

"Oh, no, thank you. I think I will stick with traditional medicine. I'm too old for such innovative approaches." Dr. Greer replied as he pulled up the sheet to cover Tracey's face.

Kathy packed her equipment and placed the black leather bag on the table to shake the doctor's hand. 'Thank you so much for your help, Dr. Greer. I really appreciate everything you've done. I am aware of the fact that you had to bypass a few rules to accommodate my requests, and I am very grateful."

"No problem, young lady. Nothing and nobody were harmed in the process, and as you mentioned, the autopsy is already completed, so I don't have to worry about compromising any important evidence. When will you download the photos?"

"I was going to bring my laptop, but my computer

at the studio in much newer, and I prefer to download the images on that one."

"Well, let me know if anything turns out, although I hope you won't be too disappointed if you find less than you expect, Ms. Spencer."

"Maybe so, Doctor, but I have to give it a try."

Dr. Greer nodded and walked Kathy to the door. "Have a great evening, Ms. Spencer, and tell Lackey I said hello."

"I certainly will, Dr. Greer. I'm on my way to meet him for dinner right now."

"Enjoy your evening, Ms. Spencer."

The moment she left the room, Dr. Greer closed the door behind her, and she headed out toward the reception area. As she walked, she tried to follow the mental map of the place which she had drawn upon her arrival.

By the time she reached the restaurant's parking lot, it was only a few minutes before seven, and Kathy was happy to see Tom's car was already there. She pulled up right beside him and rolled down her window. Tom smiled widely the moment he saw her.

"Hello, Beautiful!"

Kathy beamed, and felt relieved that right now, in this moment, their differences seemed to have evaporated like fog on a sunny morning.

"Do you want to follow me, or would you prefer to leave your car here and go together?"

"I'm not sure…where is the restaurant?"

"It's only a block or two north on Capital."

"I think it's better if I follow you. That way we don't have to drive back here to pick up my car."

"That's a plan. The restaurant is in the mall complex."

"Okay. You go ahead and I will be right behind you."

They left the parking lot, Tom leading the way, and they drove to a strip mall adjacent to the main shopping center. Kathy parked her car right beside Tom's and he came around bearing an armful of white roses.

Kathy felt a knot in her throat, and her eyes moistened with tears of relief. "Oh Tom…you old, adorable fool…what are the flowers for?"

"Nothing in particular. I just want to apologize for

the last few days – I've been as tight as the cord of a violin, and I know I haven't been fair to you."

Kathy raised herself on the tip of her toes and pasted a kiss on his lips. "I've been the same way Tom, and I owe you an apology too. I shouldn't have allowed my personal feelings over a case you're working on get the best of me."

Tom wrapped his arms around her as they stood outside the restaurant. "It was my fault, Kathy. I got you involved to start with. I guess this is the reason why mixing business and personal life is not a wise thing to do."

Kathy laid her head on Tom's chest, and thought about telling him of her visit to Dr. Greer, but she decided against it. So what if her professional curiosity led her to do something out of the ordinary? She did nothing wrong, and Dr. Greer didn't seem to have a problem with it. She was pretty sure Dr. Greer would eventually say something to Tom, and the issue of meddling with police business would certainly come up, but there was no reason to spoil a perfectly good evening.

"I'm starving, let's go in." She said as she pulled herself away from Tom's embrace and took his hand into her own.

"Mmm, me too. I hear they have amazing shrimp and grits."

"Oh, I love shrimp and grits! Let's go."

The hostess saw them to a table in the far corner of the room and brought over two glasses of iced water and two menus. Tom glanced at the menu while they waited for their server; when she arrived and introduced herself as Patsy, he handed the menu back. "Shrimp and grits for me. Thank you."

Kathy handed over her menu also. "The same for me please."

Patsy the waitress left and a faint trail of orange blossoms followed her as she went to the kitchen to call the orders.

"So, how was your day?" Tom asked as he lifted his glass to take a sip of water.

"It went great! To tell you the truth, it really started improving after you called. I was a little worried before that."

"You were? Why?"

"I guess old ghosts are hard to bury, Tom. When I saw you distancing yourself from me, old feelings of impending doom showed their ugly face again. I thought I was completely healed from my relationship with Andy, but when I couldn't reach out to you my insecurities kicked in, and I'm ashamed to admit that I feared our relationship was doomed also."

"And that's why I got you this today." Tom pulled a small box from the pocket of his pants and placed it in front of Kathy.

Kathy's eyes widened. "More surprises? Goodness, this is beginning to feel like Christmas." She opened the box to find an exquisite gold bracelet with a single charm attached – a camera.

"Oh Tom…it's beautiful!"

"Do you like it?"

"Oh my, how could I not? It's a stunning piece."

"I love you, Kathy."

Kathy reached her hand across the table to touch Tom's hand. "I love you too, Tom."

The waitress arrived with two piping hot dishes

filled to the rim with shrimp and grits. Sliced mushrooms and bacon bits were arranged as a flower around the outer edges of the plate.

"This looks amazing," she said as she dug her fork into the grits.

They ate in silence for a moment, each of them deeply enjoying the culinary treat. Tom's phone rang. It was Dr. Greer.

"Lackey, it's Dr. Greer."

"Hi Doc! Is everything okay?"

"Sure! Everything is fine, but I was wondering if you could please let Ms. Spencer know she left one of her camera lenses here. I know those things can be pretty darn expensive, so I'm sure she'll be looking for it. I would appreciate it if you could tell her that I will hold it here until I see either you or Parker. Of course, if she prefers to come and pick it up, it's perfectly fine. It will be in the small box on my desk."

"Kathy was there today?"

"Yes. She didn't tell you?"

"Well…we just arrived at the restaurant. I'm sure she would have mentioned something about it before the end of the evening." His eyes locked with Kathy's, demanding an explanation.

"Well, have a great night, Lackey."

"You too, Dr. Greer."

Tom hung up the phone and placed it on the table. His eyes had turned a shade darker each minute of the conversation.

"You care to tell me what's going on, Kathy?" He asked in a tone that was not friendly or even slightly understanding. In fact, Kathy was sure she could detect a note of annoyance in it.

"I had to try this, Tom. It has nothing to do with Alexis. As you know, I have studied iridology, and I am the proud owner of an iriscope which I've never had the opportunity to use before. My goal was to see if images last captured by the eye leave a print anywhere in the eye of the victim."

"I thought you mentioned you were done with Tracey's family."

"I am, Tom. I'm only curious. Photography is my deepest passion, and I've been thinking of asking Dr. Greer's permission to take pictures for a while. I'm sorry."

"I'm sorry too, Kathy. Even if you stepped across the line a bit, I thought we could at least be honest with each other."

"I wasn't trying to hide it, Tom. I was going to tell you about it."

"Oh yeah? When were you going to do that, Kathy? You've had plenty of chances."

Kathy could feel tears ready to spill from her eyes. "I don't know, Tom! I was scared to tell you."

"And so you damn well should be!"

"Tom, you're making a scene," Kathy whispered when she saw several heads turning in their direction. "Can we talk about this at home?"

Tom scanned the room and lowered his voice. "I'm sorry, I didn't mean to yell. It's just that you should know better than to interfere with police work."

"I wasn't trying to interfere, Tom, and I meant it when I said that I have no further connection with Alexis and her family. Her father told me to butt out in no uncertain terms."

"Why did he do that?"

"Because I believe what Alexis has been trying to say, Tom, and even if the whole thing sounds insane I know she is not lying when she talks about her friend Lily." She put up her hand as if to stop Tom from interrupting. "Look, I know that you don't believe her story either, and I can't fault you for that, but there is something strange at work, Tom. You saw the photos, right? Well, that's not the only thing that's happened. Books are falling from my shelves at the studio, magazines are flipping open, and the topic is always the same – motherhood, children, adoption. And do you want to hear the craziest thing of all? When I used photo shop software to enhance and fix up the bridal package I've been working on, I must have inadvertently erased the mother of the bride from the shots – how, I have no idea. I've been trying to place all of these pieces together but I can't seem to find a way to create a picture that makes sense; no pun intended."

Tom didn't say anything. He pinched the bridge of his nose and fixed his eyes on the glass of iced water.

"You know that I am a rational person, Tom, and I don't jump to conclusions, but some of this stuff is not right."

"I agree with you on that, Kathy, but I am trying to run an investigation, and I sure as hell cannot use ghost pictures and children's imaginary friends for evidence."

"Would you be able to use a photograph as evidence, Tom?"

"What kind of photo?"

"Dr. Greer agreed with me that science doesn't support the possibility of being able to retrieve the last image recorded through someone's eyes, but it can't disprove it either. Do you remember the special camera I own, the one I told you was over three thousand dollars but I was able to buy for five hundred?"

Tom nodded.

"That camera is not a normal camera. It is a special device used in iridology, and it is used to detect illness in the body. It uses special technology that enlarges the iris to the point that you can see even the smallest speck in it."

"What does this camera have to do with the case I am working on?"

"You see, Dr. Greer said that images are not actually

seen by the eye but by the brain; when the eye captures an image, that image is transferred to the brain by optical nerves. This explains why people with certain brain injuries are unable to see even if nothing is wrong with their eyes. Taking all that at face value, what if the image the eye captured leaves some sort of print somewhere?"

"Like a fingerprint?"

"Exactly! Could it be possible that if such a print exists it can be lifted?"

"We are bordering sci-fi, Kathy."

"You're right, Tom, but keep in mind that when Edison came up with the idea of the light bulb, that was probably considered borderline science fiction, too."

"Did Dr. Greer agree to let you take photos?"

"Not at first," Kathy grinned, "but I convinced him."

"Well, where are those photos?"

"They are still in the camera. I will download them to my desktop computer at the studio first thing tomorrow morning."

Tom sighed, then he took Kathy's hand into his and

looked deeply into her eyes. "You are one stubborn woman, Kathy Spencer. Let's see what comes out of this, but if you don't find anything, you must promise me that you are going to put this case behind you and let the police deal with it."

Kathy raised her hand and lifted her chin looking ahead. "I promise."

They both burst into laughter, neither of them sure if the spontaneous reaction was spurred by relief or anxiety. Tom stretched across the table and grazed Kathy's lips with a kiss. "I love you, Kathy."

"I love you, too."

They made small talk while they continued to enjoy the meal, and before they knew it, their plates were empty and the bottle of white wine they had decided to order after they started eating was almost gone; their stomachs were full and their minds were lulled by a feeling of general wellbeing. They left shortly after that, each driving their own cars, and they went straight home where they finished an already wonderful evening with a breathtaking session of lovemaking. Tracey's killer was still on the loose, the clues were getting stranger by the minute, but Tom and Kathy were finally singing the same song. They fell asleep holding each other, and right before drifting off Kathy said a small prayer of gratitude – her relationship with Tom was as solid as ever, and there was nothing at all they couldn't face as long as they were together.

Chapter 15

Most of the nurses were busy tending to patients when the man slipped quietly into Shannon Brinkley's room. He had been pacing the hallway, his eyes cast down on a clipboard he pretended to read anytime someone passed by. He was glad to have found a supply closet which also included scrubs – while most of the staff knew the majority of individuals on the hospital's payroll, volunteers changed often, and he was able to move around without being noticed.

Shannon lay in her bed, her face as pale as an antique porcelain doll minus the painted make-up and her hair pulled back away from her face into a lateral pony-tail. Life support machinery kept her body alive;

the multiple beeps which appeared to be swallowing the silence of the small room were a confirmation that her vital signs were stable.

The man moved quickly around the bed and slowly closed the blind – as long as he didn't move too much, the thin wall separating the room from the nurses' station would offer enough cover to get the job done before anyone suspected his presence.

His eyes searched for the IV line among all the tubing connected to Shannon's body and when he found it he grinned satisfied as he reached into his pocket to retrieve a syringe while holding the intravenous tube in his other hand. He pierced the rubber tube with the needle, and was getting ready to shoot the fluid into the line when he heard movement behind him. The sudden sound made him jolt and he instinctually turned around to lock eyes with a middle-age nurse sporting a thick layer of gray eye shadow and a pearly pink lipstick that was surely created with a fresh-cheeked teenager in mind.

"What are you doing in here, Sir?"

The man tried to pull the syringe from the IV line

but the needle was stuck into the rubber tubing, so he dropped the syringe and jumped over Shannon's bed. Shannon, unaware of anything that was going on in the room, remained unresponsive. He quickly opened the door and ran down the hallway.

"Sir! Come back here! Sir!"

The nurse's panicked tone attracted attention and within seconds several other nurses and the doctor on duty were circling around her, trying to find out what happened and saturating the small space available in the room. One of the nurses saw the syringe still attached to the line, so she carefully extracted the needle paying attention not to plunge the content into the tube connected to Shannon's hand. "Whoever that was, he was trying to inject something inside the IV line of this patient."

All eyes turned toward the nurse, and the doctor stepped up to take the syringe from her. He looked at the small amount of fluid contained inside of it, but he couldn't make out what it was. He wrapped the syringe in a paper towel he found near the sink. "I will send this to lab, so we can at least find out what he was trying to inject. I think we should call the police. We don't know what's inside the syringe, but this guy was up to no good."

The doctor gave quick orders to vacate the room so that Shannon could rest and not be disturbed by all the noise such a large crowd generated.

"Why don't you take a few minutes, Nurse?" He gently suggested to the nurse who surprised the man in the room, when he noticed her hands were a bit shaky.

"Thank you, Doctor. I would like that. Maybe I can go to the cafeteria to fetch a cup of tea. It will calm my nerves."

The doctor, a young man who looked wiser and more in control than his age would suggest, smiled brightly. "That's a great idea. I'm sure the police will need to ask you some questions as to what you saw when you entered the room. Did you see the man clearly?"

"Somewhat…he was short and with dark hair. He had a surgical mask over his face and he was wearing scrubs. I think he was a volunteer."

"One of *our* volunteers?!"

"I couldn't be sure, but I think I glimpsed at a name tag which displayed the name of the hospital."

The doctor shook his head. "Sometimes I wonder how well we screen people that walk in and out of this place. Well, go get your cup of tea, Rosalynd. I'm sure the police will be here to ask questions soon enough."

The nurse left and the doctor called the security guard who was still outside the room. "Hey!"

The security guard looked around to be sure he was the one being summoned, then he quickly walked up to the doctor. "Yes, Sir."

"I need to go down to the lab. I want you to stay in Ms. Brinkley's room until the police arrive. Nobody is allowed in here, not even family." The doctor's voice was kind but firm and the officer agreed without delay. "I'll be here, Sir. Take your time. I will make sure this room is off limits to everyone."

The doctor locked the door merging into the hallway and the security guard stood by the door adjacent to the nurse's station.

"I will be back soon. Make absolutely sure no one comes in here."

"I will, Sir. Don't worry."

With the doctor gone and the nurses dispersed once again to take care of other patients, it wouldn't have been too hard to get back into the room and finish the job, but now the security guard was in the room and the only way in was through the nurses' station, so the man knew his mission had failed this time. He wrapped the scrubs he wore into a ball and stuffed them into the backpack he was carrying. There was no place inside the hospital that was safe enough to get rid of them, so he had no choice but take them along and burn them when he got home. Once again in his regular clothes, he put on the same baseball cap he wore when he walked in and stepped out of the man's room. He scanned the hallway for anyone who might have been around when he went in, but all he saw was an orderly mopping up a spill on the floor near the elevator. He wasn't sure if he had seen the same man before, but he wasn't too concerned about him – the young man continued mopping without even raising his eyes from the stretch of floor he was working on, so he was fairly sure he hadn't paid any attention to anyone walking in and out of the restroom. He walked briskly toward the stairs; fast enough to get out of the place before being seen and slow enough not to draw any unwanted attention. In no time he was on the lobby level and he exited through the sliding door. He took a deep breath which filled his lungs with fresh air and sunshine, but he didn't feel any better. He had once again failed his mission. Today he hit his second strike, so he was quickly running out of chances. Shannon was still alive – holding her soul with her teeth but to his dismay still very much of this world. He had lost two rounds but the game wasn't over yet. He would try again, and this time he would make sure all obstacles are taken care before moving forward with his plan. After all, he thought as he got in his car, third time's always the charm.

#

Kathy held her breath while she waited for the images from the EyePix Handheld to be uploaded on her computer. Her heart was pounding in anticipation and her mouth was dry. Nothing she could do about her heart, but she knew a good cup of coffee could take care of the rest. The photos finished uploading just as she got ready to stand up from her chair. A burst of color exploded across the screen, as the photos opened, one beside the other. Kathy could hardly believe the clarity, especially since Tracey's eyes appeared very cloudy to the naked eye when she took the shots. Although a milky film was visible over the surface of both eyes, she could distinctly make out the colors at the outer edge of the iris; unfortunately, the pupil was so dilated that the predominant color Kathy could detect was faded black; it was as if the void of death had expanded until it was able to squeeze the light Kathy was sure had sparkled from Tracey's eyes when she was alive. She stared at the two pools of blackness rimmed by a thin circle of marine blue and tried to focus on their depths. She noticed a color inconsistency in the center of both pupils, but made a conscious effort to not get too excited. She moved her magnifying glass over the pupils and clicked to enlarge the portion that appeared lighter than the rest – the first disturbance looked like a sling-shot with a curved stem. The image in the other eye was even more abstract, and it appeared as a small, irregular circle. Kathy stared at both images until her eyes started burning, then she averted her gaze to the window hoping to see something that would distract her. She didn't see anything interesting, but she stood up, stretched and walked toward the window anyway. She unlatched the lock and pulled the lower pane until she felt a warm wave of air hitting her chest. It was hot outside but she took a deep breath and held it in – the warm moist air filled her lungs and made her feel alive. She looked at the large poplar tree a few feet away from her window and noticed leaves moving -- a small bird emerged from the leaves and flew to a nearby branch. Kathy wondered if the bird had a nest hidden in the tree and said a small prayer of protection for the baby birds waiting for their mother to come back, if indeed any were tucked in the thick foliage. Her mind wandered to how she would feel if she had to leave her children unattended and vulnerable to all sorts of threats, even for a short while. Did the mother bird worry about her babies while she was out looking for food? Kathy was not an expert ornithologist, but she was fairly sure she had read somewhere that birds raise their offspring as a couple, and when one parent is out the other one is always nearby. The thought of a daddy bird watching over his babies made her smile. Sometimes she wished humans were more like animals – if something that weighed less than two ounces could understand the importance of having two parents, how could we be so nonchalant about raising our children? *Many American children are lucky to have one parent...*

That random comparison offset the pleasant feeling she had felt washing over her just a few moments before, and she suddenly felt sad. She thought of her daughter, and of the bond they shared, and felt a strong urge to call her just to hear her voice.

She looked at the clock on the wall and calculated that Caroline was probably still in class, so she made a mental note to call her later, before leaving the studio for lunch. She returned to her desk and looked at the magnified shots of Tracey's eyes. She sent all of them to the printer and poured a cup of coffee while she waited for them to print. When the first one came out she looked at it to see if she could notice anything different than what she had detected on the monitor, but she strange image still looked like a sling-shot – an even bigger sling-shot now, since she had printed each of the shots on a full page. The remaining shots from the left eye showed more of the same, while all the ones from the right eye showed the strange circle she had seen before. She shook her head and laid them side by side on her desk before she took a sip of her coffee to help her swallow the disappointment she felt. She wasn't sure what to expect when she took the photos, but she had been positive that something was going to show up. Now she had no idea what that something should be, and she was fairly certain that a sling-shot was not the last image Tracey had seen before leaving this world. And what about the dot? What could that possibly be?! She suddenly felt as if she had wasted her time, and maybe Tom was right – along with time, she had probably also lost her mind. No matter how long she stared at those pictures, all she could see were a sling-shot and a circle. So much for her forensic photographic skills! She cringed at the thought of Tom and Dr. Greer laughing at her. She had secretly hoped to blow their minds with her findings, but as it turned out, the only mind that had cracked was her own. Her self-doubt was working overtime right now, and she felt as if she had let everybody down – herself, Tom, the snowy-haired doctor, Alexis, and most of all, Tracey. There was no image of the killer that was miraculously captured and retained by Tracey's eyes, and that meant two things: She was going to look like a fool, and Tracey's murderer would remain at large, at least for the time being.

She clicked off the file on her computer and pinched the bridge of her nose as she waited for the programs to close. Her mobile phone rang the moment the screen went dark.

"Hello"

"Kathy. It's Tom."

"Oh, hey Tom.."

"You sound about as excited as I am right now. What's happening?"

"Not much." She didn't want to disclose her disappointment yet; not even to him. "Just working on a boring project. Nothing special."

"I thought you were going to upload those photos

you took yesterday."

"I will do that sometime today. I was busy this morning. What is going on with you? Why do you sound so bummed out?"

"We have a warrant for the arrest of Jack Little, but when we got to his place he was gone, and today someone tried to kill Shannon Brinkley at the hospital. I don't think I will be home for dinner."

"Oh God…do you think it is the same man?"

"It sure sounds like him – short and dark-haired. The nurse couldn't see much more since he bolted from the room the moment she got in, and she couldn't see his face because he was wearing a surgical mask."

"Wow…"

"Wow is right. We had a chance to get him the first day we went to see him and we let him go. I won't hear the end of this."

"You couldn't have known, Tom."

"You're right, but that lack of intuition screwed us up."

"I'm sorry, Tom."

"Yeah, me too. Well, look, I have to go. I love you."

"I love you too."

Kathy hung up the phone and tried to dial Caroline's number but got her voice mail, so she left her a message and gathered her things before going to lunch. She inserted all the printed photos inside a folder which she labeled 'Tracey' and placed it on her desk near the pencil holder. She grabbed her purse and went out the door, looking forward to getting outside in the fresh air. When she stepped outside the building she looked up at the branch of the poplar tree to see if she could see a nest, and just as she did, the small bird she saw earlier flew in and landed on the outer edge of it. As expected, a different bird took off from the branch and she just knew it was the father. The babies were safe, warm and cozy near their mother while daddy went to fetch a snack for himself. Kathy turned away from the tree and walked toward her car. In that moment, she wished that all human children could be just as lucky.

#

It was almost eleven o' clock when Tom finally got home. His feet were hurting, and his tie by now felt more like a noose than an accessory; it was on nights like this one that the job as a tow truck driver his sister insisted he should take didn't sound all that bad after all. He peeked into the living room on his way to the bedroom and saw Kathy stretched out on the couch reading a novel.

"Hey Beautiful!"

Kathy lowered the book on her lap and took off her reading glasses. "Hi! I'm not even going to ask how your day went."

"Good idea. My day couldn't have been crappier."

Kathy got up from the couch and followed him as he walked into the bedroom. "That bad, huh? From what you said on the phone it did sound pretty horrific."

"Yeah…if one of the nurses hadn't walked in, Shannon Brinkley would be dead right now. Whoever the perpetrator was, he tried to shoot some unidentified substance in Shannon's IV line. We are waiting for the lab results, but I doubt that this guy had vitamins in that syringe."

"Do you think he is the same guy who was stalking Tracey?"

"I'm not sure. From information we found at his place, we assumed the guy is in Missouri, but who the hell knows? He could be at the North Pole baking poisoned cookies for the elves, and we wouldn't know it unless one of them turns up dead."

"Would we actually find that out?" Kathy tried to joke to lighten up the vibe, but one quick look at Tom's face told her that he was in no mood for playing around.

"Would we find *what* out?"

"If one of the elves was dead. Never mind, it was just my attempt to bring a smile to your face. I failed miserably."

"It's not you, Kathy. I'm just tired and a little frustrated. I feel like I am running in circles around this case, with no real breakthrough. Some new random fact pops up every day, and I get excited, only to get disappointed when nothing pans out."

Kathy could understand that feeling today more than ever. "I hear you. I was so hopeful about being able to lift images from Tracey's eyes that I didn't realize it was a reality only in my imagination."

Tom could detect Kathy's disappointment in her voice. "You couldn't get any images?"

Kathy shrugged. "Well, I got *some* images, but they are nothing like I expected. To tell you the truth, I am not sure what it is that I expected, but I certainly didn't bank on a sling-shot and a dot."

"Is that what you found?"

"Yes, and I'm pretty sure Tracey didn't confront a kid who was playing with a sling-shot in the woods, so I'm afraid my theory is for the birds."

"I'm sorry Kathy. It did sound like a far shot, though I have to admit it was an intriguing possibility. Even Dr. Greer rooted for you."

Kathy smiled. "He is a nice old fellow. His hair is so white it's almost blinding. He makes me think of Santa Claus – I find myself waiting for a gift when I'm talking to him."

"Dr. Greer is a good guy. He refuses to retire, but we are all kind of happy about that."

"I can see why."

The ring of Tom's mobile phone interrupted the

conversation, and Tom rushed to the table near the door where he had left it when he got home. "I'm sorry. I'm just going to see who it is."

"Of course…"

Kathy heard a muffled sound in the hallway and a word Tom's mother would have rewarded with a double dose of soap in the mouth, had she heard it – Tom had stubbed his toe in the door frame as he turned too fast on his way to the table. He almost growled into the phone.

"Lackey!"

"Lackey, it's Parker."

"Yeah…"

"Look, man, I know it's late, but I figured you would want to know this. I was getting ready to leave when an e-mail from the lab came in. The blood type found on the shirt in Brad Johnson's trunk matches Tracey's. It's too early for DNA results, but at least we know something."

"What?! Are they sure?"

"Yeah, pretty sure…"

"Damn! He was being arraigned today on the drug charges, right? I was going to check on that but I got sidetracked with everything else that happened."

"The judge denied bond. It's kind of unusual in a case like that, but I guess we were lucky. He is still at the county jail."

"Good! Do you think he is asleep right now?"

"I'm not sure, but it might be a bit late to pay a visit tonight. Why don't you get some sleep and we'll go tomorrow?"

Tom could feel the weight of his eyelids, and after having changed into pajama pants and a T-shirt, he couldn't even envision getting dressed into work clothes again. "You're right. He is not going anywhere tonight, anyway."

"And Lackey, the results from the lab at the hospital just came in also…"

"And? Do we know what the substance is?"

"Yeah…arsenic. In its deadliest form."

#

Donald Russet picked up a photo of his children from the bedside table and tried to mentally go back to the beautiful day they all had shared at the lake. Those kids were nothing short of amazing, and not a day would go by that he didn't thank his lucky star for the blessing of having them in his life. Mark was smart as a whip and he got wonderful grades in school, and Sarah was such a lovely little girl that Donald didn't doubt for a moment she would become, some day, a wonderful, compassionate doctor. Here they were – his future. He stared at their sunny faces and felt like crying. What happened to him? Why didn't he stop before it was too late? Helen was certainly not a model wife, but she was a good mother, and Donald should have remembered that before he made the mistake that ruined everything.

He brought the picture to his lips and kissed each smiling little face, his tears smearing the thin layer of dust that had collected on the glass of the picture frame. He gently placed the frame back on his bedside table and opened the drawer to pull out the revolver. He placed the cold mouth of the gun between his lips and almost gagged when his tongue tasted the cold metal. He turned his head to look at his children one more time, then he pulled the trigger, and all the pain he felt until that moment left his body attached to the brains that exploded against the bedpost.

Chapter 16

Rose Howard stirred a pot of black bean soup while Alexis rested in her room. She wasn't keen on black beans herself, but since the soup was Alexis's favorite meal, she decided it would make a great dinner. Alexis was doing better – after being released from the hospital in Raleigh, she came home to a sweet surprise; knowing that her granddaughter was crazy about cats, and aware of what the little girl had been through, Mike's mom had given her a very special welcome-home gift: a tiny orange kitten. Kathy wasn't keen on cats either, but at this point she would have agreed to adopt a tiger, had she been assured that it would help her young daughter heal. Alexis had been sitting in the living room empty-eyed when her grandmother walked in and hugged everyone, and she didn't seem at all excited when she was told to close her eyes so that Grandma could bring in a special gift, but the moment she heard the first meow, her eyes snapped open and she sucked in her breath. Grandma put the kitten on her lap and asked her to find a name for it. To everyone's dismay, Alexis didn't say anything for several minutes and just sat quietly, stroking the kitten's silky fur without uttering a word. But right when everyone's smile began to fade, Alexis brought the kitten's tiny body to her lips, gave him a kiss and almost yelled: "Petey. His name is Petey!"

The kitten's loud purr was momentarily drowned by the collective sigh that was heard around the room. Mike hugged his mom, and Rose decided that she was going to love cats.

From that moment on, Alexis seemed livelier. She still spent several hours each day being quieter than Rose liked, but as the psychiatrist suggested when they brought her in for her first appointment yesterday, healing from the trauma of losing a sibling requires some time, and should be allowed to run its course. Alexis didn't talk about Lily at all since she started communicating again, and Rose was happy about that – she still hadn't told Mike about her dream, and she didn't think she ever would. Mike had been a rock all throughout this ordeal, but even he had his limits.

She gave the soup one final stir, and was ready to turn off the burner, when the phone rang. She covered the pot with a glass lid and grabbed the receiver at the end of the counter.

"Hello?"

"Hey Love, it's me."

"Oh, hey," Mike's soft, even voice made her smile, "I'm just fixing supper – black bean soup."

"That's Alexis's favorite. She is going to like that, and hopefully she won't try to share hers with Petey the cat."

"It was brilliant of your mother to bring over that kitten. Alexis did a real one-eighty when she saw him."

"She sure did. These are the times when I truly love my mother."

"It makes two of us. I don't think Alexis would have

snapped out of her stupor as easily if she hadn't fallen in love with that kitten."

"I agree. Well, look, I'm on my way home. I only need to stop and get some gas and I will be right over."

"It sounds great. Alexis and Petey have been in her room for the last few hours. I thought of going up there, but I want to give her the time she needs. Dr. Harding suggested that giving her some space to sort things out is the best thing we can do to help her right now."

"I agree with that. She has been through a lot, and she needs time to absorb the shock. I'm glad she is not talking about Lily or that woman in North Carolina – hopefully all that will soon be part of the past."

Rose didn't respond. The last thing she wanted to do now was to generate friction between Mike and herself. She felt bad for Kathy, and she made a mental note to give her a call the next few days. "Yes, I should go and set the table. I will see you when you get home."

"I'll be there shortly. I love you."

"I love you too." She meant it with all her heart, and that was probably the biggest reason why she felt so guilty at the thought of not being completely honest with Mike.

She pulled out her best dishes from the china cabinet, and even arranged a small placemat on the floor beside Alexis's chair, on which she set a small bowl of kitten food for Petey.

She had just finished getting everything ready when she heard Mike unlocking the door.

"I'm home!"

His voice always had the power to make her feel relaxed.

"I'm in the kitchen, Mike! Why don't you go change and call Alexis while you are up there? Tell her to bring down Petey too – I have his supper waiting also."

"We'll be down in a minute!"

While she waited for Mike and Alexis to come down, she opened the door and stepped out on the deck. The recent storms had caused a lot of debris to blow around, and it all seemed to have collected on the floor of their deck, but she didn't feel up to sweeping right now, so she sat on one of the lounge chairs and tried to relax. The last few weeks had thrown her into a spin, and she needed to ground. There were many emotions she hadn't explored yet, but she didn't feel at liberty to completely feel until she knew Alexis was okay.

Mike opened the door from the kitchen and poked his head out.

"I thought you said Alexis was in her room."

"She is. She was, at least. I didn't see her coming down. You didn't find her in there with Petey?"

"I found Petey and he nearly assaulted me the moment I walked in. I think he was lonely and wanted some attention. But Alexis wasn't in there."

Rose's face darkened. "I am sure she didn't come down. She has to be in there."

"The window in Alexis's room is closed, but the one in our room is wide open…"

Rose felt her heart sink to her stomach. "Oh my God…do you think she got out?"

Mike shook his head. "Alexis is scared of heights. Even if it is possible to get down from there, I don't think she would have had the courage."

"Call the police, Mike! Something isn't right!" Rose's voice was bleeding panic, and even if she tried her best to remain calm, she was beginning to hyperventilate.

Mike didn't even question the request. He ran to the phone in the kitchen and dialed 9-1-1 while Rose ran through the house frantically calling her daughter's name.

After alerting the police, Mike went outside to wait for the patrol car and he walked around the back of the house to check the bedroom window from the outside. The grass didn't appear disturbed at all, so he continued walking until he passed the laundry room window and felt cold air trickling out. The lock was unlatched and the pane hadn't completely come down to seal the cold air in.

"Rose! Come outside!"

Before he could call again, Rose came running around the corner and into him.

"Was this window unlocked earlier?"

"No. I was in the laundry room a few hours ago, and I am pretty sure it was locked. It was closed, at least. I would have felt the warm air coming in if it wasn't."

Before either of them could say another word, a

patrol car pulled into the driveway and they both rushed to it. Neither one saw a cigarette lighter bearing the emblem of North Carolina State University hidden in the grass just a few feet away from the window.

#

The first thing that Tom noticed when Brad Johnson was escorted into the visiting room was how the young man no longer looked like a college student – now he looked tired, confused and, to an extent, afraid. His hands shook lightly as he placed them on the table to support himself as he sat down.

"Thank you for seeing us, Brad. We have a few questions to ask you."

"Ask away, Lieutenant, but you are wasting your time."

"I appreciate your concern, Brad, but there are a few things we need to clear up. You have the right to have your attorney present during this conversation. Would you like to call him?"

"No, I've got nothing to hide."

"Okay…first of all, can you tell us how a T-shirt stained with Tracey Newman's blood ended up in your trunk?"

"I don't know! I've said the same thing to ten other people already. I don't know!"

"Do you recognize that shirt as your own?"

"Yes…no…I mean, it is a plain white shirt. I have shirts like that, but I don't know for sure that one is mine."

"How could someone else's shirt be in your trunk, Brad?"

"I have no idea! But sure as hell I didn't put a bloody shirt in my trunk!"

"Can you think of anyone who would?"

"No, Lieutenant. I have spent the whole night thinking about this. I can't think of anyone. I know there are probably a few people who don't consider me their best friend, but I don't think they would go so far as framing me for murder."

"Can you tell me who these people are -- the ones who don't like you very much?"

"Well…you've been digging up stuff, so it should

be of no surprise to you that the old man who was banging Tracey doesn't exactly love me; neither does Jack Little -- he had it bad for Tracey. And I know that she-man that lives with Shannon didn't like me either because she knew that Shannon had a soft spot for me, and she won't stand for Shannon liking anyone. Of course, Shannon is part of that crowd too, since she had romantic hopes for us but I always turned her down – most times, at least."

"What do you mean by that?"

"Nothing, really. There was never anything substantial between me and Shannon."

"Did you have sexual relations with her?"

"Just once. We were both drunk."

"Did Tracey know about this?"

"No, she didn't; but as I said, she was seeing someone else too. That story between me and Shannon is ancient history."

Tom thought back about Jack Little's words. According to Little, Shannon probably killed Tracey because she liked Tracey's boyfriend. Shannon was now lying unconscious in a hospital bed, but that didn't mean she couldn't have murdered her friend. Mary Townsend even mentioned that Tracey drove her car and brought it back dirty and dented – where did she go? And then, there was the matter of the insurance policy.

"What did you know about Tracey's life insurance policy, Brad?"

"I knew that Tracey had life insurance, and she had listed me as her beneficiary in the beginning. She was going to change that after we broke up."

"I see. Was Shannon aware of the amendments Tracey was considering?"

"Yes, I think so."

"How did she feel about that?"

"I'm not sure, Lieutenant."

"How did *you* feel about it, Brad?"

"I guess I was a little upset about it at first, since it was a clear sign that Tracey had finally decided she wanted me out of her life."

"Did you kill Tracey, Brad?"

"No, Sir, I didn't. And I didn't put that shirt in my trunk either."

#

"It's pretty messy in there, Lieutenant." The young officer widened his eyes and lightly nodded as he ushered Lackey and Parker inside Don Russet's bedroom. "His wife found him when she got home from work."

Don Russet's home décor spoke volumes about his social standing, and it painted an even clearer picture of what the hospital administrator had to lose had his relationship with Tracey Newman surfaced to public knowledge. Situated on an acre of green grass in the northwestern corner of the city, and surrounded by large privacy walls, the home had a style of its own. The wrap-around porch galleries were reminiscent of a French Colonial style, but the interior was spacious and each room opened to a hallway, something not typical of French Colonial homes. In so many ways, the property reminded Tom of its owner – traditional on the outside with a few surprises waiting on the inside.

Don Russet's body was lying on its back and the neck appeared twisted on the side – the blow originating from his mouth had whip-lashed him and left him frozen into an unnatural position. The cherry wood of the headboard was dark with dried blood and speckled with gray matter, and a broken photo frame containing a picture of children lay on the floor at the bottom of the bed skirt, probably knocked over by the man's arm as it flung back after pulling the trigger. The gun was on the floor just a foot or so away from the picture frame.

Tom walked closer to the bed and conducted a first examination of the body. Rigor mortis hadn't fully set in yet, but it was very cool to the touch. Dr. Greer would be able to pinpoint the time of death a bit more accurately, but in Tom's opinion Don Russet didn't die too long before his wife found him.

"Where is Mrs. Russet?"

"She is in the kitchen with her sister. She is taking it pretty hard." The young uniform replied nodding and widening his eyes once again. Tom wondered if he did that for emphasis or if he had a nervous tic.

"Thank you. Dr. Greer should be here momentarily. I am going to talk to the wife."

Helen Russet looked disheveled and older than Tom expected. Her bottle-blond hair which was cut for volume appeared pasted to the sides of her head, and her skin was a sick shade of gray with green overtones. Her hands trembled as she tried to bring a cup of tea to her lips, and her eyes were filled with tears.

"Mrs. Russet? I am Lieutenant Lackey, with the Raleigh Police Department."

She inhaled loudly and turned her eyes toward the door to take in the first image of the man who had spoken. She acknowledged him with a nod, and he took her gesture as an invitation to join her at the table.

"I am sorry for your loss, Mrs. Russet."

"Yes, having young children to raise alone makes it a huge loss."

"Have you found a suicide note, Ma'am?"

"None. He didn't even have the decency to let me know why."

Tom swallowed the discomfort he felt in his gut and nodded condescendingly. "Not all suicide victims do, unfortunately. It's possible that he didn't plan it and just acted upon a sudden impulse."

"But nothing was so wrong in our lives that he should have felt compelled to kill himself, Lieutenant! Why, why would he do something like this? It's a miracle my children weren't with me when I came home."

"It would have been tragic, Ma'am. I'm glad they weren't. The medical examiner will be here shortly to confirm the time of death and pronounce him dead."

"Not too much need to pronounce him dead, is there? Any idiot with an IQ of five could tell he's dead."

"I know, Mrs. Russet, but we have to follow procedures, especially since Mr. Russet didn't leave a note."

Mrs. Russet's eyes opened wide. "You're not thinking that he was murdered, do you?"

"No Ma'am, I am not thinking that at all – in fact, it is pretty obvious he took his own life, I think."

"Yes, I would think so."

"Did Mr. Russet have an insurance policy?"

"I think so. We started one when we first bought the house, both of us."

"Who are the beneficiaries?"

"The children, of course, and each other. Why?"

"Just routine questions, Mrs. Russet."

There were many questions Tom wanted to ask Mrs.

Russet, but this moment didn't feel like the right one. The woman appeared genuinely distressed, and there was no reason to cause any additional suffering. He wanted to know if Don Russet's wife knew about her husband's relationship with Tracey Newman, and he allowed his mind to wonder if she would still be this upset over his demise had Tracey gone to see her the day she left the hospital after being fired. No matter what she knew, her husband was gone, and her children were left without a father – any mother would be upset about that, even if her feelings for her husband were not infused with undying love. If she knew, and she feared being publicly humiliated, her worries were over and she could be seen from this day forward as a respectable widow entitled to a nice chunk of life insurance.

"I think this is all, Mrs. Russet," Tom said, right before Dr. Greer entered the room.

"I am sorry for your loss, Ma'am. Lackey, may I speak to you for a moment?"

Tom followed him into the bedroom where the technicians were still working on the body to prepare it for its final trip away from home.

"It seems that everyone in town is using the same gun lately. The one that killed this guy is exactly like the one that killed Tracey Newman."

"No shit! Are you serious?"

"Yeppers. I wouldn't joke about something like this."

"Parker!" Tom called out to his partner who was standing by the bathroom door talking to one of the techs on the scene.

Parker looked in his direction and raised one finger to let Tom know he heard him; he wrapped his conversation with the young woman he was talking to and headed toward Tom and Dr. Greer.

"Yeah? What is it?"

"Did you look at the gun Don Russet used to do himself in?"

"Not yet. Why?"

"Look at it, and then tell me it isn't weird that he blew his brains with a gun which is exactly like the one used to slay Tracey Newman."

"No way!"

"That's what I said too."

"We'll need a ballistic report."

"Can you please take care of that, Parker?" Tom replied while he reached into his jacket pocket to retrieve his mobile phone.

Parker agreed and walked off, and Tom took the call.

"Lieutenant, this is Officer Marion in St. Louis. I called the department and was told that you are out on a case, but when I explained it was an emergency they provided your mobile number. I hope you don't mind."

"No problem. What's happening?"

"A missing person's report was filed today. It's a child related to someone who was found deceased in your state."

"Alexis?! Alexis Howard?"

"Yes, Sir. Her parents found out she wasn't in her room at dinner time, and they searched the area but the kid wasn't found. We understand that you are looking for a man who might be involved with the case, and there is speculation that he might have traveled to the St. Louis area. One of our men also found a cigarette lighter near the window we believe the girl exited the house from. The lighter bears the emblem of North Carolina State University."

"Oh God…" That was all Tom could say. Could the pictures of Tracey's family found in Jack Little's apartment be more than a coincidence? Were some of those pictures of Alexis?

"We are looking around here, and of course we issued an Amber alert a short while ago. We are hoping that you can maybe check on things from your end."

"You bet. I'm going to check out Little's place right now."

"Thank you. Her family is very distraught."

"I believe it. Please keep me posted if you find anything."

After hanging up, Tom got Parker's attention and called him to where he was standing. "Alexis is missing. She is Tracey Newman's little sister. I am going by Little's apartment to see if I can find anything."

"Damn! What a filthy bastard! Do you want me to go with you?"

"I don't think it's necessary. I'm just going to take a quick look at the place, and maybe talk to Mrs. Jenkins if she is around."

"I am going to stay here until Dr. Greer leaves, then I will report back to the station. Call me if you plan on going in."

After Tom left, Mrs. Russet went outside to one of the rocking chairs on the veranda and dialed a number from her mobile phone. "Hey, I can't talk for long, since the police are here, but Don is gone. That good-for-nothing finally did something right and killed himself. The police believed that Don and I were happy and that I am heartbroken over his death -- they had no idea of what that bastard put me through. He and his little whore both got what they deserved."

Chapter 17

Henriette Jenkins was watering her flowers when Tom pulled up in front of Jack Little's apartment, and he was happy to see that the sick plant she was tending to was finally starting to show signs of recovery and new growth – the leaves looked stronger, and their color had changed from puke green to a healthy emerald. Tom wasn't sure why such an insignificant detail made him smile, and he promptly decided that watching life of any kind thrive after several hours spent dealing with death at its worst was the welcome change he needed to shake the feeling of finality and embrace the pleasure of new beginnings.

"Good evening Mrs. Jenkins."

"Good evening, Detective….I'm sorry, I'm no goo' wi' names. You was here da otha' day with them two people."

"Lackey. Lieutenant Lackey, Ma'am."

"Yes, I rememba' you."

"I see your plant is doing well, Mrs. Jenkins. My mother always said that plants like good people."

"You is a good young'un, if you rememba' what you mama says."

"Yes Ma'am, I try. You haven't seen your tenant back the last day or two, have you?"

"No, Sir. I seed a woman goin' in, though."

"Was it the same woman who came with us the other day?"

"I dunno. My eyes ain't good no mo'."

Tom knew that he should call Parker before going in, but if Jack Little or this mysterious woman had taken Alexis inside this place, there wasn't a moment to lose. Following procedures was important – that much he had learned in his many years on the force – but common sense and gut instinct were sometimes even more important.

"You haven't seen a little girl being brought in, have you, Mrs. Jenkins?"

"A chil'? None that I've seen, but I go to bed early, so maybe I didn't see her. I didn't know he has a little girl."

"He doesn't. I need to go back inside the apartment. Is it okay with you?"

"It don' botha me none. Turn off the light when you leave."

"I will. Thank you Ma'am. I have a key."

Mrs. Jenkins didn't reply, and went back to water her recovering plant, humming an old spiritual song while Tom quickly climbed the few steps and opened the door with a copy of Mary Townsend's key.

The apartment was smoldering hot and an unpleasant odor of mildew attacked Tom's nostrils the moment he walked in – he hadn't noticed such a pungent smell the last time he was at the apartment, but that was probably because at the time the air conditioner hadn't been off for long. With most of the appliances unplugged, the silence in the room was unnerving and almost unnatural for someone used to the white noise of electro domestics, and it was only interrupted by a constant drip in a nearby sink. The blinds were closed, giving one the feeling of being trapped into a pocket of void untouched by the urban scene on the other side of the sealed windows.

Tom moved around carefully, his hand firmly gripping his gun. To his disappointment, there was no sign of Jack Little – even if he was aware that finding him here with Alexis was wishful thinking, his heart had held on to the slim hope. He glimpsed at the kitchen and saw that the pantry door cracked open, so he went to open it all the way, but nothing seemed out of place. He left the kitchen and headed for the back rooms, briefly inspecting the bathroom on the way – again, everything looked as abandoned and as tidy as the last time he was here. When he entered the bedroom, however, he thought he heard a faint sound and his heart jumped to his throat. "Little, are you in here? If you are, come out with your hands over your head where I can see them!" He listened for sounds, but all he could hear was the faucet continuing to drip its redundant song.

He looked around the room for anything that could

indicate a human presence and he noticed a little corner of black fabric on the floor at the other end of the bed. He kept his gun pointed and walked closer, and for a moment he thought of calling Parker, but as he walked around the bed he saw that the protruding black fabric was part of a small backpack lying right beside a baseball cap. He pulled a pair of gloves from his jacket pocket and slipped them on before touching the backpack. Inside, he found a set of medical scrubs and a piece of paper with Shannon's room number. "Holy shit!" He thought out loud, "it *was* Jack Little who tried to kill Shannon…"

He reached inside his jacket to pull out his mobile phone, but before he could dial the number for Parker he heard another muffled sound, this time behind him. He turned around quickly and pointed the gun in the direction of the sound, but it was too late. Before he could see anything, he felt a tremendous blow on the side of his face, and everything went black.

#

Kathy hung up the phone and looked at the clock – ten-thirty at night. Where could Tom be? When she last spoke with him earlier in the afternoon he said that he was going out on a call and would probably be later than usual getting home, but being this late without a phone call was very uncharacteristic for him. There were many times when Tom had to stretch his hours to meet the demands of his job, but he always diligently called because he knew Kathy would worry. Tonight he didn't call – the last time Kathy heard from him was around five o'clock, almost six hours ago. She hated to disturb him at work if he was busy, but anxiety was quickly setting in, so she dialed the front desk and was glad when Lana Briggs – one of the few officers she had previously struck a friendship with during a Christmas party – answered the phone.

"Hi Lana, this is Kathy Spencer, Tom Lackey's girlfriend."

"Hey Kathy! Long time no see. How are you?"

"I'm doing great, thanks; I hope you are. I am calling to see if Tom is still at work. He called me around five to say he was going out on a call and I haven't heard back from him."

"That's strange…he and Parker went on a call together, but Parker came back several hours ago and already left for the day. Do you have his mobile number?"

"I'm afraid I don't, unless I can find it in Tom's old address book."

"I don't think it would be in there, Kathy. Parker got a new number not too long ago. Hold on, let me get his number for you."

Kathy waited until Lana came back on the line and gave her Parker's number, she thanked her friend and hung up. She keyed the number and pushed the talk button, and was grateful when Parker picked up.

"Parker, this is Kathy Spencer, Tom Lackey's girlfriend."

"Hi Kathy, is everything okay?"

"I hope so. I am sorry to call so late, but Tom hasn't gotten home yet, and I am calling to see if you might know where he is."

"I haven't seen him since about seven tonight, Kathy. Have you tried calling the station to see if he's still there?"

"Yes, and I spoke with Lana Briggs. I hope you don't mind that she gave me your number. She hasn't seen him at all, so I don't think he went back to the office after the call you went on together."

Parker thought for a minute before he spoke. "Hmmmm…he said that he was driving by a suspect's house to see if he was back in town, but he was only supposed to check the place from the outside and maybe talk to the landlord; it wouldn't have taken him this long."

Parker's words made Kathy's blood congeal in her veins. "Is the suspect the guy who was harassing Tracey Newman?"

"You know about him? You might not want to share that any further, since Lackey isn't supposed to talk about police business with anybody."

"I wouldn't tell another soul but you, Parker. Isn't this the guy who's a suspect in the hospital attack?"

"Wow, Lackey really has a loose tongue."

"Never mind that, Parker; is he?"

"Yes. You haven't heard it from me, though. You

probably also know that Lackey was concerned about him being back with Tracey Newman's little sister. She disappeared today, and we found a receipt for a bus ticket for St. Louis in this guy's apartment."

Kathy felt dizzy. "Oh my God...is Alexis missing?"

"Oh, you know her too?"

"I took care of her a few times while she was in Raleigh, since she has a passion for photography. How long has she been missing?"

"Since earlier this afternoon. We got a call from St. Louis because we are working on her sister's case."

"Where does this man live?" Kathy asked, frantically searching for a pen and a scrap of paper to write down the address.

"I'm sorry, Kathy, but I am not at liberty to give you the address. I'll tell you what...I'll go and I will call you as soon as I find out something."

"Please, Parker, don't forget. I just know that something isn't right."

After ending the conversation with Parker, Kathy couldn't stop pacing the floor in the kitchen. She was too nervous to sit and too upset to stop moving. What if something happened to Tom? How would she cope with that?

When the phone rang, her heart exploded in her chest, and she could barely hear the other voice on the line.

"Mom, are you okay?"

"Yes, Honey, I'm sorry. It's Tom. He hasn't come home yet, and his partner said that he went alone to a suspect's house earlier today."

"Oh my God! Are you serious?"

"I wouldn't joke about something this serious, Caroline!" The moment her snapping words left her lips, she apologized. "I'm sorry, Sweetheart. I didn't mean to reply the way I did. I'm just upset."

"It's okay, Mom. I understand completely. Let me get off the phone so you can keep the line free. Call me as soon as you hear something."

Kathy hated to shut out her daughter, since the few times a week they spoke were precious to her, but she was entirely too distraught right now to participate in a conversation of any kind. "I will, Sweetie. Sorry again."

"Don't mention it, Mom. I love you."

"I love you too."

She ended the call and looked for the news channel on TV. Most of the segments were about city management and the impending drought which was typical of North Carolina this time of year; nothing important caught her attention, so she turned off the set and tried to focus on the novel she had been reading. She read the same page twice, without being able to retain a single sentence, so she put the book down and went to make a cup of coffee – she didn't need the caffeine, but a warm beverage might just be what the doctor ordered right now. With the TV off, the silence in the room was deafening. Kathy normally loved being alone, and she treasured her quiet moments, but right now she would have given anything she owned for the phone to ring; unfortunately it didn't. As soon as the coffee finished brewing, she poured a cup and went outside on the patio to sit on one of the new loungers she and Tom bought three weeks ago. The night was still, and a lone bird who seemed to have his days and nights mixed up sang a melancholy tune from a branch nearby. An ambulance siren screamed in the distance, and Kathy closed her eyes and whispered a prayer.

#

Parker pulled up in the parking spot directly in front of Jack Little's apartment and looked around for Lackey's car. There were three vehicles parked in the small lot, including one with flat tires and a cracked window, but Lackey's car was nowhere in sight. He wondered which of the units was Mrs. Jenkin's residence, and he damned himself for not having that information handy. Lackey was the one who used to keep everything with him, while Parker left his work life at the office every time he went home for the night. He called the night desk to see if someone could retrieve the information for him. Lana Briggs answered the call.

"Lana, it's Parker. Could you please go to my desk and see if you can find my notes from the last few days? They should be in a small stack by my computer. I need the exact address of Mrs. Jenkins, Jack Little's landlord. I think I circled her name on the notes, so it shouldn't be too hard to find."

Lana Briggs put him on hold for a few minutes, then she came back on the line and gave him the address.

"Thanks a bunch. I might call back in a few to get someone else to join me here."

"Do you know where Lackey is? His girlfriend called a while back looking for him."

"I'm looking for him too. She called me after she spoke with you. He missed his regular check-in, but knowing how Lackey resents not having personal space to follow his leads I am not surprised that his absence didn't alert a search for him."

"Do you need reinforcement, Parker?"

"I'm good for now. I'm going to talk to the landlord. I hate to wake her up at this time, but I can't think of anything else to do."

"Okay. Keep me posted, Parker. If I don't hear anything back from you within thirty minutes I am going to send a car."

"Good idea, Lana. I will call right back."

He got out of his car and squinted to see the dirty plaque with the unit number that allegedly belonged to Mrs. Jenkins. When he found it, he knocked on the door several times before a sleepy-eyed Mrs. Jenkins answered from the other side of the closed door.

"Police, Mrs. Jenkins. I just need to ask you a question."

Mrs. Jenkins opened the door, and Parker needed all the self-control he could master to keep his face impassive. Mrs. Jenkins's hair was wrapped on large rollers that in the semi-dark hallway light looked like coiled pink snakes, and her withered body was barely covered by a skimpy magenta nightgown which was visible through the open robe she was wearing.

"Do you know what time it is, young man?"

"It's very late, Ma'am, I'm sorry. I am looking for an officer who came by here earlier today. Have you seen him?"

"The detective that was here earlia'? Yes, I saw him. His ca' was still here when I closed ma blinds." She wiggled her neck to see around Parker, half-exposing a sagging breast as she did that. Parker wanted to look away and he couldn't, and for a moment he thought about people who don't want to look at accidents but can't take their eyes off the mangled cars as they drive by.

"His ca's gone. He gone, I reckon."

"Did you see anyone else go into the apartment, Mrs. Jenkins?"

"Nah, but it don't mean not'ng. Me and my boyfriend was having a romantic dinna' and I wasn't lookin' outside."

Parker tried his best to keep his running imagination from painting pictures in his mind, and he just nodded to shoo the thoughts away.

"I might have to go inside the apartment, Ma'am. Is it okay?"

Mrs. Jenkins sighed heavily. "I'm in my nigh' clothes. Let me get the key."

"Take your time, Ma'am. I have to call for someone to go in with me. It will take a while."

"A while? How long's that?"

"I don't know. In fact, can you just give me the key? That way I won't bother you any more, and I can just put it back into your mailbox."

"That's goo'. Let me get it for you."

She stepped away from the door for a moment and came back with a key which she handed to him. "Here you go. Be quiet, so you don't wake nobody."

"I will. Thank you Ma'am, and goodnight."

Mrs. Jenkins closed the door and Parker went to his car to call for someone to join him. After trying to dial Lackey's number without luck several times, he laid his head against the headrest and waited. A patrol car pulled up within ten minutes.

Parker led the way to Jack Little's apartment and opened the door with the key that Mrs. Jenkins gave him. Even before they went inside, they both saw a faint trail of dried blood starting from the doorstep and leading toward the bedroom. The trail led to a larger blood stain beside the bed, and when Parker leaned down to inspect it more closely, something else caught his eye: Right beside the bed, half-hidden by the bed skirt was Lackey's mobile phone.

#

Brad Johnson laid awake in his cell, his mind working overtime to come to a decision. The only way for him to get out of jail was to destroy the life of the only woman he ever loved. Erin Winthrow was his alibi; she was also the non-happily married wife of one of the most prominent men in town. She and Brad were together the night that Tracey died, but he couldn't tell the Lieutenant about her without breaking the bond of trust he and his lover had. Erin had two small children and a very controlling husband who wouldn't think twice about taking her babies away from her if she publicly humiliated him. Brad couldn't do that to her, and if his silence meant that he was going to serve time undeservingly in exchange for her happiness, then he was willing and ready to continue on the same path. He heard his roommate snore and he sighed. How had things spiraled down this way? He had no idea how that shirt had gotten into his trunk, but he was sure it wasn't there the day before he was pulled because he had just gone to clean his car that morning on his day off. Someone had to have put it in there between that afternoon and the next day before he got out of work.

His stupid addiction had taken him further than he ever expected, and he couldn't believe he had lowered himself to selling drugs. He wasn't a dealer, and he had really tried hard to curb his need for pills after Tracey could no longer provide them for him, but withdrawal and desperation had quickly set in, and he wasn't thinking straight. The money he was earning wasn't enough to support what he needed, and he had agreed to sell a bit on the side.

But if someone was trying to frame him by putting the bloody shirt in his trunk, how did they know he was going to be busted that afternoon? Who could possibly hate him enough to follow him around and know of his whereabouts? Did that someone listen to his conversations on the phone?

His mind was spinning, and he felt nauseated. He had to figure who this person was, and he didn't know where to start. He didn't want Erin to sacrifice her life for him, and he knew that she would do just that if he went to trial.

#

Mike Howard tried to keep himself busy by re-organizing his garage. Growing up with a neat-picking father taught him to do just that, and he could almost hear his old man's words ringing in his ears as he worked: *If your life is falling apart, organizing what you can will help you remain in control.*

Mike didn't feel in control at all, but he continued to arrange bolts and nails as he desperately tried to keep from falling apart. He cleaned drawers and shelves, and he nearly burst into tears when he found Alexis's sand toys neatly stored inside a box behind the weed eater. Where was his little girl? Why was God doing this to him? Rose wasn't very religious, and Mike always felt a bit uneasy about this side of her, but right now he began to wonder if she wasn't indeed right – how could a righteous God allow a little girl to disappear, or a young woman in her blossoming years to be senselessly murdered?

A tiny meow coming from the other side of the closed door wiped those thoughts from his mind, and for a moment he was grateful to the kitten for now allowing him to indulge such blasphemous ideas. He opened the door and let Petey in to wander around in the garage while he worked. Petey rubbed against his legs and purred loudly, before he climbed over a cardboard box set near his oversize tool box, and sniffed around. Mike watched him for a few seconds and then went back to separating nails by size. Petey jumped from the box onto the table and continued his inspection, using all the grace a cat could master until a small cockroach sped from under a small stack of papers and raced over one of his paws. All of a sudden, Petey was all paws, and in a few strikes he knocked all the bolts and nails off the table, as he desperately tried to catch his elusive prey. Mike cursed under his breath, and he gently removed Petey from the table and put him back in the house. He had worked on those nails and bolts for the good part of an hour, and seeing them all spread on the floor made him want to scream out of frustration. He swept them up with a small broom he kept hanging by the tool box and opened a drawer of the shelf near the table to put them in there until a later time when he could sort them out again. When he opened the drawer, something metallic clung against the back of the enclosure and he dug his hand in to see what it was. When he pulled out his hand and looked at the object, he felt his knees buckle up. Clutched in his hand was his father's cigarette lighter, the one he had misplaced and could no longer find. Instantly, a conversation he had with Alexis rang through his mind and his heart began to race. *"Do you remember the lighter you lost last month, Daddy? The one that belonged to Granddaddy?"*

"Sure I remember. What about it?"

"It's in the tool drawer in the garage."

"How do you know that, Alexis? Did you see it there?"

"No. Lily told me to tell you it's there. You put it there when that salesman came up our driveway to sell you lawn treatments and you forgot about it."

Alexis wasn't with him when the salesman came; she was in her room playing dolls by herself. The man had come through the yard while he was organizing a box containing his father's belongings and he had almost stepped out of the garage holding the lighter. Since he was wearing a pair of gym shorts with no pockets, he threw the lighter in the open drawer and forgot all about it after the salesman left and Rose called him in for lunch. Alexis couldn't have seen him putting the lighter in the drawer, and yet she knew it was in there. Lily told her, she claimed. Something else of importance nudged at the edges of his mind, and when it surfaced, Mike gasped and had to hold on to the table to keep himself from falling. Alexis also knew of Tracey's pregnancy, before anyone else knew. He dug his nails into the cover of the work table and took a few deep breaths to steady himself; he laughed hysterically and then he cried, as he crumbled to his knees and realized that no amount of organization could save him from falling apart right now.

Chapter 18

When Parker returned to Jack Little's apartment to see how things were progressing, two patrol cars and an unmarked car occupied three of the eight parking spaces designated for the residents, and four other spots were occupied by unidentified vehicles which Parker assumed belonged to residents. Mrs. Jenkins was standing outside despite the late hour, and Parker was glad to see her completely dressed this time.

"Hello, Mrs. Jenkins, you're up late I see. Or early…"

"I dunno what's happenin' to the world, Detective. In my day, now, you didn't hear of this kind of nonsense."

"Maybe you should go inside, Mrs. Jenkins." Parker felt awkward preaching at someone her age, but this wasn't a good part of town and an elderly woman had no business standing outside alone at this hour, even with several officers just a few doors down.

"I'm fine, fella. I got to wait for the tow truck to take this car right here. I tell residents all the time that I don't want their friends parkin' in my lot, and look here – this car don't belong to nobody who pay rent in this place."

Parker's instinct was on full alert. "This car doesn't belong to one of your residents? Could it belong to one of their friends visiting them?"

"I got eigh' apartments and eigh' spaces. One each resident; no mo'. Friends ca's is not allowe'."

"Wait, Mrs. Jenkins, hold off the tow truck. Let me check this plate first."

"You do that, Detecti', but you get this here ca' out of my property."

"We will, Mrs. Jenkins. I promise."

Parker jotted down the license plate number on his pocket-size notepad and walked back to his car. He called in the number and waited for a name to go with it. His hopes of hearing that the car belonged to Jack Little were quickly shattered when the plate was matched to a man by the name of Eduardo Carlos.

He rushed back to Mrs. Jenkins. "You don't have a tenant by the name of Eduardo Carlos, do you?"

Mrs. Jenkins shook her head. "No, Sir, I su' don't."

"Have you ever seen anyone going up to Mr. Bernardini's place?"

"Yes, I have. He has a small man who see him from time to time. They look like bruddas, if you ask me. And a woman too."

"Did this man look like Mr. Bernardini?"

"Yes Sir, I just done told you that."

"Did the man and the woman you saw go in together sometimes?"

"Not sometimes. All the time. Only today, I saw first the woman and then the man goin' in alone."

"He was here today?"

"Yes Sir. I saw him this afternoon."

"Thank you Mrs. Jenkins. I promise that the car will be removed by morning." Parker said as he got in his car and started the engine. Maybe Eduardo Carlos had nothing to do with Tom's disappearance, but the only way to find out was to ask him directly.

#

Kathy sat at the kitchen table and ran her fingers through her hair. Almost fourteen hours later now, she still knew nothing of Tom's whereabouts. Parker never called back, and Tom's mobile phone was still turned off. She felt in her heart that something happened, and yet her mind refused to accept the possibility. She rubbed her forehead with her thumbs and tried to focus on the photos spread out on the table. A slingshot and a dot – what, if anything, could they possibly mean?

Her phone rang and she jumped before automatically turning her head to look at the clock on the stove – seven o' clock in the morning. "Hello?"

"Kathy, it's Parker. I still don't know where Tom is. His car is gone, but we found his mobile phone inside Jack Little's apartment…"

Parker's pause infused a double shot of anxiety into Kathy's veins. "Parker, you're not telling me everything."

"We also found some blood stains, Kathy."

Kathy swallowed a mouthful of bile before she could answer, and felt faint.

Parker tried his best to sweeten the blow. "Kathy, we don't know it's his blood. It's just an assumption. We also found a car which doesn't belong to any of the tenants. I went to the address of the owner, and nobody is there. I'm still here, hoping that maybe he will come home and I can ask him a few questions. According to the landlord, a man was seen going up to Jack Little's apartment this morning, so I am banking on the fact that the owner of the car and the guy who went to see Jack Little are the same person."

"Can you not get in there, Parker?"

"Not without a warrant or without the person who lives here letting me in."

"I'd like to show you some pictures, Parker. They might be relevant to the case."

"What sort of pictures?"

"They are shots of Tracey Newman's pupils. Before you discard the idea, please hear me out -- some of the photos show a slingshot, and others a circle."

"What the hell does that mean?"

"I'm not sure, Parker, but those may have been the last images that Tracey Newman saw before she died."

"Bring them by the station in about an hour, Kathy. I should be there by then."

Kathy didn't know why she suddenly felt better, but she suspected that Parker's unexpected acceptance of this possibility was a factor. She gathered the photos and put them back inside the folder, before heading to the bathroom to take a shower.

#

Parker looked at his watch – eight o' clock in the morning. He doubted that Eduardo Carlos was coming home. He left a business card stuck in the door and was getting ready to leave when an elderly man sporting a checkered flannel shirt and high-water trousers came up the stairs and almost ran into him. His choice of clothing seemed odd in this blistering heat, but in his long career on the force Parker had seen even stranger things and he readily decided that the old man probably suffered from low blood pressure. He probably didn't know Eduardo Carlos, but there was no harm in asking.

"Say, Good man, would you know the man who lives in this apartment?"

"Yago? I sure do. Who wants him?"

"No, I'm sorry, we must be talking about different people. The name of the man I am looking for is not Yago, but Eduardo Carlos."

"That him. His name is Eduardo, but his friends call him Yago. With a 'Y'."

Parker didn't want to even know the reason why someone would choose such a nickname, so he asked another question instead. "Do you know where Yago is right now?"

"He probably at his girlfriend house."

"Interesting. You wouldn't know her name by any chance?"

"The name escapes me, but I know where she lives."

"Yeah? Where is that?"

"1420 Wintry Lane. I know it because I had to take Yago there a few times, when his car broke down."

"Thank you, Sir! I really appreciate your help. If you see Yago with a 'Y', tell him that Sergeant Parker would like a word with him."

"Sergeant Parker? Is Yago in trouble with the law?"

"No, he's not. We're just old friends."

"Oh good. I don't like cops too much myself…"

At other times, Parker would have inquired further as to why this old man had a problem with the police, but right now he was in a hurry, and he couldn't waste any time indulging conversations unrelated to the case; besides, his mind was already working overtime to figure out how the man could wear those clothes in this blistering heat without breaking into a sweat. He thanked the old man again and headed to his car. More suspects were floating up to the surface, and Parker knew that the game was becoming more complicated by the minute. He wanted to go straight to the girlfriend's house, but a quick look at his watch told him that Kathy was probably already on her way to meet him at the station, so he postponed his plan until after her visit.

#

Mirna Thompson had just clocked in and taken her place behind the glass window at the ticket counter of the bus station in downtown St. Louis when she spotted a little girl sitting alone. She was very small and delicate, and Mirna – a grandmother of three – felt instantly irritated at the fact that the little girl's mother would have left her there alone, even if she was only down the hall visiting the restroom. Did that woman not watch the news? – Small children are taken every day, sometimes even under their parents' eyes. She made a point to watch over the little girl until her mother came back, and to keep a better eye on her she decided to close her window and pretend to be organizing paperwork; she certainly didn't want to get distracted and miss anyone with malevolent intentions approaching that child.

The little girl hugged her knees, and laid her head on them, her small backpack on the seat next to her.

Mirna watched as her tiny eyelids fluttered and her left hand reached out to dig inside the pint-size luggage. She pulled out a small brown teddy bear and placed it between her head and her knees. Mirna looked at her watch – almost nine –o'clock, exactly twenty minutes since she clocked in – and the child's mother was still gone. She had enough of this nonsense. She stood up and walked out of the booth, determined to find out why the little girl was left unsupervised for so long. She slowed down her step as she approached the row of seats, hoping not to scare her.

"Sweetheart," she called gently, "are you okay? Where is your mommy?"

The little girl looked up with sleepy eyes, and took a moment to focus on Mirna's face, but her voice was clear and infused with resolve. "My mommy is at home. I am going to see Kathy."

"What do you mean your mommy is at home? Who's here with you?"

"My friend Lily."

"Well, where did Lily go?"

"She's here. We are going to see our friend Kathy in

North Carolina."

"That's nice. Why don't you come with me, Sweetie?"

"Thank you, but my mom always tells me I shouldn't talk to strangers."

Mirna smiled. "I'm not a stranger; my name is Mirna, and I work here. I can get you some lemonade or some Coke if you want."

The little girl's eyes opened wide. "Can I have Sprite?"

"You certainly can. Come on."

Mirna placed a protective hand over the little girl's shoulder as they walked by a homeless man laying at the edge of a corridor. The smell of urine, disinfectant and sweat, all combined in one disgusting package, lingered in the air.

The little girl crunched her nose. "It stinks in here!"

"Yeah. Bus stations are not a good place for little girls, especially when they travel alone."

"Where are we going?"

"To my supervisor's office. She will help keep you safe."

They walked together through a door that opened on a series of cubicles, and continued to one of the larger enclosures.

"Wow, this place looks like a beehive!"

Mirna laughed and knocked on the glass door. When she saw her supervisor waving her in, she opened the door and led the little girl inside.

"Who have we got here?" The woman asked smiling.

Alexis took charge of the conversation and readily introduced herself. "My name is Alexis. My friend Lily and I are going to see our friend Kathy who lives in North Carolina."

"I see. How old is Lily?"

"I don't know. She is a girl like me."

The blond woman arched her eyebrow, and she and Mirna exchanged a look.

"Why don't you wait here a minute, Alexis? We'll be right back."

"Okay. Can I have my Sprite now?"

"Of course, Honey. Let me get one for you." Mirna walked to a small cooler at the far corner of the room

378

and got a can of Sprite.

While Alexis was busy opening her drink, the two women stepped outside. Mirna spoke first. "I think we should call the police, Lois. It sounds like we have a little runaway on our hands."

The other woman nodded. "Please call from Derrick's office while I keep her entertained."

#

"Sorry I'm late, Kathy. I had to stop for a cup of coffee on my way in. I had no sleep last night."

Kathy sat in the chair across from the desk and smiled. "It's okay. I guess it makes two of us not sleeping last night."

"So, what photos were you talking about on the phone?"

Kathy opened her case and pulled out the folder containing the photos.

"Here they are. I also included a few shots I have taken at my house; I'd like to know if you see the same thing I saw in them." She lined all the photos on the desk, starting with the ones of Tracey Newman's face.

"Holy crap! If I didn't know better, I'd say this is a woman screaming."

"Look at it closely, Parker. Do you know this woman?"

Parker put on his reading glasses and took a better look. His mouth opened as he focused on the image, and he raised his eyes to meet Kathy's. "What is this? Did you photoshop these?"

"No Parker. I took those shots around my house to make sure my camera wasn't broken. Who does the woman look like?"

"Well, I'll be damned, Kathy. She looks like Tracey Newman."

Kathy could easily detect the shock on Parker's face, and she watched him as he swallowed repeatedly. "Now look at these – Dr. Greer let me take some photos of Tracey's eyes with my iriscope."

"Your iris-what?"

"Iriscope. It's like a special camera that holistic doctors use to detect illness in the body by identifying irregularities in the iris of the eye. When I took shots of

Tracey's eyes, of course, her pupils were completely dilated, so I didn't think anything would come out, but I got these." She pointed at the line of photos featuring the slingshot and the small circle. "According to my theory, those are the last images that Tracey saw before dying, but unfortunately I can't make them out. She wouldn't have looked at a slingshot before dying."

Parker sat back in his chair and was quiet for a few minutes. Kathy could not read what he was thinking, but she could almost see imaginary little wheels spinning in his head. He picked up one of the photos and put it under his desk lamp; he turned on the light, and studied the image carefully, then he looked up at Kathy."

"What if this is a charm or a pendant that was hanging on someone's arm or neck, Kathy?"

That thought never occurred to her, but the image of Tracey seemingly pointing to a necklace on the bathroom counter in one of the photos flashed through her mind. And what about the small circle? She wanted to ask Parker that, but was afraid to break the spell of possibility that was opening in his mind.

"A charm of a slingshot?"

"No, but it could be a pendant with someone's initial! A letter "Y' rather than a slingshot. Look, I've got to go, Kathy. I will call you later. Forgive me if I can't walk you out – do you mind if I keep this photo?"

Kathy shook her head, still recovering from the surprise of Parker's reaction.

Before she could say anything, he was gone.

#

The first thing that Tom noticed when he woke up was the smell of mildew and naphthalene that pervaded the room. His head was hurting and he could taste something salty on his lips, but when he tried to move, a wave of pain shot across his entire face and he grimaced. It was pitch black in here, and hot as Hades. He couldn't move his hands or his feet, and he felt wet material from his shirt sticking to the sparse hair on his chest.

Suddenly the light came on, and felt as a knife jabbing at his eyeballs. Someone else was in the room but Tom couldn't move or turn his head to see the figure insinuating toward him. He could hear the steps on the concrete floor coming closer and he wondered if the shallow breaths he was taking were going to be his last.

The man walked in front of him, and he and Tom locked eyes for a moment.

"What do you want from me? Why am I here?"

The man's laughter was malicious. "You have a way of getting in my business, Lieutenant, but we are taking care of that today."

"Who are you?"

"My friends call me Yago. Are you my friend, Lieutenant?"

Tom didn't reply.

"Everything would have gone well, you see, if Shannon Brinkley didn't start poking her nose into things she had no need to get into."

Tom knew he had to buy time if he hoped to survive. The knife protruding from the man's right hand was definitely a good incentive to bring the gift of gab out of him.

"What did Shannon do?"

"Too bad for her that she found out something she

wasn't supposed to know. And besides, she isn't very nice to Mary."

Tom already knew the answer to his questions, but he asked anyway. "So her overdose wasn't accidental?"

The man laughed, the sound of his voice filling every pocket of this humid, forsaken place. "Accidental? I wouldn't think so, Lieutenant. It wasn't too hard to slip some pills into her drink."

"Did you kill Tracey Newman?"

"I was going to, you see, and then that bitch got away. But she died anyway."

Tom was confused by that statement. "What do you mean by that?"

Yago's teeth reflected the light coming from a single light bulb hung on the ceiling. "You are too curious, Lieutenant, and curiosity unfortunately killed the cat."

#

Parker turned on his lights and siren as he punched the gas. He sped through the beltline traffic and was glad that he had at least avoided the rush-hour congestion. When his mobile phone rang, he thought of not answering, then changed his mind and clicked the talk button along with the speaker.

"Parker."

"Sergeant, this is Lana Briggs. St. Louis called and asked to speak to Lackey – they have Jack Little in custody."

"No shit! That's great. Did they leave any other information?"

"No, they just said to call back."

"Hold on to that number for me, Lana. I'll call back soon."

He ended the call and pulled up in front of the residence, not sure if he had the right address. The home was pristine clean, with flowers in the yard and a white picket fence. He parked in the driveway and walked to the door, all along admiring the delicate pansies planted in the flower bed running the whole length of the walkway. He knocked twice and waited for someone to open, but there seemed to be nobody home. He knocked again and then walked around the back of the property praying not to meet a guard dog – an accident from his youth had left him wary of pooches of all sizes. The back yard was just as manicured as the front, with grass so green and fresh-looking that Parker had to fight the urge to lay in it.

He was ready to turn the corner and get back around to the front when he thought he heard something. He listened carefully but no other sound came through. He took one more step, and another muffled scream pierced the classy silence of the neighborhood. This time he knew he hadn't imagined the scream. It was a man's voice, and although he couldn't be sure it was Tom's voice, his gut instinct told him it was. He had to get inside. All the doors were locked, and none of the windows were open, so he stopped for a moment and tried to gather his thoughts. He was aware that Tom's life was in his hands right now, and any mistake could be fatal.

Chapter 19

Shannon had no idea of where she was when she first awakened. She tried to focus on her surroundings but her eyelids felt exceptionally heavy and she could only keep them open for a few seconds at a time – although there wasn't much light filtering through the blinds, to her aching eyes it felt like a breath of fire. Her muscles felt like heavy weights, and her first thought blended with a memory from her childhood when she had tried lifting the heavy grocery bags from the trunk of her mother's car to prove her strength.

Something was stuck in her mouth, preventing her from calling out. She desperately tried to raise her arm to remove the object in her mouth but was too weak to do so. Her body felt numb – she had only felt that way once before, after waking up from a particularly scary dream and being unable to move; if she remembered correctly, the term her friend Amy used to explain the episode was something along the lines of sleep paralysis, although right now her mind was too foggy to be sure.

She wanted to close her eyes and go back to sleep, but something deep inside of her told her to remain awake. She remembered dreaming a lot while she was asleep, and many of her dreams were of Tracey. She allowed those memories to flood her mind now that she was awake, and could feel tears stinging her eyes. Tracey was her best friend, and Shannon loved her like she never loved anyone else in this world, and yet she allowed fear to get in the way. Mary didn't like Tracey because she was jealous of her, and never missed a chance to accuse her of wrongdoing, even when Tracey wasn't around to defend herself. After Tracey was found murdered, Mary was the first suspect on her list. She remembered laying awake at night, waiting for Mary to killer her too, but Mary never did – in those moments,

Shannon thought that Mary was enjoying this game of cat and mouse she was playing with her, and felt empowered by simply scaring her and keeping her in control. And unfortunately, Shannon was so emotionally abused that she believed many of the lies Mary told her, including the fact that Brad was possibly Tracey's killer. Brad had a problem with addiction but he wasn't a murderer. And what about when she accused *her* of murdering Tracey – because on the same night of the murder Shannon had taken her car and brought it back with a dent? What Mary didn't remember was that she had attacked her that night, and Shannon had fled grabbing the first set of keys she found on her way out; once she got outside, she noticed that she had the wrong keys, but she couldn't go back upstairs to get her own. She instead peeled off the parking lot, crying too hard to see clearly, and hit the corner of a mailbox a few blocks down the road. The rain was blinding but Shannon didn't care – getting away was all she cared about. She sped out of the edges of town, and drove aimlessly through country roads until she was too exhausted to continue, then she pulled into a muddy field, locked her doors and slept for a few hours. When she went back home the next day, Mary wasn't there, and Shannon cleaned the car the best she could, but some mud was still stuck on the undercarriage. Mary came back around lunch time, and the moment she walked through the door, Shannon knew she was in trouble. Mary's face was dark and swollen like the clouds of a violent storm, and Shannon promptly asked for her forgiveness. A few days later, Tracey's stepfather called and informed her of what happened. Mary was home and listened to the conversation from the phone in the bedroom; the moment Shannon hung up, Mary accused her of killing Tracey because of a family dispute Tracey had caused. The absurdity of the accusation made Shannon burst into spontaneous laughter -- yes, she was upset, but she would never kill someone she loved like a sister over something so insignificant. Unfortunately for her, that burst of unchecked emotion led to a beating. She wished she never met Mary, and her mind floated back to the day she first saw her.

At the time, Shannon needed extra money to cover her car payment, and had taken a job as a barmaid at

Green Olive, a bar Mary often frequented. Shannon hated to work there; she couldn't stand the starving looks she got from some of the men that lurked by the pool tables, and was ready to quit one night, when one of those men tried to grab her. Mary was there to save the day – she yanked the man from behind and threw him over the pool table; he was too drunk to react, and surprise was the only thing that registered in his inebriated brain. He looked at Mary with a grin on his face as he tried to lift himself up, and made the fatal mistake of calling Mary 'sweet cheeks'. Mary didn't take it as a compliment; she gave him a hand to help him stand up, and when he did she punched him square in the stomach, knocking the wind out of him. His friends watched without uttering a sound, one man barely whispering that 'it wasn't cool', but one fiery look from Mary was all he needed to swallow the rest of his complaint.

After the men left dragging their injured friend along, Mary walked up to Shannon and asked her if she was okay. Shannon was grateful, and a part of her was in awe of Mary's strength and white-knight attitude. They became fast friends, and from that point on Mary was there every night until closing to make sure nobody else would mess with 'her Shannon' as she soon nick-named her. Of course, word spread fast and nobody did – Shannon could have walked naked around the place, and men would have focused on the cue ball; a cute woman chained at the ankle to a bulldozer was way too much trouble to toy with on a night out with friends; in fact, if a new patron went in, it didn't take long for the older ones to brief him on the dangers he might encounter.

In the beginning, Mary seemed nice. She and Shannon ate together several times, especially after Mary was fired from her daytime job and had a lot of time on her hands. Shannon wasn't sure why Mary lost her job, but anytime she asked, Mary replied that she was working with a bunch of sissies with no balls, so she decided not to pry any further.

During their lunch outings, Mary told Shannon a bit about her life and didn't hide that she had little trust in people. Her own mother abandoned her and her brother when they were very young, and even if she re-appeared in their lives several years later, Mary had already closed that door. Never would she trust that woman again. Her mother had tried all she could to mend her relationship with the two children, but neither of them were interested in her repentance. After one particularly violent exchange, Mary had pushed her mother's boyfriend against the wall, and told him to get lost. The two – mother and boyfriend – seemed to have gotten the message, and Shannon thought they were finally gone. It wasn't that she didn't like them, and in fact, many times she felt bad for Mary's mother, but Mary was always angry after she saw them and Shannon hoped they would finally give up. The last time they stopped at her apartment, the day before Tracey disappeared, Shannon was in the shower and she heard Mary yelling at them. She locked herself in the bathroom and waited for them to leave before she got out, but as soon as they left Mary started banging on the door asking what was taking so long, and she had to let her in. It was the first time Mary hit her in the face. Until that day, there had been a few times when Mary grabbed her too hard, and even once when Mary ripped her pink shirt off her body because – according to her – it was too sleazy, but she never really hit her until then. After her mother left, Mary was like a pressure cooker waiting to explode, and Shannon was terrified. Mary's violence had escalated over time, and some of its poison insinuated through crevices of their life together in such a way that by the time Shannon realized she had a problem she was too scared to do anything about it.

A sharp wave of pain shot through her head, and Shannon shut her eyes to make it go away. Memories continued knocking at the edge of her consciousness, and although she tried to push them away to rest for a moment, they wouldn't leave her alone. She remembered looking for the key to her storage unit and being unable to find it, so she asked Mary to go pick up another one at the management office. The next day, she went to store a box of books she planned to donate and noticed that her belongings appeared disturbed. Not many people would notice something so insignificant, but for Shannon it was a huge thing – being an overly organized person had served her well in many occasions and hurt her in others. This time, her obsession with neatness had cost her dearly. She opened the boxes to make sure everything was still as she had left it, and found a pair of bloody boots in one of them. A small voice inside her head suggested that whoever put those boots in the unit was the same person who killed Tracey, and of course, Mary was the number-one candidate among her suspects. Panic overtook her entire being, and she put the box back and locked the unit before going back to her apartment to think. Mary had left for work earlier and was probably due to return around seven – three hours from now – so Shannon spent the next hour trying to decide whether she should call the police or pretend she hadn't seen anything.

Her nerves were so raw that she almost screamed when someone knocked on the door. She looked through the spy hole and saw Mary's stepfather – Mary's mother wasn't married to him, or even engaged, but that was how he liked to introduce himself. Mary was gone, so she felt it was safe to open; in fact, maybe she could explain to him what was going on with Mary, and he would make sure he and his girlfriend stayed the hell away.

She let him in and invited him to sit and he accepted enthusiastically. He mentioned that he was driving through the area when his car started overheating, so he wondered if it was okay for him to stay a spell while the car cooled off. Shannon didn't see anything wrong with that and offered him a drink. She poured two glasses of Coke and brought them back to the living room where he was sitting. He took it and smiled warmly, making sure to thank Shannon profusely. They talked about Mary for a while, and Yago expressed his wish to see his girlfriend reunited with her children; he said that he understood how Mary and her brother felt, and he was elated that Mary's brother Jack was at least amenable to discussing the possibility of his mother being a part of his life. He also said that no matter how long it would take, he was ready to support his soon-to-be fiancée, and that he was proud of the fact that she was doing all she could to make up for the time she had missed with her children – to her, seeing her babies happy was a mission she would stick to for the rest of her life.

After taking the first sip of a second large glass of Coke she just poured, Shannon had to use the bathroom, so she excused herself and left Yago in the living room while she ran to empty her bladder. When she came back, they picked up the conversation from where it left off, but it wasn't long before Shannon started feeling really tired. She wanted to ask him to leave, but her innate sense of hospitality prevented her from doing so. She laid her head on the back of the couch, and gradually slipped away. The last thing she remembered was Yago asking her how she felt, and the rest was a complete fog. The realization of what happened suddenly exploded in her mind, and even if her body didn't cooperate fully, the adrenaline rush pumped enough steel into one of her arms for her to grab the tube inside her mouth and yank it out. She felt a searing pain in her throat and nose, but she didn't care. She tried to scream but her throat was on fire, so she ripped the tubes from her body in hope that they would set off an alarm. When the nurse and the police officer on duty ran into her room, she sat up on the bed, and with a raspy voice she announced: "I know who killed Tracey Newman."

#

Mike and Rose Howard had nearly given up hope when the phone finally rang to announce good news. An employee at the bus station had found Alexis waiting to board a bus headed to North Carolina and she called the police; the moment the call went through, it was immediately routed to the detectives investigating Alexis's disappearance who rushed to the bus station and were relieved to find out that their case had a happy ending.

Mike burst into tears a few seconds into the call, and Rose – not knowing what upset her husband so much – immediately froze into a state of deep panic. If she were to live to the ripe age of a hundred, Rose would never forget her husband's face when he hung up and the words 'she's alive' sputtered from his lips almost drowned by the tears he could not stop. That was when Rose's icy wall shattered and she fell on her knees praying and crying, her whole body shaken by a quake of powerful sobs the epicenter of which was smack in the middle of her heart. They hugged and cried, laughed and kissed, and then walked together to the car, each supporting the other through yet another crippling wave of emotion.

Mike sped down the highway, too happy to think about tickets or accidents, and when they arrived at the bus station, he pulled straight into a handicapped spot to save time – if $100 was all he had to pay to see his little girl five minutes sooner he was more than glad to open his pockets and hand out a bill.

The practically ran inside, their legs fueled by love and a never-before-felt sense of joy, and they nearly crashed into an overweight security guard clad in an ill-fitting uniform.

"Sir," Mike asked the security guard, "Our daughter was found at the station today. Can you tell us where the director's office is?"

In spite of his lack of caring about his personal image likely caused by a minimum-wage salary and long hours spent ensuring the safety of a place that didn't do him any favors, the young man smiled and shook their hands. "I'm Officer Fines. Follow me. I'll take you to meet your daughter."

The young man walked with a different dance in his step, and led them to a small cluster of offices where one policeman in uniform and one in civilian clothing stood waiting. Satisfied to finally have done something of importance in his day – playing a part in reuniting a lost child with her parents was the work of a hero in his book – the young man bid his goodbye and left wearing a smile that was so bright it stole the attention from the quarter-size stain on the front of his shirt.

The detective who met Mike and Rose shook their hands and told them how happy he was that their daughter was safe, and then he ushered them into the manager's office where Alexis was sitting on an overly stuffed chair sipping a can of soda and munching peanut butter crackers.

The moment Mike and Rose stepped inside, Alexis sucked in her breath, something she always did when she knew she was in trouble; but this time, Mike and Rose were too happy to reprimand her, and both nearly dove on her and squeezed her into a sandwich hug.

"Mom! Dad! I can't breathe!" She said laughing, enormously relieved to realize that her parents weren't even thinking about punishments. "Where's Petey?"

"Petey is at home, Sweetheart," her father replied as

he quickly brushed tears from his eyes – happy or not, he had a tough-daddy reputation to uphold. "He missed you a lot. We all did."

Alexis arched her brow and looked at both of her parents' faces, a bit confused by their less-than-typical reaction. "But aren't you mad at me?"

Rose smiled and hugged her tightly. "Mad? We are madly happy that you are okay, Alexis. Why were you trying to go to North Carolina?"

Alexis cast her eyes down to meet the floor and balanced herself from one foot to the other. "I wanted to see Kathy. She understands me, and…"

"And what, Alexis?"

"Nothing. Never mind." Her little face was suddenly sad, the weight of the emotions battling inside of her too heavy to bear alone.

Mike kneeled down until his eyes met his daughter's. When he spoke, his voice was soft and laden with regret. "I found Granddaddy's lighter, Alexis. It was exactly where Lily said it was. I am so sorry I didn't believe you; I hope you can forgive me, and I hope Ms. Kathy can forgive me too, for being so ugly to her. I was

401

just hurt and under stress, Alexis, and I know it is not a very good excuse, but I am asking you to please accept my apology."

Alexis's eyes widened as far as her lids could open and as soon as she was able to process the words she threw her tiny arms around her father's neck, squeezing as hard as she could. Rose burst into tears and hugged both of them; crying felt good right now and for once, it was for a happy occasion. She doubted she would ever tell Mike about the dream she had at the hospital, but never again would she fail to listen to her daughter.

They thanked the officers and hugged Mirna Thompson who stood in the corner crying her eyes out, then they walked out of the bus terminal holding hands.

Before she got in the car, Alexis hesitated for a moment and Mike asked her if she was okay.

"I'm fine, Daddy, but I think I lost something that belongs to Ms. Kathy. I was playing with a lighter I found on a table in her studio while I was there, and I accidentally put it in my backpack. I wanted to bring it back to her but I lost it. Do you think it was important to her, like the one that belonged to Granddaddy?"

"There is only one way to find out, Alexis. Let's go home and call her."

"Daddy…" Alexis said in a small voice, sadness once again darkening her delicate features, "I was going to see Kathy to tell her something important that Lily said."

"Yes? What is it, Alexis?"

"The people who killed Tracey are going to kill Ms. Kathy's boyfriend if someone doesn't stop them."

#

Mary Townsend lay in bed staring at the ceiling. She missed Shannon, and knew that if Shannon lived, she would have some serious changes to make. Of course, there was a possibility that Shannon would go to jail, if it turned out that she was indeed involved in Tracey's murder. Could her Shannon be a killer? Everything was possible of course, and in her own troubled life Mary had learned not to trust anyone completely. Starting from her mother, the relationships she forged in her life always left her stranded. The worst one to date was certainly the relationship she had with the foster father who raped her repeatedly, and Mary held her birth mother responsible for it – had she not abandoned her at an early age, Mary wouldn't have been in that predicament. After years of abuse, she was finally old enough to run away and make it on her own, but her view of men was forever damaged, and her anger was so intense she felt overpowered by it. She dated a few girls after that, and enjoyed intercourse with them; for once, she didn't have to lay in the darkness crying and hurting. None of the girls she dated ever captured her heart, until she met Shannon. Knowing that Shannon saw her as a hero allowed her to bask into the sunshine of her heightened self-image. Shannon was everything she ever wanted – she was beautiful, kind and gentle, and most of all, she needed Mary. Shannon wasn't able to harm a fly – or was she?

The arrow of a painful doubt pierced through the fibers of her consciousness and spread like wildfire. She sat up in bed and ran a hand through her hair, unable to shake the feeling of foreboding in her heart, so she got up and went to the living room. She sat on the couch and looked for the TV remote, cursing loudly when she couldn't locate it. She turned on the lamp beside the couch and got on her hands and knees to see if it had fallen on the floor, but something sharp went through her knee and she involuntarily screamed. When she lifted her knee she saw a drop of blood erupting from a tiny puncture wound, so she ran her hand over the carpet to see if she could find what pricked her. Her hand came into contact with a small hard object and she picked it up to look at it. It was a small diamond earring, one of two that her mother had given her the last day she saw her. Mary laughed when that gift was given to her, and her anger came forth in waves. She clearly remembered throwing the closed box on the floor in the kitchen, and her mother's boyfriend picking up and opening it to ensure the earrings were still inside. Mary told them both to leave and never come back, and when they did, Yago was clutching the box safely in his hand, with both earrings in it. How could one of those earrings be on the carpet right now? Had he come back to the apartment when she was gone?

Thinking about her mother's boyfriend made her

even angrier, probably because she knew her mother had chosen his company all for the wrong reasons. Her mother never actually came out and said it, but his resemblance to Mary's brother was so uncanny that Mary was sure her mother was dating him only because she felt closer to her lost son that way.

Suddenly she thought of something...the cops had mentioned that the man who tried to kill Shannon at the hospital was Jack, but Mary knew Jack was not in town when the attack occurred. She hadn't told anyone, but Jack had found some photos of Tracey he felt were particularly beautiful when he cleaned his bedroom closet, and had taken them to a photo shop to have them copied – he didn't want to separate from them, but he also wanted her family to have them, especially the one of Tracey and her little sister together. He didn't want to send them in the mail, so he bought a bus ticket to bring the photos in person; according to what he told Mary, it was his chance to also apologize for his past behavior. He never meant to scare Tracey, and he wished to express to her family how much he truly loved her. Actually, Mary thought that he loved Tracey too much, and if she had any doubts before, they were quickly wiped off when she saw the creepy shrine to Tracy in his apartment. Mary never went to Jack's place, even if she had a key, and she was just as surprised as the two detectives who went in with her.

Jack was gone when Shannon was attacked, and yet the man who attacked her fit his description. Yago! How could she have not thought of him?

She sprang from the floor and ran to grab the phone to call the number hand-written on the back of Lieutenant Lackey's business card. She was greeted by an answering machine and slammed the phone down. She had to warn the Lieutenant before someone else got hurt, but first of all she had to get some answers, and the only place she could find them, she was sure, was at her mother's house.

Chapter 20

Parker had been a police officer long enough to know that under no circumstance he should put the life of a hostage in danger, and Tom's agonized scream meant that he wasn't alone; the worst thing he could do was to alert the other person of his presence. He got in his car and moved it to the next block, and thought about calling for reinforcement but decided against it – he never before went against procedures but in this case the hostage was his friend. He practically ran back to the house and looked for a way in, and cursed under his breath when he found that all the doors were locked. One look at the kitchen window made him want to scream for joy: The glass panes weren't properly aligned which probably meant that the lock wasn't fully engaged. With a moderate amount of pressure, the lock gave in and the pane slid up creating a passage way for Parker to enter the house.

The kitchen was deserted and he couldn't hear any sounds from anywhere in the house, aside from a grandfather clock loudly ticking away in the living room. Using the wall for cover he inched toward the doorway and scoped the room adjacent to the kitchen – it was furnished exclusively with antique pieces and a baby grand piano set at an angle in the far right corner. The blinds were closed to shield away the heat of the day, leaving the room in a semi-darkness which conferred an even more austere feel to the ambience.

With his gun drawn, Parker made his way through the room and came to a small door situated directly across from the staircase. He put his ear to the door to listen for sounds coming from the inside, but everything was quiet. He tried the handle and was happy to find that it wasn't locked, so he turned it as softly as he could and cracked the door, but before he could open it fully, the mouth of a gun appeared from the doorway across the foyer and Parker froze.

A figure suddenly appeared behind the gun, only a few feet away from Parker. "Drop the gun, brother."

Parker didn't argue, and let his gun fall by his feet.

"Put your hands behind your head and open the door, then start going down the stairs slowly."

Parker did as instructed and was grateful that the stairs weren't completely dark. The man moved behind him, keeping the gun so close behind his head that Parker thought he could smell the scent of metal. When they reached the bottom of the stairs, the man pushed Parker into a darkened corner toward a figure whose face was bathed in crusted, darkened blood. It didn't take him long to recognize the man.

"Oh my God...Tom..."

The man watching the scene stood smiling, one of his hands clapping against his wrist. "Well, aren't you the smart one, Detective? You found us after all. That's really too bad that you won't be able to tell anybody."

He made Parker lay on the floor and removed the handcuffs from his back pocket, then slid them across his wrists and snapped them shut.

With his face pushed against the floor, Parker didn't immediately see the other figure descending the stairs, but Tom did, and his breath caught in his lungs. Illuminated by the single light bulb on the stairs, her face appeared even uglier than Tom remembered when he saw Yvonne Fowler the first time at the warehouse of *Caldwell & Sons* . He was sure she was the same person who called him and accused Brad Johnson of the murder.

"Oh my, look who came to visit! Two fine officers from our wonderful police department." She said with an affected smile that accentuated the deep lines in her face and made Tom shiver.

"Yes," Yago picked up her line and carried it forward, "we should offer them some tea, Sweetheart. After all, we *are* in the south and we can't forget about hospitality."

Tom tried to move but his hands were tied so tightly behind his back that his arms wouldn't even budge. He licked his lips to moisten them and when he spoke his voice came out as a cracked whisper. "Why? Why did you kill Tracey?"

The woman burst into bitter laughter. "Why? I thought you were smarter than that, Lieutenant. Tracey Newman was a whore who used my son and then dropped him like a hot potato when she was done with him. She accused him of stalking her and blocked him from even talking to her. Do you know what her rejection did to him?"

Tom was confused. "Your son? Who's your son?"

"Oh, so you haven't connected the dots yet, I see. My son is Jack Little, the man everyone suspects of killing that little slut. He even tried to change his name and start anew, but you couldn't leave him alone."

"Your son has a shrine in his apartment with photos of Tracey. What do you call that if not insanity?"

Yvonne's face contorted into an angry, twisted mask, as she raised her foot and kicked Tom in the mouth. "Be careful about what you say, Lieutenant. My son wasn't a stalker. His only sin was to love that woman; God only knows why. I was the one who encouraged him to create that little corner of happiness. Being near that woman made him happy and that's all I cared about."

Parker couldn't move, but he turned his face to the side to take a better look of the woman. Tom shook his head. "But why? If you didn't like Tracey, and you felt she deserved to die, why did you support his love for her?"

"You couldn't understand, Lieutenant. My son loved her and she rejected him."

"Why do you feel so responsible for your son's relationships, Yvonne?"

The look on Yvonne's face changed from angry to sad. "Because I was never able to protect him and make him happy when he was a little boy. Now is all I have."

The woman was mad, of that Tom had no doubt, but he couldn't understand how her boyfriend could support her ideas. He shifted his gaze to look at Yago standing beside Yvonne; nothing registered in his eyes but sheer adoration for the woman. Why? Maybe if he could understand his motive he could find a way to play on his emotions and find his way back to freedom.

"Do you agree with all this, Yago?"

Yago nodded, his eyes still focused on his beloved. "Yvonne is like the mother I always wished to have. I wish my mother could have loved me enough to look out for me. I support everything Yvonne does."

So there was a catch – like Yvonne's children, Yago grew up without the safety net provided by a caring mother, and when he met Yvonne he fell in love with her mission to be there for the children she was hoping to reunite with. Maybe, if he found a way to show Yago a different side of Yvonne – maybe the side of her *abandoning* her children at a young age – he would be free from her spell.

"So your mother left you too, Yago?"

Yago's face hardened. "Yes. Drugs were more important than I was."

"Was that what happened to you, Yvonne? Did you get involved with drugs and gave up your children?"

"No! That's not the way it played out. My children were ripped away from me."

"But why, Yvonne? Did social services come in?"

"I...I went to jail for something stupid. I was caught stealing from the store I worked at. It was a long time ago."

"So you chose material things over your children?

You knew you were going to lose them if you got caught."

Anger spread across Yvonne's face and her hand reached into her jacket pocket from which she pulled out a small .45 and pointed its mouth directly toward Tom's face. That unexpected turn of events convinced him that it was best to change his tactics. Yvonne's face was streaked with pain so intense Tom feared she would shoot at any moment.

"That's enough, Lieutenant! I loved my children, and I was only stealing to give them what they needed after their fathers left us penniless. But someone like you would never understand what it is like to struggle and to wonder how you will feed your children the next time they cry because they are hungry. My boyfriend at the time was a drug addict, and he split after I was arrested. When the police found drugs in my house, they assumed they were mine."

"I understand, Yvonne. You were only doing what any loving mother would have done."

"You're right, Lieutenant. And that's why that woman had to die, and her little boyfriends had to suffer."

A sudden realization hit Tom square in the chest. "Did you put the bloody T-shirt in Brad Johnson's car?"

Yvonne sneered. "That's a dumb one right there, so that was an easy job – Brad Johnson is too cocky to even lock his vehicle. It wasn't hard. Just as it wasn't hard to intercept his call to his little dealer and find out where he was meeting him to make his purchases."

It was all clear now -- all the puzzle pieces were finally in place.

"Why don't your children want you back into their lives, Yvonne?"

"They blame me for everything that's happened in their past, unfortunately. They don't understand that everything I've ever done has always been for them. My hope, Lieutenant, is that someday they will finally see the light; and for that to happen, I have to be free. I'm sure you can see why you and your friend here cannot leave this house alive."

\#

Mike Howard was glad Kathy's number was still programmed into his mobile phone, although he suspected that if he didn't, Alexis probably had it committed to memory. He dialed the number and waited for her to pick up, a little concerned about being able to keep a straight voice despite the knot in his throat threatening to choke him. When Kathy answered, his heart pounded at the beat of shame.

"Kathy, this is Mike Howard. How are you?"

A little surprised to hear his voice, but eager to know how Alexis was faring, Kathy replied with excitement and disbelief intertwined into a near-whisper.

"I'm doing well, Mr. Howard; how are you?"

"We are doing well, now that Alexis has been found. She ran away to catch a bus headed to North Carolina."

Worried by the possibility of being accused of this latest evil, Kathy raised a hand into the air as if silently trying to stop Mike in his track with her gesture. "I knew nothing about this, Mr. Howard. I complied with your wish and interrupted all communication with Alexis when you asked me."

"I know, Kathy, and I am calling to apologize for

my rude behavior. I was very upset that night, and to tell you the truth, I was scared to death. Tracey wasn't my biological daughter, but I loved her as if she were; I was already grieving her loss when I felt threatened by the possibility of losing another child to emotional withdrawal."

The words coming from the phone weren't making things right, but they helped Kathy accept the reasons behind Mike Howard's behavior; as a parent, she felt empathically connected to him, and right now she could feel his pain and wanted to cry.

"I understand. You don't owe me any apologies. You only did what any caring parent would have done in your place."

"No Kathy. A loving parent should have cared enough to listen to what his daughter was trying to say, and I don't know that I will ever be able to fully forgive myself for not having been there for Alexis when she needed me most."

Kathy was a little taken aback by this open-heart admission – what was Mike trying to say?

"You did the best you could, Mr. Howard.

Unfortunately, it is very hard to accept certain things that aren't part of collective knowledge."

"You are right, and that's why I should at least have listened to people who had that knowledge, or at least owned the ability to keep themselves open. When we were still in North Carolina, Alexis told me about a cigarette lighter which I had misplaced – she knew exactly where it was because Lily told her. Lily also told her about Tracey's pregnancy and about the fact that more than one person was involved in her sister's murder, and of course, I didn't believe any of it. I blamed it on her overactive imagination and left it at that."

Kathy was holding her breath, eager to know where this conversation was heading and hungry for any additional words coming from Mike.

"A couple of days ago I found that cigarette lighter, Kathy. It was in the exact place Alexis told me about; of course, I suppose it is possible she could have seen it, but Alexis never goes into the garage on her own because she doesn't like insects very much, and furthermore she wouldn't have gone to look into my toolbox. When I found my father's cigarette lighter, I also thought about what Alexis said concerning her sister. She couldn't have known of her pregnancy, and the fact that she did made me very uneasy, even the first time she mentioned it. I don't think I even processed it in my mind that night – I just chose to brush it under a carpet of ignorance in favor of things I could tangibly accept."

Kathy was crying openly now, her tears running unchecked down her cheeks, and her chest rising violently to contain the sobs that wanted to burst out and be heard.

"As you can see, I do owe you an apology Kathy. I wanted to believe that our daughter was slipping away because of some strange influence you bestowed on her; I was looking for a scapegoat."

"Alexis never wanted to upset anyone, Mr. Howard," Kathy said in between sobs, "she was just trying to help. She has a gift – an unusual one, I grant you – but a gift nonetheless. It has often been speculated that children's imaginary friends are spirits that find a way to communicate with them because children don't pass judgment and are able to remain open to unknown things. Lily is a spirit, Mr. Howard. I don't know who she is or why she chose to connect with your daughter, but I believe that she was there to support Alexis through her painful ordeal."

"I understand that now, and Lily will never be a forbidden name in our home again. Please forgive me Kathy; I can only pray to God that Alexis will find it in her heart to forgive me someday, too."

"I have no doubt she will, Sir. Alexis loves you, and nothing will ever change that."

Mike Howard was doing his best not to burst into tears, and Kathy heard someone else talking to him on the other end of the line.

"Alexis would like to talk to you, Kathy. Is it okay if I put her on the line?"

"Of course! I would love to talk to her."

When Alexis's tiny voice came through, Kathy felt as if someone just injected her with a dose of sunshine.

"Alexis! How are you Sweetheart?"

"I am doing well, Kathy. How are you?"

Kathy wanted to respond that she wasn't doing well

at all, and that she was worried sick about Tom, but Alexis wasn't the right recipient for that kind of talk – this poor little girl had been through enough.

"I am doing great, Alexis, thank you for asking. I've missed you."

"I've missed you too, Kathy. I have your lighter, the one you kept on your desk at the studio; I think I accidentally put it in my backpack when I packed my things. I was trying to bring it to you, but I couldn't."

"Oh, Alexis…don't worry about that lighter. I think someone left it at my studio, and you can keep it if it reminds you of your time here."

"Really? I will treasure it."

Kathy wanted to hug her through the phone. "But tell me, Alexis, how are you feeling?"

"I am feeling great now that mom and dad believe me. They understand that Lily is real; did you talk to them about that?"

"No, I didn't; they understood on their own, and you should really appreciate the effort they are making with this."

Oh, I do! And you should see how big Petey is

getting!"

"Petey? Who's Petey?"

"Petey is my kitten. My grandma gave him to me. He sleeps with me."

"That's wonderful, Alexis. Kitties make great friends, don't they?"

"They sure do!"

"I need to let you go, Alexis. Thank you so much for calling me. I hope you will continue to stay in touch."

"I will Kathy, but I haven't told you the most important thing I need to share with you."

"What is it, Alexis?"

"The girl who killed Tracey...she is really mad, and she is going to kill your boyfriend."

Kathy froze. "Did Lily tell you that, Alexis?"

"Yes. She said that this woman is mad because her babies don't want her, and she thinks Tom is an obstacle."

Kathy's head was spinning. *Who is this woman threatening Tom? Is she trying to kill him now?*

"Did Lily give you a name, Alexis? I know it is a lot

to ask, but please try to ask her."

"She already did, Kathy. She said that her name is French or something…it starts with a 'Y'…yes! Yvonne – that's what she called her."

"I have to go, Alexis. Please ask Lily to pray for Tom and for me."

"I will Kathy, I love you."

"I love you too, Sweetie. I will talk to you soon."

She clicked off the call and tried to call Parker, but his phone rang without an answer. Frustration and fear embraced one another inside of her and she burst into sobs so violent her whole body was shaken by them. Tom was in danger. Lily had said so, and Lily didn't lie.

#

Rose Howard drove in front of St. Francis Catholic church several times before she could make up her mind to stop and go inside. She hadn't been to church in many years, even if as a child she was very active in her home church. The hypocrisy and the underlying corruption she had detected over the years had gradually eroded the foundation of her beliefs, and once she moved from New York City, where not going to church on Sunday was equivalent to social suicide for a young Catholic girl raised in the *Famiglia* mentality, her days sitting on a pew were numbered. Yet, even after all these years, she still could tap into the feeling of peace her young heart experienced when she walked through the doors of a church. Right now she needed to rekindle that sense of peace, and most of all she needed to bury her feelings of guilt in regards to her dead children.

She finally parked and looked into the rearview mirror to check her appearance before getting out of the car – an old trigger probably buried deep in her subconscious from her childhood, when her mother overly fussed about looking one's best when preparing to meet the Lord.

She walked through the heavy wood door and immediately went to cross herself with holy water, then curtsied in front of the crucifix over the altar and filed into one of the pews toward the back of the chapel. She sat for a long time, her eyes taking in the perfect beauty of her surroundings and her soul lulled by the quiet peace reaching out to her like the hand of a loving mother. For the first time in many years – and especially since the horrible storms that had ravaged through her life the last few weeks – Rose felt like she had finally come home.

She closed her eyes and tried to process the feeling – waves of different emotions washed through her and she was flooded with love pouring straight from her heart.

Our Father, which art in heaven,
hallowed be thy name.
Thy Kingdom come,
thy will be done,
in earth as it is in heaven
Give us this day our daily bread.
And forgive us our trespasses,
as we forgive them that trespass against us.
And lead us not into temptation,
but deliver us from evil.
For thine is the kingdom,
the power, and the glory,
for ever and ever.

Amen.

"...deliver us from evil." Guilt is the second evil after fear...it was time to let everything go – her guilt over aborting Lily, and her fear of having caused Tracey's death by not protecting her enough. She knew that tradition calls for confession to deliver one's heart from sins, but she had become comfortable enough in her own personal relationship with God over the years to feel confident about unburdening her soul without the help of a stranger.

"Please forgive me Father, for I have sinned. I have allowed a moment of panic to write the story of my life for many years. I ask forgiveness for not bringing Lily into this world. I know a life is always precious, even in the direst of circumstances, but at the time I was scared and I didn't feel that I could be a good parent. I am human and I make mistakes, but I am not a bad person and I have beaten myself down long enough. I trust in your divine wisdom and I ask for forgiveness. If I know that you have forgiven me, I will be able to forgive myself. I fear now that my sense of guilt was the trigger to bring upon Tracey's murder – I didn't want the first child, and the second child was taken away from me. If your judgment is against me, Lord, I am prepared to live with that pain forever, but I am humbly asking you to grant me healing."

She stood up, unaware of the tears that had freely washed down her face and went to light a candle beneath the statue of the Virgin Mary.

"This candle is for you, Lily. I am sorry I wasn't ready to be your mommy. Fear ruled my thoughts and I never thought of the wonderful opportunity I was granted to bring such a bright angel into this world. Please forgive me, and thank you for being there for your sister when she needed you most. Mike and I, we didn't understand, and we chose to keep our minds on shut-down to push away the pain when Alexis needed to be comforted. But you were there for her, and I don't think I have words to express my gratitude to you. I wish I could keep you here with us, but it isn't right – you're an angel, and like all angels you should not be bound to this earth. I love you Lily, and I hope that if you ever choose to come back to Earth, you will be happy and free."

As her words ended, Rose felt a weight lift off her soul. Until that moment, she had no idea how heavy the chains she had been carrying were. She remained on her knees in front of the Virgin Mary, her eyes closed to allow the final debris of those old feelings to leave her heart, then reached into her pocket for more money to buy another candle.

"This one is for you, my beautiful Tracey. You had a whole life ahead of you, and I will never know what it is like to hold your children and to see you grow older; for that I am sorry, but I am also grateful for the time I had with you. You were one of the brightest angels, and even if you were only in my life for a very short time, you have given me more joy in those few years that many receive in a lifetime. Go in peace my love, and rest among the most beautiful stars."

Rose's chest shook with sobs as she let go of her daughters. The tears came furiously and copiously and she lost track of the time she was in the church. When she stood up she felt light-headed but her heart was at peace; she had suffered an unimaginable loss, but her living daughter was still here for her to take care of, and she pledged to dedicate the rest of her life to her happiness.

She picked up her purse from the floor and wiped her eyes, then slowly walked outside. The sun was bright and she instinctually brought a hand over her brows to shield away the excessive light. Across the street, she saw a young woman with blond hair reaching her hand out to a younger girl wearing piggy tales. Rose watched them walk away together, smiling and talking before turning into a side street she never before noticed when driving through the area. She crossed the road and came upon the street, but when she looked up she saw that it led to nowhere – what looked like a street from a distance was instead a curve a few feet deep bordered by open woods. Rose stood there for a while, knowing in her heart that the two girls were rushing to meet the light of the sun filtering through the trees.

#

Alexis sat at the desk in her bedroom rubbing Petey's silky fur, and she smiled when he pushed his little head into her hand so forcibly that he caused the cup full of pens resting near her arm to fall. The sound of the pens scattering on the desk scared him enough to make him jump out and seek shelter under the bed skirt.

"Oh Petey…look at the mess we made. Let's pick them up before Mommy or Daddy get in here."

She picked up the pens and colored pencils she saw on the desk and got down on her hands and knees to look on the floor for some she knew were missing. She was taken by her task that she didn't notice Lily in the background, resting against the door.

"Alexis, I came by to say goodbye."

Alexis turned around a bit surprised. "I didn't know you were here, Lily. I'm sorry, I didn't mean to ignore you – Petey made me spill all the pens on the desk." Alexis stood up and placed the orange pencil back into the cup before Lily's words had an impact; when she finally processed the message, she looked up at her friend wide-eyed. "What do you mean you came to say goodbye? Where are you going?"

"Where I should have gone a long time ago, Alexis. I am going home."

"But where's home? Will you come back?"

"I'm afraid not. Or maybe I will someday, but we probably won't see each other any more."

Alexis's eyes filled with tears. She already lost one sister, and now she was ready to lose the best friend she ever had. "But why, Lily? Aren't you happy here?"

Lily smiled, but her eyes betrayed a shadow of sadness. "It's not that, Alexis. I am happy when I am with you, but this is not where I belong. My place is very far away from here, but I couldn't go back until I fixed something that was broken."

"What did you have to fix, Lily?"

"A broken spirit that was left in chains. I had to wait until the chains were loosened and the spirit could fly free."

"I don't understand, Lily. Whose spirit was it?"

"It doesn't matter any more. It is fixed now and she will never feel the weight of the chains she was carrying."

"Was it Tracey?"

"No, but Tracey is fine by the way. She knows that her killer is going to be brought to justice and for that she is grateful; she is ready to go home too."

Alexis was crying openly now, her heart shattering while she wrapped her arms around herself in a gesture of comfort.

"How can I live without you, Lily?"

"You will be fine. Maybe you can ask Mom to adopt or at least foster a child nobody wants. That way you will gain a sister or brother, and that child will finally feel the love of a family."

"Mom and Dad wouldn't do that."

"You don't know that, Alexis. Maybe you can suggest it to them yourself, and you might be positively surprised by their answer."

"But I don't want a new sister or brother! I want you..."

"I live in every little girl and boy who's not wanted. If you give your love to them, you will offer that love to me, and even if I am far away I will be able to feel it and send you back my own."

Lily's image began to lose density at the edges and soon Alexis could see through her. Her heart ached but something inside of her told her that no matter how badly she wanted Lily to stay, she had to let her go.

"I will always love you Lily! You are the best friend a girl could ever dream of, and to me you are like... like..."

"A sister?"

"Yes! Just like a sister!"

"Then continue to see me that way, Alexis, and know that I will always love you and watch over you."

A spitting sound made Alexis turn her head to see Petey looking twice his size, his kitten fur sticking out to scare away the intruder.

"Oh, Petey, you don't have to be scared. It's just Lily."

She picked Petey up and hugged him tight, her hand gently wrapped around his underside. When she looked back up, Lily was gone. She sat back at her desk, put Petey down and buried her head into her folded arms while she allowed tears to flow free. When Petey rubbed against her head and purred, she raised her head and then scooped him up and kissed him gently.

With Petey still in her arms, she opened the door and headed to the bathroom to wash her face; as she walked out into the hallway she felt a light breeze brushing against her, followed by a giggling sound. In spite of her pain, she smiled – Lily had finally made it home.

#

Rose dried her eyes as she parked her car in front of the grocery store. She was exhausted but her heart was soaring. She finally felt free – free from the past, and free from the guilt that kept her soul is bondage for a long time. There was one final thing she had to do before going home, and she knew that she wouldn't be completely at peace until she did. She knew the police had tried to contact Tracey's father without much luck, but Rose knew where to find him. After his latest marriage had catapulted into a disaster, Frank Newman had decided to say goodbye to the outside world. He had come to see her once before he left for the mountains, and asked for forgiveness for all the wrong turns in their marriage. Rose didn't want to hear his words of repentance, her wounded ego still enshrouded in a cloak of self-righteousness, and she asked him to leave. Before he left her doorstep to disappear forever, he left one number no one else knew, and begged her to keep him informed about what went on in Tracey's life. Of course she never did, her anger blinding her from seeing him as a father who loved his child despite his faults.

Now that her anger toward herself was allowed to dissipate, her anger toward Frank was following right along. He wasn't the best husband, but he loved Tracey, and he had the right to come visit her grave. She dug the number from the small pocket in her purse and noticed that her hands were shaking when she dialed the number. She closed her eyes and swallowed when he answered. The conversation was strained at first, but the moment that Rose mentioned what happened to Tracey, a long silence was followed by cleansing tears. If love wasn't enough to unite them in this life, loss had come to join their hands in a lifelong marriage of parental grief. They spoke for a long time, and Frank asked if it was okay for him to visit the grave soon.

"You don't have to ask, Frank. Tracey was your child too, and I am sure she would love for you go by her grave. Please, do stop by the house when you do, and I'll fix lunch. It's time to let bygones be bygones."

Chapter 21

"I believe what you're telling us Ms. Brinkley, and I really appreciate your willingness to help, but we already have a suspect in custody."

The detective standing in front of Shannon Brinkley's bed had a patronizing tone, which drove her mad. He was short and stout, wearing an ill-fitting suit that didn't flatter his figure at all, and his face seemed unnaturally pasted to the collar of his shirt, as if someone had forgotten to draw a proper neck. His lips were curved upward toward his cheeks, fostering an involuntary smile that made him look like a clown without make-up – Shannon never liked clowns, and she liked this man even less. She asked for Lieutenant

Lackey when she first spoke with the guard on duty, but this man was sent to talk to her instead, and he wouldn't give her any information on how she could get in touch with the detective in charge of Tracey's case. She thought of calling Mary to ask her for the number she knew was at the apartment, but she wasn't ready to see Mary yet; it was as though the time she was asleep had granted her clarity, and she was now ready to stand up for herself and move forward. She shook her head and lay back on her pillow. Even if she felt better, she was still weak and it didn't take much to tire her.

"No, I don't think you understand, Sir. I said that I know who killed Tracey Newman."

"So do we, Ms. Brinkley. Bradley Johnson was taken into custody for the murder of Tracey Newman."

Shannon sat up on the bed automatically, any remnant of the fatigue she felt a few seconds ago devoured by the words spewed from the clown's mouth.

"Whoa! Wait a minute…Brad is a junkie, and God help me if I say this, he was probably not a good boyfriend for Tracey, but he is no killer!"

"I assume that you didn't get to read the papers in

here, Ms. Brinkley. Mr. Johnson was arrested after a bloody shirt was found in his trunk. The blood was positively identified as Ms. Newman's."

Confusion registered in Shannon's eyes. "What? But that's not possible…"

"Why would you say that, Ms. Brinkley? Can you offer Mr. Johnson an alibi?"

"I can't, but I know who can."

The detective narrowed his eyes and cocked his head on the side. "Oh? And who's this person?"

"Erin Winthrow. Brad was with her the night of the murder."

"If you are correct, Ms. Brinkley, why didn't Ms. Winthrow come forth to help him, or why didn't he mention her name himself?"

"It's not Ms. Winthrow, Detective; it's Mrs. Winthrow. She is a woman married to a prominent figure in town, and she has small children. I'm sure she has reasons to not wish to be identified publicly, and Brad would not betray her this way."

"Even if his life is at stake? I would imagine that anyone with an alibi would be quick to deliver any name that can save him."

"Not if that someone is in love, and Brad is in love with her."

The detective looked at Shannon intently as if trying to detect anything on her face that wouldn't support her statements.

"If Brad had a bloody shirt in his trunk, somebody put it in there, and I know exactly who."

"Okay, let's hear it…"

"Yvonne Fowler is a woman who worked with Brad, Detective. She is also the mother of a man who was obsessed with Tracey, and she hated Brad because she felt that Tracey left her son for him."

The detective's attention was piqued, and he sat on the chair adjacent to the bed with his shoulders slouched toward Shannon. Confident that he was willing to listen now, she continued. "As you know, someone tried to kill me…"

"Wasn't that attempted suicide?"

Shannon shook her head vehemently. "I wouldn't kill myself, Detective. Someone tried to kill me, and that someone is Eduardo Carlos—though he goes by the nickname Yago—Yvonne's boyfriend."

"Why would this Mr. Carlos want you dead, Ms. Brinkley?"

"I am not completely sure, but it might be connected to the fact that earlier that day I found something which was possibly connected to Tracey's murder – a pair of work boots splattered with blood that were hidden inside my storage unit."

The detective arched his brow. "Yes, I have read about those boots in the case file, but how do you think they got in there?"

Shannon sighed. "My roommate is Jack Little's sister and Yvonne Fowler's daughter. They could have picked up a key from my apartment when they came to visit. The same day that I was fed an overdose of drugs, Eduardo Carlos came by the apartment with the excuse that his car was overheating. I offered him a drink while he waited for the car to cool off and he accepted. I poured drinks for both of us, but I got up to use the restroom at some point during the conversation, and shortly after I went back and finished my drink, I started falling asleep. I'm afraid I am unable to tell you what happened next because I lost consciousness."

The detective was deathly silent, and although he didn't give any signs of either believing or disbelieving Shannon's story, he seemed to be considering it at least.

"Where do Mr. Carlos and his girlfriend live, Ms. Brinkley?"

"I don't know where he lives, but Yvonne Fowler lives at 1420 Wintry Lane. My roommate shared her address once while we drove by the neighborhood."

"I will send a car to check it out, Ms. Brinkley. Thank you for your cooperation."

He put his small notebook into the inside pocket of his jacket and prepared to leave when Shannon called asked: "I am not trying to pry into business that doesn't concern me, but why can't I speak to Lieutenant Lackey?"

"He and his partner have been away on an investigation I assume. They haven't been in the past couple of days."

"So you don't know when they will be back?"

"I'm afraid not, Miss, but I will be happy to record your statement."

He left and Shannon closed her eyes. This detective didn't inspire any trust, and she wondered if any of her words had made a difference, but she was too tired to worry about it now. She tried to clear her mind and to rest her eyes for a few minutes, but before she knew it she was asleep.

Meanwhile, Detective Quince got into his car and scanned the notes he had taken in Shannon's room, his mind considering the possibility that Shannon Brinkley was right. If she was, an innocent man was awaiting someone else's trial. And suddenly, Lackey's and Parker's absences seemed strange too; of course, their job allowed for them to go off on different tangents as they followed a lead, but in all the years she knew them, they never did that without at least notifying the desk. Maybe the Brinkley woman was still hallucinating from her long sleep, but Quince had also learned long ago to trust his gut instinct. He picked up the radio and called in. "This is Quince. I need a patrol car to meet me at 1420 Wintry Lane to check out a suspect. I will let you know if I need additional back-up."

He sped out of the hospital's parking lot and headed

toward the beltline. He was probably chasing a white fly, but experience taught him that no lead was ever to be ignored.

#

Yvonne Fowler cocked the gun and pointed it at Parker who was still laying face down on the floor. Tom tried to distract her.

"Why do you want to shoot him? He hasn't done anything to you. He is not even working on this case. If you want to shoot someone, shoot me and let him go."

Parker wanted to turn his head to look at Tom, his heart swelling from the senseless sacrifice his friend was willing to make, but knowing that a gun was ready to spit lead on his head froze him on the spot. For a moment, he thought of something his father always told him when he was little and they lived in the country. *If you see a dead possum, son, shoot him anyway, because those varmints only pretend to be dead sometimes, so predators will leave them alone.*

Parker wanted to play the opossum game, but he

doubted Yvonne Fowler would buy it – she was crazy, but not stupid. If anything, the idea of being an opossum made him want to laugh, and he knew that hysteria was quickly setting in. In the face of death one can laugh or cry, but what's the fun in going out holding on to a Kleenex?

In his prone position, Parker didn't see a shadow moving behind Yvonne and Yago, but Tom did. Tom kept his face impassive, and his resolve to buy time multiplied exponentially.

"I'm serious, Yvonne. Take me. I am the person in charge of this case and I am the one who would be arresting you. I'm sure Parker is willing to negotiate with you and offer you silence in exchange for freedom."

Yvonne burst into mad laughter. "You can't be serious, Lieutenant. Really? Do you actually expect me to trust the system or anyone who works for it after the system is responsible for leading me to this moment? If they hadn't taken my children away, neither one of them would hate me for the pain that someone else caused them. I will never believe in the system again, and both of you are a part of it."

Before Tom could say another word, the gun went off and Parker's body jolted from the floor. Blood spurted from his head onto Tom's face and chest and for the first time in a long career dealing with death and criminals, Tom's stomach gave out. He turned his head to the side to vomit, just as another gunshot went off. In his heightened state of panic, he thought he was the one who was hit this time; or maybe he was already dead and he didn't know it – it happened, right? He had seen movies and psychic shows claiming that the dead sometimes don't know they are dead. But he wasn't the one hit. As the sound of the shot still lingered in his ears, Tom saw Yvonne Fowler grab her chest, before crumpling on the floor like a puppet with severed strings. Yago threw himself over her and screamed an agonizing howl which didn't seem human, but his pain was to be short lived: One more shot exploded through the basement, and Yago joined his beloved on her journey with no return.

Mary Townsend walked out of the shadows, the smoking gun still clutched angrily in her right hand. She stepped closer to her mother and kneeled beside her as the woman got ready to take her last few breaths. Tears were running furiously down her face, as she took her mother's bloodied hand and squeezed it. "I'm sorry Mom. I know it is not natural for a child to shoot her parent, but it is also not natural for a mother to abandon her children, and you did."

Yvonne tried to speak, but her voice drowned in the gurgling sounds coming from her throat. She tried to squeeze Mary's hand back, but she could barely feel it any more. She locked eyes with her for one last time, hoping that Mary could forgive her. Mary started to pull away, but at the last second, she laid her head over her mother's chest and sobbed. "I loved you Mother. When I was a little girl, and I was scared to death every time my foster father came into my room, I fantasized that some day you would come to save me. In my mind, I had painted a fable as to why you had left us, but as I got older I knew it was just my imagination. You never cared about me and Jack, no matter what you say now. You can spend your last few minutes on this Earth blaming everyone else for your shortcomings, but you know that you can only blame yourself. Thanks to you I have become a monster, and God is my witness that maybe now I will be able to let go of the anger I have felt trapped inside of me since you left."

"Fo-rgg-iiii-ve meee…..I looove you." Yvonne did all she could to say those last few words.

"I forgive you Mother, because I think your mind was first eaten up by drugs even if you denied it, and then by anger, and you weren't thinking straight."

Yvonne's mouth twisted into a pained smile, and she gasped for breath. Her eyes rolled back and her body was shaken by a powerful seizure. When her muscles relaxed, Yvonne Fowler was gone. Mary looked at her mother and Yago lying by her side, his arm still protectively wrapped around her shoulder, and closed her eyes to delete this last image of them from her memory. She was standing up when the door of the basement slammed open and three officers led by Quince came down the stairs with their guns drawn.

"Freeze! Drop the gun and put your hands on your head where we can see them!"

Mary looked at them with vacant eyes and did as

she was told. One of the officers handcuffed her while two others ran to assist Tom. Their horrified faces when they looked at Parker lying on the floor in a pool of blood told Tom that these young fellows would not forget this moment any time soon.

Mary was led upstairs and to the patrol car waiting outside, and Tom, finally free, took a moment to feel steady on his legs.

"Jesus, Lackey...what were you and Parker doing over here?"

"Pretty much the same thing you did, but you were surely more successful than we were."

"Why didn't you call for reinforcement? That's procedure, you know..."

"Yeah...I know. I went to Little's apartment and Eduardo Carlos was there, ready to ambush me. He is the one who took me here."

"Eduardo Carlos?"

Tom pointed at the dead man on the floor. "That's him. He was Yvonne Fowler's lover."

Quince shook his head. "Shit! Then the Brinkley woman wasn't lying!"

"What do you mean? Did she wake up?"

"Yeah, she did, and she asked for you; but since you were missing in action, they sent me to talk to her. She told me that Yvonne Fowler's boyfriend tried to kill her by overdose."

Tom closed his eyes and allowed these last bits of news to fall into place.

"It all makes sense now. Yvonne Fowler confessed to killing Tracey Newman. I guess she thought I wouldn't tell a soul."

Quince helped Tom upstairs and as they emerged into the foyer, Tom could hear sirens quickly approaching. He sat at the kitchen table for a moment, waiting for the paramedics to check him out, and ran a hand through his hair.

"Have you got a phone on you, Quince?"

"I sure do, Buddy. Do you need to call someone?"

"Yes. I need to call Kathy. I'm sure she is worried sick about me by now."

#

Brad Johnson tried to focus on a paperback novel he got from the cart circulating through the cells, but his mind was elsewhere and he couldn't concentrate. He read the same sentence several times but could hardly retain any of the words, so he folded an ear on the page and closed the book. He stared at the ceiling, and listened to the sound coming from the corridor. He could hear inmates screaming, doors clanking and guards laughing in the distance – same sounds, different day. It was like time was on hold in here; seconds merged into minutes and minutes into hours and days, and the only way to really tell the passage of time was by the pattern of meals being passed into the cell from the small window on the door. Dried eggs and wooden bacon meant the day was just beginning, while chili accompanied by brick-style corn bread could be served both at lunch or dinner but were more often a treat reserved for lunch. Dinner often consisted of an unidentified mess of soup that looked and smelled like dirty dish water, served with rolls and mixed fruit.

A clinging sound at his own door made Brad jolt. The soup had already come by a long time ago, which meant that it was nearly bedtime. Who could want anything with him at this time?

The door opened to introduce an officer who was almost as tall as the door frame.

"You're getting out of here, Johnson."

Brad looked at the man suspiciously. Even if he had never been in jail before, and nothing really bad had happened to him during his current stay, he heard enough stories in the past to make him wary of anyone who walked into his cell.

"I am? Where am I going?"

"You're going home, I reckon."

"What?! What happened?"

"I'm not sure. I was just told to come and take you to the processing room for discharge."

"But...but...can I ask anyone a few questions?"

"Yeah. There is a lady waiting for you outside."

"A lady? Who's that?"

"I don't know. I guess you'll find out soon enough."

The guard led Brad to an office where he was allowed to change into civilian clothes before signing discharge papers; then a different man led him across a doorway into a neon-lit office where a policeman and Erin were waiting. The moment he saw her he wanted to cry. He didn't know why exactly, but the emotions pouring from his heart were so intense and overwhelming that even swallowing repeatedly didn't stop the tears from flowing. Erin stood up and ran into his arms.

"But why, Erin?"

"I got a phone call from your friend Shannon. I was scared to death, but she made me see how just how selfish I was being. I couldn't allow an innocent man to rot in jail to save my reputation, Brad. Especially if that man is the man I love and hope to spend the rest of my life with."

"But what about your children?"

"The children will go with me. Once I explain the type of verbal abuse and emotional withdrawal I was exposed to – we were all exposed to – there is no judge in the world that will stop me from being with my babies. It was time for me to finally grow up and be the woman and mother I know I can be."

Chapter 22

Kathy stretched her legs and smiled when her foot touched Tom's warm leg. She wrapped her arm around his chest and breathed in the cologne he splashed on his body last night after taking a long warm shower. Since the paramedics were very adamant that he should receive medical attention and maybe a CAT scan after suffering a concussion, he rode with them on the ambulance and Kathy picked him up from the hospital. She couldn't describe her feelings when she saw him in the triage unit – she wanted to cry, laugh, scream, and most of all, she wanted to hold him and never let him go. She hadn't told Tom yet, but a couple of weeks ago she received a job offer from a national magazine, and although she thought of throwing the idea out at the time, right now taking the job didn't seem a bad decision at all – in fact, it felt like the perfect opportunity to start a new chapter. She wondered how Tom would feel about the possibility of relocating but was sure that after seeing his long-time partner losing his life in front of his eyes was probably going to help make up his mind; after all, Tom hinted at changing careers many times, and this could very well be the turning point. She didn't want to discuss her plans last night when they finally got home, but her excitement at the prospect of creating a new reality for her and Tom was growing by the minute and she knew it wouldn't be long before those fantasies came pouring out of her in the form of words.

She wrapped her leg around his and tried to wake him up, but he didn't even budge, so she quietly got up and went to brew some coffee. It was a beautiful morning, and although it was promising to be another scorcher, the temperature was still fairly mild at this time of day. As soon as the coffee finished brewing, she poured a cup and brought it outside to the patio where she sat under the umbrella she recently purchased. The air was thick with humidity already, and the light breeze felt like the breath of an angel riding a steamy cloud. The Poplar tree in the backyard was loaded with emerald green leaves and when Kathy looked at it, she almost gasped. The last time she had been out here, the leaves were barely beginning to sprout, their tender green only a promise of the majestic splendor they would achieve just a few weeks later. Just a few weeks later – to Kathy the last few weeks felt like a lifetime. So much happened in such a short time; so many people lost their lives at the hands of fear and human weakness, and so many others saw theirs changing forever, profoundly affected by the events that took place. She felt that she and Tom were at the verge of a change – their relationship had been challenged by this latest investigation, and she almost lost him, but the wild ride had finally come to a stop and they were now ready to walk together toward the future. She filled her lungs with the sweet morning air, the scent of Honey Suckle a luscious treat that lingered in her nose long after she exhaled. She loved North Carolina, but she felt that her time here was over – she and Tom could relocate to a small town somewhere, and she could support both of them with her photography until he found a new job, hopefully away from crime and danger.

She was so taken by her thoughts that she almost forgot her cup of coffee. She took a large sip and held it in her mouth for a second before swallowing, as if the powerful flavor could inject her with the courage to tell Tom she was ready for a change.

She was about to take another sip when she heard the sliding glass door open and saw Tom still wearing shorts and a T-shirt waving at her. She smiled and waved her hand back, then padded the chair beside her to invite him to join her outside.

"Good morning Sweetheart! Did you sleep well?"

Tom ran a hand through his hair and sat, and Kathy automatically reached out to touch his bruised cheek and swollen eye.

"This looks so painful, Tom…"

"It is painful, but it will heal. On the other hand, there are parts of me I doubt will ever heal." His voice was tinged with the color of sadness, and from the intensity of his tone she could tell the color of his pain was blood red.

"I know, Tom. Or actually, I don't. I can't imagine being there to see a friend die."

"You said it, Kathy. A friend. For a long time, I only saw Parker as a partner, and to tell you the truth, I didn't even like him very much. He was always abrupt and moody, but in the end, he died trying to save me. How can I forget that and start healing? The moment I close my eyes, I see his face, and then I remember the times I wished he wasn't my partner, and guilt kicks in. If he wasn't my partner, I would have died."

A single tear ran off the outer edge of Tom's left eye, and he wiped it quickly, but not quickly enough; Kathy saw it and her heart broke for him. Losing a friend is hard enough without guilt getting in the way, so she knew Tom was in for a long healing process.

"Tom…I've been thinking about something…"

"What is it?"

"You have mentioned leaving your job many times, although I know you were not ready for it and you were only venting out frustrations. But what do you think about considering that possibility now?"

"Leaving my job?" Tom's eyes widened as he tried to absorb the impact of Kathy's words. "But what would I do? Police work is all I know, and to tell you the truth I think I would be bored without it."

Kathy covered his hand with her own. "Just leave it at that for now, Tom; just think about it. I have had a job offer from a big magazine and if I accept we'll be able to relocate anywhere we choose – the pay they are offering is surely enough to support a move."

"Wow…that's a huge change, Kathy. I don't know what to say. I don't want to hold you back from realizing your dreams, but I've never left North Carolina and I can't even imagine what life would be like elsewhere."

"It's not a decision I have to take right now, Tom. Just take your time and think about it. I promise you that I will not pressure you one way or the other. In fact, I am going to step inside to get another cup of coffee. Would you like one too?"

Tom nodded, his mind still chewing the surprise Kathy just delivered. Kathy got up quickly and disappeared through the sliding glass door, and Tom was left there to think. He had dreamed of this day many times – of when he and Kathy would be financially stable enough to make choices for their future together – but he never really believed it would arrive. Now, it was suddenly here, and he wasn't sure what to think of it. He knew that even if he remained a police officer he would never be the same, as not too many people can watch a friend die in front of them and move forward as if nothing had happened. Both he and Parker knew that dying on the line of duty was a threat that loomed over their heads anytime they went in to work, but intellectually processing the risk didn't lessen the impact of such a profound and scarring loss. Parker was a family man and very involved with his daughter; Tom felt a tight squeeze around his chest when he thought of how his daughter would take his untimely death. Was it worth it? Was a job worth the life of a good man? He thought about Kathy and how she would feel if he had died instead of Parker, and he knew that even if she never asked she would be immensely relieved if he quit his job as a police officer. It was definitely something to think about. And of course, he was proud of her – she was a superb photographer, and this was her time to shine. He wanted to support her and yet he was terrified at the prospect of walking away from a profession he merged with for so long. He closed his eyes and saw Parker, his old pal, the friend who had laid his life on the line for him, and he wished Parker could have walked away too. It was too late for Parker, but not for him, and as Kathy came back outside carrying two cups of coffee he felt a slight twinge of hope breaking free from its prison of guilt and pain -- maybe a radical life change was just what the doctor ordered.

#

Mary Townsend walked to the visiting room and sat across the glass from Shannon. When she first entered, Shannon could barely recognize her – she looked smaller than how she remembered her, and her hair was slightly longer and more feminine; but the thing about her that kept Shannon in a spell was her eyes; they were no longer filled with anger, and for the first time in her life Mary looked like a lost little girl.

"Hi Shannon..." Mary was surprised to see her, "I didn't know you were out of the hospital."

"I wasn't. I checked myself out this morning when Detective Quince came by to see me and told me what happened. How are you Mary?"

Mary shut her eyes for a moment and tears escaped them. "I am fine. I am finally free from everything – I am free from my mother, but most of all I am free from myself and from anger, and I am happy that you no longer need to live in fear of me. I cannot tell you how sorry I am, Shannon. Believe me when I say that I love you and that every time I scared you I hated myself for it but couldn't help it. I had no control over who loved me or left me when I was a child, and I had no power against the man who raped me repeatedly when I was no more than a little girl – I wasn't going to let anyone be in charge again, and I couldn't bear the thought of being abandoned by anyone else. There is something else I need to share with you...something you will probably find sick and completely twisted. You look a lot like my mother did at your age, so when you loved me I felt like she was loving me and I was a happy child again; when you resisted my attention I felt like my mother was abandoning me all over. Do you remember the night we met your friend from high school? I know you had no interest in her, but just seeing you so captivated by her tales of times gone by made me feel like second option – I was second option to other priorities where my mother was concerned. I never meant to hurt you Shannon. I do love you, and if I never see the light of day out this place again, I wish you a happy life. Find someone who can treat you right and can respect you for the beautiful person you are."

Mary turned her face away and quickly wiped the tears away. Shannon was sobbing openly, her heart breaking for a friend who had inflicted her own pain on her, yes, but had also avenged her twice.

"Maybe you won't be convicted, Mary. When the jury hears what happened they will probably understand."

Mary smiled through her tears. "No, Shannon, they won't. To them I will look like a monster with no conscience who committed the ultimate crime, and maybe I am just that, but I guess I will have to wait for God to judge my actions. I hated her, Shannon. I hated her with everything I had in me; I blamed her for everything that happened to me and to my brother Jack. I just hope that he can move on now, and be free from the ghosts that haunted both of us for a long time."

"I will find Jack, Mary, and talk to him. I promise you that no matter what happens to you, I will look out for him."

Mary nodded, tears running freely down her face. "Thank you Shannon. You're a good girl. I hope that some day you will be able to forgive me for the pain I've caused you and you will be my friend. I never meant to hurt you – I just didn't know how to love you."

"I know, Mary, and I have already forgiven you. As far as being your friend, you will never have to worry about being abandoned again."

Shannon lifted her hand and placed it on the glass, and Mary raised hers to touch it. They couldn't physically feel each other's touch, but for the first time they were truly connected through the heart.

#

Brad Johnson and Erin Winthrow got out of her gold Toyota Camry and hugged. She opened the back door of the car and let out her children, and she lovingly reminded Hannah – the younger of them – to be careful about the flowers. Jimmy filed out of the car behind his sister and fussed at her for getting out too slowly.

"Be patient, Jimmy," asked him smiling, "Hannah is trying to make sure the flowers don't break."

"But why do we need to carry flowers to this park? I don't see a playground anywhere – not even a swing set!"

Brad laughed and ruffled the little boy's hair. Jimmy reminded him a lot about himself at that age, and he silently pledged to be there for him as he grew up. He was aware that Jimmy already had a father, and he was okay with taking any scrap of time with him that he could; he didn't want to steal the spotlight, but he hoped that Jimmy would come to love him some day. Erin answered Jimmy's question in a calm and firm voice that instantly tamed the little rebel inside of her tiny son. "We are bringing these flowers to honor the memory of a friend. Her name was Tracey, and she died not too long ago, just beyond those trees. The park is allowing us to place a small cross marker there and the flowers, so that's what we are going to do now. I expect you to be at your best behavior when we approach the place where she became an angel; are we clear, Mr. Jimmy?"

Jimmy stuck his hands in the pockets of his red shorts and shifted on his feet while he looked down at his scraped knees. "Okay Mom. I promise, but I still think we should have taken the flowers to a park that had a play area; this Ms. Tracey would have liked it better."

Erin smiled and they all walked toward the trail leading into the woods. When they reached the area where Tracey was found – still marked by a piece of yellow tape left behind after the police wrapped the investigation – they stood around solemnly, Hannah proudly holding the flowers, Jimmy kicking a small pebble with his shoe and Brad and Erin closing their eyes to wish Tracey a happier journey than the one she left behind. Erin took the flowers from Hannah and handed them to Brad, who laid them on the ground while blowing a kiss into the air. "Goodbye Tracey. Our paths only crossed for a short while, and not in the healthiest of ways, but you were a good person and I will miss you. Rest in peace, Sweetheart, and awe the angels with the songs humans weren't fortunate enough to hear."

Erin wiped tears and arched her brow as she looked at Brad. "Songs?"

"Tracey loved to sing. She could play guitar and her voice really was beautiful. She wrote a few songs that are probably still at her apartment."

"Wow, that's nice…maybe we should go look for them, Brad, and have them framed for her family."

Brad looked at Erin with adoration in his eyes. "I have made a lot of mistakes in my life, but I must have done something right to deserve you. I have made a decision, Erin, and I was going to tell you tonight over dinner, but I might as well tell you now. I have a problem with addiction, and no matter how hard I try on my own, I don't think I can kick it, but while I was in jail I spoke with a counselor who told me of a local program I can sign up for. The program lasts for thirty days, and their rate of success is impressive. If you are okay with it, I will check myself in tomorrow, and by next month we can really start a new life, free from the past and from anything else that can get in the way. I don't think I will have a job when I get out, but I will find something else. I promise you right now, in front of Tracey's memorial that I will make a good life for us."

"Oh Brad…of course I am okay with it! I love you so much!"

"Good then, we can go home, after I ask you one final thing."

"Yes? What is it?"

Brad got on one knee and took a small box out of the pocket of his shorts. He opened it in front of Erin to show a tiny diamond that even in its small size captured some of the sunlight filtering through the trees and sparkled in colors of fiery red and cool blue. "This is only a promise ring, Erin, because without a job it is all I can buy at the moment, but I promise you that if you accept to be my wife some day, I will honor you and love you and I will get you a ring much prettier than this one."

"Oh my goodness, Brad….of course I accept…I…I

didn't expect this. I don't know what to say."

"We have a long road ahead of us, Erin. You will need to get a divorce, and we might be in for a nasty custody case, but if you can wait for me for one month, I promise I will never leave your side again." He turned toward the children and was happy to see they didn't mind to make eye contact with him. "I promise you both that I will never stand in the way between you and your daddy. I love your mommy, but your mommy and daddy were already not happy together before I came along. I will support anything you choose in life, and I will be content just to be there for you if you need me."

Hannah appeared a bit surprised but he didn't detect any resentment in her eyes. Jimmy looked for more pebbles to kick and Brad gently touched his shoulders. "Did you understand what I said, Jimmy?"

"Yeah, I did. I only have one question. Does your house have a playground?"

"Not yet, Jimmy, but I will build one just for you."

They all laughed together, and hugged, before saying goodbye to Tracey and walking back to the car. A light breeze blew through the trees and gently ruffled the leaves, just as a songbird flew on a nearby branch and delivered a soulful melody. Jimmy stopped on his track and turned around, his eyes as big as saucers. "Did you hear it, Mom? Maybe that was Miss Tracey singing one of her songs."

Chapter 23

Kathy rubbed Petey's silky fur while the kitten knitted her abdomen. She was glad to have worn a pair of jeans rather than the light cotton skirt she had planned to wear initially, since Petey's nails would have gone right through the thin material of the skirt.

"So, what do you think of Petey, Kathy? Do you like him?"

"He is adorable, Alexis. I am sure he makes a wonderful playmate."

"Yeah…I don't have Lily anymore, you know?"

"Oh? Where did Lily go?"

"She said she had to leave but she would always watch over me. I didn't understand what she meant, but she left before I could ask her."

"Sometimes, people only cross our lives for a short while, Alexis, but the time we have with them is priceless. Lily was a good friend to you, and she was a good friend to me. She helped us both and I think we will always remember her with love. As long as you keep someone in your heart, they will always be alive – you won't be able to see them with your eyes, but if you remember the good times you had together, they are right there, always waiting for you. Love and friendship don't know boundaries of time or space."

Alexis nodded, and swallowed a knot in her throat to stop herself from crying. Petey crawled up to Kathy's neck, and arranged his tiny body over her shoulder for a quick nap. His warm fur, combined with the softest purring sound Kathy ever remembered hearing, came together to form a powerful cocktail of instant peace. Kathy picked him up as gently as she could and placed him on the cushion beside her; Petey stretched and his whiskers twitched before he fell back into the type of deep sleep only a kitten could fall into. Kathy stood up and ran her hand over Alexis's hair.

"Why don't you rub Petey for a little while, Alexis? I am going inside for a second to see if your mom needs help with dinner."

She walked into the kitchen where Rose was busy stirring something that smelled delicious. Kathy and Tom hadn't had anything to eat since they first arrived at the airport this morning, and she was starving. Rose saw her coming in and smiled in her direction while she continued stirring.

"Thank you so much for coming, Kathy. I know Alexis is on a cloud right now. She couldn't wait to show you Petey."

"I am glad you invited us, Rose. Tom has been having a hard time the last week, and I am confident that a change of atmosphere is going to be good for him."

"He almost got killed....Jesus...that woman was crazy."

"Yes, she was. It is very sad to know what led her to madness."

Rose's eyes filled with tears. "I understand her a little, you know? When I first found out about Tracey's death, I locked myself into my own darkness, and I was not willing to get out of it until I realized that my other child needed me. Yvonne lost both of her children, so she remained trapped into her own pain."

Kathy nodded. "I can't even wrap my mind around a loss so deeply devastating. I just wish she could have gotten help on time. Now one of her children is in jail and the other one is missing."

"He is not missing, Kathy. He was released by the authorities here in St. Louis and he called us. He apologized for his behavior and asked if he could bring flowers on Tracey's grave – we said yes."

"Poor guy…"

"I hope he will seek help to banish the ghosts of his past. Shannon said that she is going to help him find a good therapist."

"You talked to her?"

"Yes. She is in town, meeting Jack for dinner as we speak. She is staying with us for a few days."

"If Tom and I don't have a chance to see her before we go back home, please do tell her that we wish her the best."

"I will. Oh, and Kathy...thank you for being there for Alexis. I know Mike already said it, but I want to let you know how much I appreciate you."

"It was my pleasure, Rose. In time, your family will heal, and you all will be able to smile again together for the wonderful photos Alexis will take. I haven't told her yet, but I have a gift for her – a camera like the one I carry around, which she liked very much."

"Oh Kathy...thank you."

"Don't mention it. We'll give it to her after dinner."

"It won't be long then. Dinner is ready."

They walked out of the kitchen together, Rose carrying the pot of soup she prepared and Kathy bringing in the fragrant hot rolls. Mike and Tom captured the scent and appeared at the door, their faces like little boys' waiting for gifts on Christmas morning. They all sat around the table, Alexis almost running to ensure she got to sit beside Kathy. The food was delicious, and the company even better. Like all others, this storm was finally over, and it was time for the sun to shine again.

#

"I'm glad to meet you, Kathy. Lieutenant Lackey, it's great to see you again, although I have to say that I was a bit surprised this morning when Mrs. Howard told me you were here. I am sorry I was late getting back last night, but Jack and I had a lot to talk about." Shannon said as she extended her hand to shake Kathy's.

"The pleasure is mine, Shannon. I am sorry for your loss."

"Tracey was like a sister to me, and I will always miss her."

"I know. I lost my sister to cancer a few years ago, and I still feel the weight of that loss."

Rose looked at Kathy and they locked eyes for a moment. Rose didn't know that Kathy had lost a sibling, and that awareness brought home just how wonderful it was that Kathy had connected to Alexis. They had suffered the same type of loss, and they both found ways to cope in their common passion for photography.

Jack Little stood to the side, afraid to intrude, but Shannon reached her hand out to him and invited him to come closer. He hesitated at first, but joined them anyway. They all walked together to Tracey's grave,

Alexis leading the way. Each of them offered a silent prayer, but Shannon got on her knees and kissed the photo on the cross. "I am so sorry, Tracey. You were my sister by choice in this life, and I will treasure your memory forever. I have done things I am not proud of, but never because I didn't love you. Stupidity and alcohol fueled my actions, and I ask for your forgiveness."

She bowed her head and cried softly, until Jack placed a hand on her shoulder and offered his other hand to help her stand up. "Tracey was very special, and so are you, Shannon."

Shannon stood up and cried on Jack's shoulder until everyone was ready to walk back. Alexis took photos of everyone on her way out, and promised Kathy to send her a copy. As the group moved along, Tom thought how crazy life is sometimes – even the most heartbreaking tragedy hides the seed of healing and new beginnings. Several people had lost their lives, but many others had found comfort and healing in one another, and they had found the courage to slay their inner demons.

#

Kathy and Tom checked in their luggage and walked hand in hand toward the Starbucks stand inside the airport while they waited for the flight that would take them back home. Tom looked tired and Kathy was a bit concerned. He insisted that he was well enough for the trip, but the dark circles around his eyes told otherwise.

"Are you okay, Tom?"

"Yes. I'm still a little tired, and my head is still hurting some, but I think I will survive. What about you?"

"I am doing great. It was good to see Alexis, and it felt wonderful to know they are all there for each other."

"It really was," Tom agreed, "and you can call me a sentimental old fool, but I was happy to find out that Jack wasn't responsible for Tracey's murder. I feel bad for him and his sister."

Kathy smiled. "I like it when you channel the old sentimental fool. He's endearing, and I would love to spend my life with him."

"Really? Even if he works as a plumber or as a cashier at a grocery store?"

Kathy stopped walking, her eyes searching Tom's face for confirmation of what she just heard. "Tom…are you saying…"

"I'm saying that I'm too old to be a cop, and I am tired of fighting crime. It's an exciting profession when one is thirty years old, but do you know how hard it is to jump fences at my age? I am thinking of retiring, if that's okay with you. Of course, I will look for another job and you will only need to keep me for a short while, but I think that life in a smaller town is going to be cheaper anyway. I grew up in one of those, and they are great."

Kathy's happiness exploded in a smile so big she feared her face would crack. "Tom! Do you really mean it? I can take the job and we can move?"

"Yes, I mean it, even if it would be nice if you told me where we are moving, so I can start preparing."

"Alabama or Mississippi are the two available choices right now, but we can take our time deciding."

"Hmmm…good fishing in both places. Maybe we can flip a coin."

Kathy didn't care. Mississippi or Alabama, or even

the end of the world, were fine by her as long as Tom was there to share the fun.

Their plane boarded soon after, and as they left St. Louis Kathy glimpsed at the Gateway Arch, the gateway to a better life. She blew a kiss to the bridge and welcomed the symbolism – she and Tom were ready to embark on a new journey, and she had no doubt that it would be the life of her dreams.

THE END

Carrington-Smith

Sandra Carrington-Smith is an Italian-born author who relocated to the United States in the late 80's after marrying a US soldier who was serving overseas. Although writing was Sandra's deepest passion since childhood, her dream of becoming a published author had to be placed on hold for several years. Moving to a new country provided several challenges, the biggest one being the language barrier she encountered when she first arrived. In order to become fully integrated, Sandra tapped into her love for reading, and over time her vocabulary grew extensively. She gave birth to three children and devoted most of her time to raising a family. By the time she was in her late 30's, Sandra decided to revisit her old passion for writing, and penned a novel of paranormal suspense, *The Book of Obeah,* *followed* *by* a self-improvement book, *Housekeeping for the Soul: A Practical Guide to Restoring Your Inner Sanctuary.* Both titles were sold to the same publisher and released in 2010, and *The Book of Obeah* went on to win an international book award. Currently, Sandra is working on two new novels: *The Rosaries* (the sequel of *The Book of Obeah)* and *Shadows of a Tuscan Moon.* Sandra Carrington-Smith lives in Raleigh, NC, with her husband, children and three cats.